The Future Embodied

Edited By Jason Andrew and Mae Empson

Copyrights and Credits

ISBN: 978-0-9794221-1-9

Publisher's Note: We are very proud to include authors from both sides of the Atlantic Ocean. To keep the mood of the stories intact, the editors have declined to "Americanize" the English spelling of the UK authors. We trust that readers on both sides of the Atlantic will be able to adjust.

Cover by Galen Dara

Editors: Jason Andrew and Mae Empson

Table of Contents

Introduction

by Jason Andrew

The seed of inspiration that inspired The Future Embodied germinated around the dinner table during a friendly conversion between Mae Empson and myself. We wanted to collaborate together to edit an anthology that would be open to talented emerging writers and set them alongside known professional writers. We established only one hard rule: the subject of the anthology had to fall firmly into the hard science fiction genre, but nailing down the exact subject for the yet-unnamed anthology vexed us.

In the new millennium, science fiction challenges us to create new dreams during a time of embarrassing riches of technology and discovery. The average person has a smart phone that possesses infinitely superior processing power compared to the computer that helped place humanity on the moon. Writers seeking to create new stories must imagine possibilities that will change the way people live.

While we brainstormed over possible topics, Mae said something that reminded me of how new medical science completely changed my life.

After suffering through a horrible day at work, I returned home feeling quite tired. My wife Lisa noticed something wrong with my face—I was talking out of the side of my mouth, and my facial expressions weren't normal. Thankfully, she worked at a transplant center and recognized the symptoms. She immediately took me to the emergency room at the hospital.

Bell's Palsy is a form of facial paralysis caused by a pinched nerve that disrupts control over facial muscles on one side of your face. Imagine that half of your face is constantly numb and you look like the Batman villain Two-Face.

Lisa took me to the emergency room and reported my symptoms. The doctor immediately knew what to do and gave me a specially prepared shot of adrenaline, which eased some of the symptoms. He prescribed a series of medication that I had to take daily, and within three months my malady healed. Only twenty years ago, it might have become permanent.

We quickly warmed to the inspiration, and within an hour we had the title and tagline for our new anthology: The Future Embodied – An anthology of speculative stories exploring how science and technology might change our bodies and what it means to be human.

We asked for character-driven, near-future stories exploring how the trajectory of current science and technology could impact our daily lives and choices. We wanted this anthology to embody a wide range of human experience, voices, and bodies, and in particular, to credibly consider our present and future demographics. We encouraged writers to populate their stories with bodies that have been under-represented in speculative fiction, but which should be ever more present in visions of our near future–aging bodies, obese bodies, chronically ill bodies, diverse racial and multi-racial bodies, or bodies from diverse geographies.

The proper creation of a themed anthology requires mastery of a subtle art that allows for insight into the potential of raw material. We had the theme, but had no idea what the shape of the future would hold. Taking the next step, we selected two guest stars who would anchor the anthology.

Talking during my bout with Bell's Palsy was quite difficult, and I felt too tired to write. I spent a good deal of my time reading everything and anything I could get my hands on. I reread a wonderful book that speculated about how a society might deal with a massive aging population once medical technology increased the average lifespan of its citizens. *Logan's Run* felt especially compelling, as I had just turned 39 and was already expecting my wife to start chanting *Carrousel!* William F. Nolan graciously agreed to write a story for this anthology.

David Gerrold wrote my favorite episode of *Star Trek*. I do not make this statement lightly. This television series meant a good deal to my childhood. It was the one common experience I could share with my family. A number of the episodes were more fantasy than actual science fiction, such as the one with the sexy salt vampire, the return of the sun god Apollo, and my least favorite, Spock's Brain. The Trouble with Tribbles dealt with galactic politics over planetary ecology and economics. This was a human problem seen in the future, and it felt real. Many of Gerrold's science fiction novels deal with biology and economy. I was very curious about how he might deal with this subject, and he was kind enough to agree to contribute to the anthology.

We believed in our subject and in this project. Our successful Kickstarter collected $1,960 towards paying our writers. Mae and I personally thank each and every one of the 61 patrons who allowed us to chase this dream. Thank you for supporting science fiction.

The great sculptor Michelangelo once said "I saw the angel in the marble and carved until I set him free." We painstakingly read through every submission until we began to see a pattern for the project and learned what we wanted the final book to be.

Mae was the first to understand it. She theorized that the really good submissions fit into four main subcategories and that any real medical breakthrough would dramatically affect at least one of these categories:

- Parents and Children
- Jobs and Industries
- Communication and Travel
- Treatments and Complications

Once the grand picture become clear, the remaining pieces of the anthology fit into place like a giant puzzle. By the time this book sees print, a little more than a year will have passed from that fateful conversation at dinner.

The Future Embodied has more than 80,000 words worth of stories that will raise questions about what our lives might be like in the future. These stories will invite you to laugh, cry, and everything in between. After all, isn't that the point?

Parents and Children

A Memory of White Flowers

by Nghi Vo

Phan Cam stood on the narrow steel walkway that stretched over miles of oyster reefs and waited as patiently as she could for her mother-in-law to die. On the bluffs above the beach, the Nguyen family home waited for her return. It had been built when terraforming settlers first came to Hoa Trang, and throughout the two hundred years since, it had grown from a low timber building to a sprawling compound, capable of housing all forty-one members of the Nguyen family as well as their servants and the team of mariculturists that the family hosted from places as diverse as Earth, Krasivyj, and Bei Guang.

Hau had sent for a monk and a nun from Earth for his mother, and they bathed the house in the smell of incense. They both sat like saffron-swathed statues at Ngo Lien's bed, chanting softly in time with the respirator. Hau sat close by as well, but during a calm moment, he urged Cam away.

"It will be soon," he said wearily. "There is no need for you to be right here, only stay close."

Cam wished that she could reach out and stroke her husband's hair the way that she would have done if they were alone. Instead, she bit her lip and squeezed his hand before all but fleeing the room. Behind her, she imagined she could feel her mother-in-law's reproachful gaze, though of course she knew that was impossible. The Nguyen family matriarch had slipped into a coma days ago, and even her occasionally-errant daughter-in-law could not make her stir again.

The nun was also a trained surgeon, and she looked at Cam meaningfully before she left the room. The day before, the nun had first snipped and then shaved a palm-sized patch at the back of Cam's head, readying her for the surgery that was to take place as soon as her mother-in-law passed.

"Is it seven generations that your mother-in-law holds?" the nun asked politely.

"Eight," Cam replied, a touch of pride in her voice despite her anxiety. "Nguyen Doan was born on Earth."

The nun hummed, impressed. The Nguyen family were among the earliest adopters of the Chinese dragon's pearl technology, the memory implants that passed the knowledge of each successive generation on to the next. The Bei Guang branch of the family boasted eleven generations held in the mind of their clan head, Nguyen Tuan, but he was very young, and some of his predecessors had died long before their natural spans.

Hau himself held five generations of memories. It would have been more if not for a murder that his ancestors had had tried on Earth as a mass killing. In the four years since his father's death, he held those memories with the kind of grave reverence that one could expect from a dutiful eldest son, but it had not always been so easy.

When she asked him what it was like, he was slow to answer.

Instead, he touched the scar buried in his thick hair, and because they were alone, Cam could lean against him, pressing her lips to the back of his hand.

"Sometimes, I look at the main door of the house, and I remember a woman in a green tunic and white trousers standing there and waving at me. It's Auntie Truc, who set the family to weaving the oyster mats and started the reefs. She's happy to see me, only it's not me, it's my great-great-grandfather, her brother. This is before they fought over the family's holdings in Bei Guang, before she was killed in the fire."

Hau looked suddenly startled, and then he had closed his lips firmly and would say no more.

Cam had heard the rumors of that fire. Servants whispered that it was caused when an ornamental lantern was thrown, not knocked over, and that clever Truc, who by rights had more claim to the family leadership than her brother by a second wife, had found the door locked from the outside when she tried to flee. It was only a rumor, but Cam looked at her husband's closed face and came to her own conclusions.

The cool breeze from the ocean tugged at her hair, and Cam turned to put her face to it. Hoa Trang, was more than eight-five percent water, and the peninsula held by the Nguyen family took up almost ten percent of the available land. Cam still wasn't quite at her ease planetside, not after her childhood aboard her own family's merchant ships, but she was comforted by the ocean that stretched from horizon to horizon and matched the blue of the sky so well that there was no difference between them. At night, the black sky was dazzled with stars, and she imagined those stars living in the water as well, throwing back their cold light through the shivering waves and spinning with lives all their own in the depths.

She was done with off-planet travel though. As the future mother of the Nguyen clan, there would be trips to Mars to visit the university there, and to Earth as well, of course, once every ten years to make the pilgrimages to the family graves, but the boundless striving of the generation ships and the merchant vessels were lost to her. She had not thought she would miss them after her marriage ended twenty years of constant wandering, but it was a longing that crept up on her.

"You should be inside," a familiar voice behind advised. "What is it going to look like if your mother-in-law dies and they find you mooning over the water?'

Cam spun around only to be pulled into a firm embrace. Her mother was half a head shorter than she was, but as she always had, she gave the impression of someone much larger.

"Ma! I didn't think you could get away!"

Vu Hyuen made an impatient sound, stepping back and neatening her maroon tunic and narrow black trousers fastidiously. She was dressed somberly in respect to the situation, to Cam's eyes, she looked a little odd. Typically, her mother preferred lavishly embroidered brocade jackets and wide trousers when she was on leave, and of course on the bridge of the Bach Dang, she wore the commander's black jacket and slacks. In dull black and maroon, there was something almost demure about her mother.

"Sang can keep things quiet for a few days," Hyuen continued briskly. "I wanted to make sure that I was here to look in on you for at least a little while."

Cam smiled at the mention of her brother, but her face fell at her mother's reminder. Her hand went self-consciously to the shaved portion of her head, and she glanced way.

Her mother made a noise that was half-impatient and half-concerned, and she took her daughter's hand, removing it firmly from her hair.

"You are worrying for nothing," she said bluntly. "It's very safe."

"We don't do it," Cam couldn't resist pointing out. "Our family members don't walk around with generations in their brains."

"You still have the name, but you are not part of the Phan family anymore," her mother said sternly. "The Nguyen family does things differently."

Cam bit her lip, and Hyuen narrowed her eyes.

"You knew about this when we were putting together the marriage contracts," she said. "You knew that your father-in-law carried four generations in his mind when he toasted to you and your husband at the wedding. What has changed?"

Cam drew one shoulder up defensively before standing straight again.

"I am afraid that I will no longer be myself," she admitted. "Hau knows things now that make him a different person. He is quieter, and now he is more than himself. He... he is his father, and his grandfather, and the three men that came before them."

Hyuen's mouth quirked a little at that, but her eyes were bright and sharp.

“Yes, and you will be Ngo Lien, Vu Ly, Vu Truc and all of those other women as well, but you will also be Phan Cam.”

Cam would have made a face at that, but her mother took her hand and tucked it into her own arm. She was trapped, and when her mother started to stroll along the narrow bridge, she had no choice but to follow. Underneath them in the clear water, she could see the regular rectangular oyster reefs, studded with thousands upon thousands of rocky shells. Their meat fed most of the planet, the legacy of poor Nguyen Truc, whose memories were burned away to nothing.

“Look, child, do you remember what happened to your father's aunt?”

Cam blinked in confusion, and nodded.

“That's Great-Aunt Mai,” she said after a moment. “She flew the Bach Dang from Bei Guang to Earth while the power coils were malfunctioning. The engineers said that it was only by the grace of gods and ghosts that she landed at all.”

“Aunt Mai was brave and a little mad,” Hyuen said seriously. “The Bach Dang is my home, and I love it almost as much as I love my children, but I would never trust its power coils once they started to spark.”

She shook her head, and Cam smiled. She had spent most of her childhood and adolescence on the Bach Dang, and sometimes, there were days when the ship had seemed like a rebellious older sibling, constantly disobeying and giving Hyuen headache after headache.

"So you remember Great-Aunt Mai. What about my grandmother, do you remember her name?"

"Vu Thi. She was a painter, wasn't she? She did the murals on Krasivyj, the ones with all of the birds. She..." Cam trailed off, and her mother picked it up promptly.

"She ran away. My grandfather beat her just once, and it was enough. She took my father, even though my grandfather threatened to kill her. She returned to her parents and had her son formally adopted into the family. My grandfather tried to kidnap my father a half-dozen times, but then he died in an accident on Earth. That is why I am Vu Hyuen, not Tri Hyuen."

Cam shivered a little. Vu Thi was something of a legend in her mother's family, the woman who could paint birds that looked like they would fly off the wall and who had a temper as monstrous as a solar storm. She softened as she aged, however, and Cam had very, very faint memories of an ancient woman with a goblin's smile and a handful of milk candy for her when they visited Earth for the new year.

"What about your father's great-grandfather, surely you remember him?"

"Phan Loc," Cam answered with a grin. "The pirate."

Hyuen's eyes sparkled even as she pursed her lips and shook a mock-stern finger at Cam.

"Now that is not a good thing to say," her mother said. "Surely he only stumbled upon those derelict vessels. He never pulled them away from the war zones, and of course he never sold the goods to both sides."

Though there were still old-timers who could not say Phan Loc's name without a distinct and pained curl of the lip, the men and women of Cam's parents' generation lauded the old pirate as something of a hero. He was the one who had created the real wealth of the Phan family, and his wartime scavenging and profiteering had paid for the Bach Dang, the Thịnh Vuong, and the Tay Son, the foundation of the fleet.

Cam and her mother shared a quiet grin, and Hyuen squeezed her arm. Her mother was not a comforting woman, not in the way that other mothers might have been, but she had a soul as steady as rock. That rock was something you could build on.

Hyuen was the youngest commander the Phan fleet had ever seen. She took the position after the death of Cam's father and uncle in a routine shipping excursion, and through the twenty years she held that position, she had become one of the pillars of the clan. She was a woman who possessed a controlling share in the clan's stocks and whose voice had to be heard by the clan head, even if she had only married in.

"Do you remember when you first took command of the Bach Dang?" Cam asked suddenly. "When you had that horrible fight with Grandfather?"

Hyuen's eyes took on a sparkle that other women reserved for truly hilarious plays and puppies.

"You're going to have to remind me about which one," she said with a fond smile. "There were so many in those days."

“The one about bringing me and Sang onto the ship. He wanted to keep us on Earth with them...”

“And he thought he were going to because I had spent four nights straight in front of the family council arguing for command of the Bach Dang. I don't think I could even see straight that day.”

“Grandfather tried to make Auntie Thu hide us,” Cam said, squeezing her mother's arm tight.

“Yes, and I had to go tearing into Thu's private apartments to find you. She never looked at me quite the same after that!”

Cam laughed, even though there was still a catch in her throat when she remembered the terror of being lured away from the council room with Sang and then locked into Auntie Thu's closet. She and her brother had clutched each other for what seems like hours before she heard her mother's crisp stride followed by the sound of a length of iron being jammed into the door to pry it open. The wood cracked and splintered, letting light into the tight dark space, and revealing two terrified tearful children. Hyuen had taken each of them by the arm and dragged them straight back to the ship that was now, by reluctant council agreement, hers to command.

“Do you know why I'm asking you these questions?”

Cam shook her head, and her mother slapped her on the arm lightly.

“You will be all of the women of the Nguyen clan,” she said seriously. “But child, you will also be yourself. All of the stories that you have, from the Phan family, and from the Vu family, and all of us, those are a part of it as well, and that is what you will pass on when the time comes."

Cam caught herself rubbing the shaved patch of her skull again, and she was startled to feel how normal it was already. Soon there would be a fresh scar there, which would be the least of the things that she would have to get used to, but in time, it would be hers too.

They had circled back to the beach when the cry went up. The professional mourners, held in reserve for the better part of a week, began to wail, and from the highest windows of the Nguyen family home, silk banners flew down to the ground, cladding the house in mourning white.

The house looked like a float of the creamy blossoms that gave the planet its name, and as Cam started to run, she realized that she would remember this too.

Mother's Little Helpers: A Memoir

by Miles Britton

I was 16 when my sister got a tail. Thinking back, I guess I should have known. She'd been acting different for months, distant. It was the fifth summer of the African flu, I guess we were all acting a bit different. But I never thought my sister had turned mod.

Ever since graduation, Taos had stopped talking about going off to college. Most days she'd come back home from the movie theater around the corner where she worked and head straight to her room. Once or twice a week, if Dee Dee Day was on, she might come out to join Mother and me for dinner around the 3D before disappearing back down the hall like a ghost. Mother didn't seem to mind at all, not as long as Taos was home, safe.

I'm still not sure how Mother saw it. She had just gotten home from her shift at the hospital. Taos was usually in her room by then, but that day my sister must have gotten careless. Or maybe she'd just stopped caring. I was in my room, watching the latest mining moon launch on the news, when I heard the shouting.

"...Jesus *Christ* Taos how in God's name could you do such a *stupid* thing for Christ's *sake* you will never leave this apartment with that goddamn *thing* so help me..."

It's hard to imagine now, but body modification was a big deal back in those days. I can still remember the first one I ever saw. I was a freshman, my second day of high school. African flu had already hit the west coast hard by then, and almost every school within a hundred miles had closed down. There weren't enough students or teachers to fill the halls. So that year they started herding all the kids left, a few thousand of us, onto one campus. I had just gotten my lunch, and I was looking for a familiar face to sit with when I saw the commotion: a bunch of seniors, mostly boys, crowded around one of the front tables. They giggled and postured, fascinated by something at the end of the table. Through the gaps in the shoulders, I caught a glimpse of her as I walked by.

The girl had elf ears. They were huge, at least a foot long. They curved up over her head, through her hair, like the veiny, translucent wings of a bat. For a second I thought they were fake, like in the movies. But the tips dipped up and down every time she laughed. And every time she laughed, the boys laughed with her.

There were others at school, too, probably a dozen. A few had horns: goat and antelope, mainly. Another guy, he had gills cut into both sides of his neck. I could never get close enough to tell if he could actually breathe through them. By the time Dee Dee Day—beautiful, tragic Dee Dee Day—got her fox tail a year later, mods were a household word. But a word you'd whisper. There were stories at school about wild, freak parties out in the desert, about mods getting high on trypt and running around like animals. The way the kids told it, they were always naked. Possibly somebody died. I don't think half the stories were true, but it helped give the mods an ugly *allure*. They seemed to possess a kind of freedom, a kind of fuck-it-all abandon that spit at death, laughed at the absurdity of life. It was a feeling most of us growing up in those days rarely, if ever, felt. Maybe that's what attracted Taos.

"...had any idea what you were up to I would have locked every door in this apartment swallowed every *goddamn* key you hear me..."

Mother and Taos fought for hours that night. It was the worst I'd ever heard: crying, cursing, slammed doors, walls kicked, pounded. More than once Taos threatened to run away. Mother threatened to lock her up in mental institution, to cut the damn thing off herself.

Before graduation, Mother and Taos had had their share of fights. About college, mostly, with Taos wanting to go to LA to study theater like Dee Dee Day, and Mother insisting she attend the community college just up the road. But those fights were nothing compared to this. At one point I snuck out of my room and crept down the hall to spy. They stood in the kitchen. Mother had on her blue nurse scrubs, her stringy blond hair pulled back with one of Dad's old bandannas. Taos had her back to me, her hands on the hips of her short, white dress. I'd seen her wear that dress dozens of times, but I'd never seen it move like that before. I froze and stared.

The fabric below her hands, at the end of her spine, was squirming. It jerked back and forth. Like a rat caught in a sheet. I turned and went back to my room, nauseous.

I lay down on my bed. *Taos has a tail.* I closed my eyes and tried to picture it. A flash of images raced through my mind—dogs, cats, pigs, cows, lizards, rattlesnakes—each one worse than the last. I opened my eyes and sat up. My stomach turned. I tried to think of other things, anything. But my mind kept going back to Taos. Where did she get the money? Body mods weren't cheap, especially back then. Something like a horn or cat's eyes could cost as much as a year of college tuition.

That's when it dawned on me. Taos had been working at the movie theater since she was 14, all so she could save up money for UCLA after Dad died. I know she applied. She never told Mother, but she had me read over her essay before she sent it in. I also know why she stopped talking about LA altogether around May. Every other senior in her class had heard back from their schools by then. But not Taos. And she knew by then she never would. I guess I never really thought about what she would do with all that money she saved. Maybe put it toward community college. But a tail?

They were still fighting when I finally fell asleep.

Mother grounded Taos for the entire summer. From then on Taos had to come straight home from work. No more loitering with her coworkers smoking cigarettes in the parking lot. No more sticking around an extra ten minutes to catch a few scenes of Dee Dee Day's latest, posthumous comedy. No more leaving the house without Mother, period. Which meant that nothing really changed.

Mother had always been protective. As the only child of an Evangelical preacher, she grew up on bedtime stories about the Rapture and people coming home one day to an empty house, a load of laundry tumbling in the dryer, a glass of water on the counter with the ice still floating in it.

But her paranoia got really bad after Dad died. He caught the flu in the first outbreak, in the summer of '25. One day he went to work, came back home with a cough, and three days later he was gone. After that, Mother never let Taos or I stay over at friends' houses anymore. She said she couldn't sleep unless she knew we were home, safe. Which was fine by me. My best friend caught the flu a week after Dad did, and I never saw much point in trying to find another one. But pretty soon Mother would fret when we did much of anything we used to do, outside of school and work. Even just running down the street to buy a soda from the corner store meant a half-hour argument with Mother. She was afraid we'd walk out that door and never come back. I won't pretend I never considered it, even before I left her, and Earth, for good.

But, in the end, it was easier just to give in. Not for Taos, though. Never for Taos.

At the end of July we packed up the car for our annual beach trip. I hadn't seen Taos but a handful of times since their fight a few weeks back, and even then it was just a glimpse of her shadow as she swept past my bedroom doorway. I hadn't spoken to her at all. A few times I found myself standing outside her closed door, my hand raised to knock. But I never did. I'm not sure what I would have said, anyway.

The highway out to the beach was inter-controlled, so once we were out of the city Mother turned on the autopilot and swung her seat around to join us. She pulled down the foldout table and put a 3D on. Probably a bad DiCaprio comedy—Mother loved him. Supposedly he was a sex symbol back in the day, back before he gained all that weight. Now he just looked like a wrinkly, fat toad, but it was a good distraction. Taos sat in her chair and silently flipped through tabloids on her tablet. I don't think she looked up once.

We pulled up to our beach house a little before noon. It was a small, rustic cottage, with a back porch that opened up on the boardwalk. Mother's grandfather built it in the 90's, back during the housing boom. We'd been going up there every year since I can remember—it was the farthest place Taos or I had ever traveled—but it hadn't aged well. The white paint around the doors and windows was flaking off in chunks, and the roof sagged toward the back, pulling the walls along with it. The house looked like it had another year or two in it before it finally gave up for good. Mother couldn't afford the upkeep, not since Dad died.

Taos and I helped unload the luggage. The air inside the house was stale and smelled of mildew, so the first thing we did was open all the windows. There were two bedrooms, one on each side, and a couch in the main room. I took the couch and let Taos have the room, even though she had it last year.

After we'd unpacked, we all put on our swimsuits and headed down the boardwalk. The beach was empty, beautiful. Looking around, it was hard to remember that just a few years back, the same place would have been packed with people, with beach umbrellas pitched as far as the eye could see, families splayed out with their coolers and towels and bottles of sunscreen, kids building sandcastles, playing paddleball, tiny heads bobbing out in the water, laughing and splashing. But after five years of the flu, the beach was ours.

We found a good spot by the dunes to set up our canopy. I unfolded my chair under it, stuck my feet in the sand and dug my toes in until I hit a cool layer. Mother set up her lounger a few feet away by the cooler. Taos spread out her beach towel between us and laid down on her back, close enough to the roof of the canopy to get some sun without getting burned.

"What a gorgeous, gorgeous day," Mother said. She leaned back in her chair and sighed. After a moment, she sat up and pulled her sundress up over her head. She tossed it on top of the cooler.

It had been awhile since I'd seen Mother in a bikini. She was still thin, like Taos, but her body was settling into middle age. The pale skin on her stomach had started to wrinkle, sag, especially around her tattoos. The two Dali elephants, parading toward each other on their long, spidery legs, had aged the worst. They looked like they were melting into her belly button. It was probably all a little more surreal than the artist intended.

I stared out at the ocean. I had my tablet in my lap, but I didn’t feel like reading. I watched the waves lap against the sand, watched the white crests out in the middle pulsing and swelling together. I had never been on a boat before, but I started daydreaming about what it would be like. To grip the wooden handrails, the sea spray spitting against my cheeks. Just staring out into the vast, blue ocean as I bobbed up and down in the swells, like I was riding the chest of a giant, a snoring giant. I could stand behind the captain's wheel, look out into the horizon, turning that wheel in whatever direction I felt like going that day. Maybe sail away past those islands off in the distance, not stopping until I glided off the edge of the world, on past the first row of clouds, float all the way to the Moon, all the way to—

"Taos!"

Mother's voice snapped me awake. I glanced over. Mother glared down at the space between our chairs, at my sister. Taos was on her knees, half-standing up on her towel.

She had untied her sarong. It lay crumpled against her feet. At her waist, poking out above her bikini, was a puff of brown and white fur: a deer tail. It twitched up and down, like a rodent sniffing the air.

"Fuck me," Taos mumbled. She grabbed her sarong and pulled it around her waist, cinched tight a knot. She flopped down on her back and picked up her tablet. Her fingernails clacked loudly against the plastic screen.

No one spoke again for over an hour. We sat in silence, staring at our tablets, though I'm not sure how much anybody really read. After awhile Mother asked if we were hungry. I said sure, but Taos didn't even bother to look up. Mother opened the cooler and passed me a sandwich and a soda. I had to tilt my chair and stretch my arms over Taos to reach them. The sandwiches were hummus and tuna, Taos's favorite. They were wrapped in cellophane. I ate mine with the cellophane on, peeling it down inch by inch like a banana so it wouldn't get sand in it.

Mother and I ate in silence, staring out at the water. The only sounds were the muted roar of the surf and the click clack of Taos's fingernail whenever she flicked to a new page.

"I talked to Dr. Darami this morning," Mother said, as if to no one in particular. She had finished her sandwich, the cellophane balled up tight in her fist.

Taos didn't say anything. But the clicking stopped.

"He has a niece, a couple years older than you. Last year she got a..."

I held my breath. I wanted to turn to look at my sister, but I didn't dare move.

"*...thing.*" Mother rolled the ball of cellophane between her fingers. It made a crinkling sound. "Dr. Darami, he knows some amazing surgeons. They were able to remove it, completely. He said there wasn't even much scarring." She paused. She turned her head toward Taos. "Now, it's not cheap, but–"

"No."

"Now Taos, please–"

"No!"

Mother took a deep breath. She raised both fists to her mouth, held them there. She didn't move. Then she exhaled and lowered her hands into her lap.

"That's too bad, because I made you an appointment for next week," she said.

I snuck a glance down toward my sister. She had dropped her tablet. She had her eyes squeezed shut. "Cancel it."

"Taos," Mother said, calmly. "I don't believe I was asking your permission."

I'm still not sure what happened next. All I remember is that one second I was holding my half-eaten sandwich down near my armrest, and the next it was gone. Taos was on her feet. She had her hand pulled back, my sandwich gripped in her fingers.

The sandwich hit Mother on the side of the head, just above her ear. The cellophane burst apart on contact. Bread and tuna and hummus shrapnel splattered across her face, her hair, her body.

"Taos!" she screamed.

But Taos was gone. We watched in silence as she stomped down the beach toward the water.

Mother's mouth hung open. She was covered in white gunk. Splotches clung from her hair. There were speckles scattered across her chest, across the elephants drooping into her belly button.

"Jesus Christ," she muttered. She grabbed a roll of towels from the cooler. "Jesus *fucking* Christ."

I watched Taos's body grow smaller and smaller down the shore line. But she never disappeared completely. After ten minutes, she turned around and started heading back toward our canopy. I whispered a sigh of relief. Mother was still muttering to herself, dabbing at her hair with a paper towel, but I knew, from the corner of her eyes, she had never let Taos out of her sight, either.

Taos didn't stop when she got back to the canopy, though.

Instead, she walked right past us. She headed up the boardwalk without even slowing down. She had untied her sarong again. She dragged it behind her like a conquered flag.

"Taos, goddammit!" Mother called after her. "Get back here!"

The last thing I saw was the twitching, brown ball dancing above her bikini bottom.

Mother stood up and slammed her chair closed. "Leo, get your stuff."

I helped Mother pack up the cooler and gather the trash. We broke down the canopy. All in all, it couldn't have taken more than a couple minutes.

It was all the time Taos needed.

She wasn't at the house when we got back. We searched her room. Her suitcase was gone. So was her purse. The only thing she left behind was her sarong. I found it floating in the toilet.

"Get in the car," Mother said.

We drove around for over an hour without any sign of her. Only one road led from the house to the nearest town, but a wall of dead brush and abandoned houses lined both sides. There were plenty of places to hide. At one point, I looked over at Mother in the driver's seat. She had bitten down on her bottom lip so hard it was purple.

"She'll be there when we get back," I said. I'm not sure she heard me.

But Taos wasn't back at the cottage. By then Mother had a wild, panicked look in her eyes. I told her I'd go check the beach again. I went out to the garage where we kept some old bicycles. They were buried behind a mound of junk. I finally managed to pull one out that still had air in the tires.

I pedaled down the boardwalk to the beach. I headed straight toward the water line, where the sand was firmer. It was late in the day now. The sun threw long, spindly shadows of me and the bike across the sand.

I biked for what felt like an hour. I never saw another soul. I turned around and biked just as far in the other direction.

Taos wasn't on the beach.

Mother was on her ear when I got back. "Nothing? Nothing at all?" She had her head in her hands. She was still in her bikini. "Yes, but...but she *just* turned 18 last month...No, I...Yes, I understand...I realize that but...but I want her back *now*..."

I fried up some eggs when it got dark. I brought Mother a plate, but she didn't eat. She just sat there at the table, her eyes ringed red, drinking cup after cup of coffee. I fell asleep on the couch in front of the 3D. I don't think she slept at all.

She called the police again in the morning. They wouldn't file a missing persons report until 24 hours had passed, but the officer took pity on her. He promised to radio all the cars in the area to be on the lookout for a missing girl. Mother gave him Taos's description. She didn't mention the tail.

We stayed at the beach three more days. The police weren't much help. There was a report of a girl matching Taos' description hanging around the parking lot of the liquor store in town. The cashier assumed she was either an orphan or a trypter. Last thing he remembered was seeing the girl climbing in the passenger side of a black pickup truck. Or maybe a gray SUV. It was hard to tell in the dark.

And that's where the trail ended.

Mother and I left the next day. We drove back home in silence. Those first few nights in the apartment, I couldn't sleep. It was eerie without Taos. It was like she'd been replaced by a cold, suffocating void. By whispers. By shadows. Mother begged me to sleep in her room. Some nights I'd wake up, the bed shaking with her crying. After the first week, I got used to it.

A month passed. Then two. There was still no word of Taos. At some point, Mother went back to work at the hospital, and I went back to sleeping in my own room.

And we waited.

They found Taos' body six months later, in a motel room on the outskirts of LA. She was naked, stuffed under the bed. A week's worth of empty trypt ampoules littered the room. Someone had stabbed her to death with a piece of a broken lamp.

The cops never found who did it. Though I don't think they ever put in much effort. Just another trypt-related case to toss into a file full of them. And what was another death to them? What was another death to any of us?

Mother stopped going to work. After the funeral, she stopped leaving the apartment. It might not have been so bad, but she wouldn't let me leave either. If I ever got near the door, she'd start crying and begging and pleading for me to stay. When school started, I had to sneak out every morning just to go to class. I gave up after a few weeks.

From then on, Mother and I lived like rats. We never left the apartment. The Chinese place around the corner delivered all our meals. At night, we made popcorn and watched 3Ds in bed. Sometimes we laughed. We never once mentioned Taos.

With the money from Mother's savings, we could have lived like that for years. And we might have.

Then one morning, I was searching under Mother's bed for one of Dad's bandanas, when I pulled out an envelope crammed in the corner, hidden between the wall and a box of old Christmas decorations.

I pulled it out and flattened it between my fingers.

The envelope was addressed to Taos. The return address was from the UCLA Committee of Admissions. The seal had been torn open. I pulled out the letter inside, my fingers shaking.

Dear Ms. Taos McGovern,

Congratulations! It is our pleasure to inform you that the Committee of Admissions has offered you a place in the University of California, Los Angeles, School of Theater and Film Class of 2034. Both as the Dean and a former student of UCLA, it gives me great pleasure to send you this letter as... I didn't finish reading.

I left that night.

I lay in bed for hours, Mother next to me, waiting for her to fall asleep. When I was sure she wouldn't wake, I crept out of the room and grabbed her car key off the kitchen counter.

I drove straight to the Sky Mall. I knew there would be Moon recruiters there. Their ads had been all over the 3D for months.

I found the booth just inside the South entrance. There were two recruiters, both muscular guys with crew cut hair and tattoos running from their wrists to their ears. The main guy asked me if I was over 18. I lied and nodded. This was back during the REEs rush, when Chinese companies would hire anything with two arms and two legs—and even that was probably negotiable. They sat me in a chair and took a sample of my blood. They scanned it for the flu virus as I waited. Then they handed me an application without another word.

The next space shuttle left from Reno in three days. I drove back home and parked the car on the street in front of the apartment, leaving the key inside.

Then I caught the next bus to Reno.

I spent nine years on the Moon. Nine years of gray skies and desolation. Nine years of coughing up dust and waking up with the taste of gunpowder on my tongue. Nine years of cold, lonely silence.

I never pretended to like it. No miner did. The work was exhausting, numbing. Most miners only lasted a few months before they lost their nerve, or their mind. The rest of us, well, we found trypt. Beautiful, life-saving trypt.

I never once tried to contact Mother. I couldn't. I was too angry. Besides, for the first time in my life, I was free. I was finally in control of my own life. It hardly mattered if that life was barely worth living. I swore I would never go back. Not to Earth. Not to Mother.

For the first few years, she sent patches almost daily. I deleted every one without opening them. By the fifth year, the patches were fewer and farther between. By my last year, just one every few months. I guess that's when I started to miss her.

The first patch I listened to was just two minutes long. Since the company I worked for was too cheap to buy a 3D screen, her image was so flat and staticky that all I could make out was a moving, gray blur. But I could hear her voice, loud and clear.

Mother.

She said she still loved me. She still loved me, and she forgave me. Forgave me for leaving her, abandoning her. She said she could never understand it, but she could forgive. Then she asked when I was coming home.

I reached out to flip off the screen. But the next thing she said made me stop, mid-motion.

"Your brothers and sisters, they can't wait to meet you," her voice said. "They've heard all about you, Leo. They can't wait for you to come back and join your family."

Brothers and sisters?

From then on I listened to every one of her patches. It took a few months, but I finally was able to piece it all together. *They* were her new adoptive children, her trypt babies. I guess one night she was up late watching 3D, and she saw an ad about saving the sea monkeys. That's what we used to call trypt babies back then. Those deformed, premature fetuses, with those big eyes and flattened chests. Until then, I didn't even realize they ever made it out of the womb alive.

In her patches she sounded happier than I had ever heard her. The last patch I got, she had just adopted her fifth sea monkey. She was a proud mother, once again. And me, I was her prodigal son.

The REE loads were drying up by then. Companies had already begun shutting down, packing up, and heading back to Earth. The company I worked for went belly up soon after. After that, I had no choice. I was going back home.

My plan was to settle in Reno, to start a whole new life of my own.

But by then I was too deep in trypt. It took me just two weeks to blow through my payout. After that it was just me and the withdrawal. The withdrawal won without a fight.

Mother opened the front door.

At first I thought she didn't recognize me. She stared at me, not moving. Then she pushed open up the screen door and reached out to touch my cheek.

"Leo," she said. "My Leo."

She looked older. Her hair had grayed. Her face was thin, hollow, the cheeks creased with long, deep slivers of wrinkles. But the rest of her had put on weight.

She pulled me inside. The apartment was exactly as I remembered: small, outdated, clean. It was the last part that surprised me most. With five kids running around, I figured the place would be a wreck. Mother must have spent every second of her free time cleaning up after them.

We sat down at the kitchen table. She held my hand and gazed at me, still smiling. I wasn't sure what to say. After a moment she asked if I wanted a cup of tea. She said she didn't have coffee in the apartment anymore; she quit drinking caffeine after the first adoption. A few minutes later she came back with two steaming mugs.

We sipped our tea as she peppered me with questions about the Moon, mining, the flight to space. I tried to answer as best I could, but I really didn't feel much like talking about it. I had just one thing on my mind.

"Mother, I was wondering–"

"About your brothers and sisters?" Her face broke into a relieved smile. "Oh, I was so hoping you'd ask. I wasn't sure you wanted to meet them." She pushed herself up from the chair and stood up. "They've been napping, but it's probably time I wake them."

For a second I thought she was going to walk down the hallway to get them. But she didn't. Instead she just untied the sash from around her waist and pulled open her bathrobe.

It's amazing what they can do with body modifications these days.

Attached to her skin, spaced out across her stomach like dots on a die, were five human bodies. They were tiny, no bigger than fetuses, with little arms and legs poking out underneath large, round eyes. As I watched, they began to move.

The one above her left breast yawned and rubbed its face with two cupped fists. It paused when it saw me.

"Mama, who's that?" it chirped. It looked at me with big, blue eyes.

"Kyle," she said, "I'd like you to meet your older brother, Leo. He's come all the way back from the Moon to stay with us. Isn't that wonderful?"

Kyle looked at me. He yawned again and curled back against Mother's skin.

I stared at her, at the strange things protruding from her stomach. The tiny, malformed faces. The faces of my new brothers and sisters.

Mother smiled.

"You are staying, right, Leo?"

Headlong

by Sarah Pinsker

By the time David got around to flat out begging us, he really was the only kid left at school who didn't have a Pilot.

"You're a scholarship kid in a school of rich boys," I said, looking to Julie for reinforcement. "Nobody's expecting you to have everything."

I piled brown rice onto my plate before passing the serving bowl along and helping myself to the next bowl, steamed broccoli. I was on a health kick, which meant the whole family was on a health kick. David sat opposite me, his body rigid with annoyance. The food hadn't reached him yet, and he clenched his empty plate in two white-knuckled fists.

"That's all the more reason for me to get it, Ma," he said. "I'm different already. Why make me even more different? It's not like the surgery is expensive."

I cringed at the word "surgery," and he changed his approach. "Who ever heard of mothers refusing their kid something that helps him study better?"

The food made its way past Julie and Sophie. David relaxed his death grip on the dinnerware to heap rice, then broccoli, then half a chicken onto his plate. He was always served last these days, a forced measure after the night a loaf of bread disappeared before three of the four of us had gotten any. I even called him BC for a while, for boa constrictor, after I had a dream that he unhinged his jaw and ate the entire Thanksgiving turkey.

There was silence while we chewed, then David raised his fork in triumph, a spear of broccoli still impaled on the tines. "Just think of my grades, Ma! And the health benefits. I'd have more time. I could join the track team…"

I exchanged a look with Julie. We had been trying to get him out of his bedroom and away from his computer for two years. He had steadfastly refused to join any clubs or teams. His real peers were online, he'd argued. We hadn't pressed, as long as he kept up his schoolwork and came willingly to the dinner table. Lately, he hadn't maintained the promised grades.

"Let us talk it over," Julie said.

"Is that 'I want to say no, but I don't feel like fighting over dinner,' or will you really talk it over?" he asked. Sophie giggled.

"Both," I said. "New topic time. Soph, your turn. How's fourth grade treating you today?"

"My teacher farted during math."

Julie's shoulders were already shaking. I tried to hold it together. "That's it? Did you learn anything?"

David grinned. "Maybe Sophie didn't, but I guess the teacher learned not to eat beans for lunch."

"How do you know what my teacher ate for lunch?"

"I know everything," David said, waggling voodoo fingers at his sister. She looked impressed. I glanced at Julie, knowing she too was savoring this moment of normalcy.

The argument continued in bed that night. The lights had already been off for several minutes when Julie called me back from the edge of sleep.

"I understand why this is a big deal for you, Valerie," she said, making me grasp for the subject momentarily. There had been several big deals over the course of the day. After dinner, Sophie had had her first seizure in four months, breaking through yet another medication. We should have known it was too good to last. Still, Julie couldn't be talking about that, since the seizure was obviously a big deal for all of us.

"The Pilot?" I asked. She didn't respond so I assumed I had guessed right. "How could it not be a big deal?"

"Maybe it would help him in school. He's having a rough time."

"And the answer to a rough time is brain surgery? How could a kid whose sister has epilepsy ask his mother's for voluntary brain surgery? Especially one that was supposed to treat drug-resistant seizures?" That had been in the link that David had sent us the first time he broached the subject. I had been incensed. Deep brain stimulation still hadn't been approved for use in cases like Sophie's. Meanwhile some research lab had developed a modified recreational use and marketed it to the masses. It wasn't fair.

"It's only an outpatient procedure. I've read the risks and it seems pretty safe. Hell, I've considered it for myself."

I rolled over to look at her in the dark. "Are you serious? You're on board?"

"I'm open to it. I'd like to do more research, but from what I've heard it's no big deal. It might get him out of his room a little more. It won't break the bank either; we'll just have to wait a little longer on your brakes."

"And the gutter?"

"And the gutter," she said, wrapping her arms around me. "Small price to buy our kid's happiness."

"I'd be crazy to agree to this, and you're crazy to ask."

"Mm hmmm," she said, and was asleep a moment later. As always, I envied her ability to put the day aside. Worst case scenarios branched through my head for another hour before I finally fell asleep.

I tried to sort it out with a run the next morning. My runs have always helped me think. Something about the rhythm of my footfall, the rise of the road. On the days I need to find clarity, I leave my music behind. I'd marked all of our family milestones, good and bad, with actual miles. Julie's terrifyingly difficult pregnancy, the decision to adopt Sophie after David's birth, Sophie's first seizure, the endless treatment discussions. Most of these were things that Julie and I went through together, discussed and diagrammed and planned to the degree that anything can be planned. And still there were conversations that I had with myself in addition to those with Julie, nuances and personal decisions and choices of which concerns to share out loud and which to swallow. I'm sure she did the same, though I can't say when or where or how.

It's part of why I'd encouraged David to run, though he had never taken me up on it. Despite my lack of biological contribution, he's built like me, tall and lanky. He thinks like me. He retreats into his head and holes up there, unable to see his way around the obstacles in front of him.

I laced up my shoes, pulled my hair back into a ponytail, and slipped out the front gate. After a couple of impatient minutes of warm up, I broke into a jog, then an easy run. I pushed myself a little faster, trying to reach the place where my body segued into its own autopilot, where each step generated the next, and it was easier to keep going than stop. I thought about our serious children, and then I ran away from that concern. I thought about brains and their intricacies and vulnerabilities. And then I was running, and all was quiet in my head, and in the quiet I found my own answers. And then I was just running. When I got back to house, drenched in sweat, I found my family eating breakfast around the kitchen table. I gave each of them a kiss on the head, met with various degrees of acceptance and revulsion and a general agreement that I should shower.

David's Parent-Teacher night was the final straw. Julie stayed home with Sophie. The doctors had upped her dosage again, and we were hoping this time it would work. Otherwise we'd be starting over again with another medication, a fifth multi-month round of trial and error.

Why did David want his brain messed with when the best neurologists in the country still played guessing games? How could recreational surgery be so precise when there was still no surgery that would work for Sophie? It boggled my mind.

I hadn't expected to have to fight his teachers over it as well, but they were spouting the same lines David and Julie had.

"He really is getting left out without a Pilot," said his math teacher, Ms. Sloan. She was young, probably closer to David's age than mine.

"How so?" I asked.

"It gives them more time to study. Dedicated time."

I shifted in the narrow chair. Math teachers had always made me feel stupid. "I don't really understand how it does that. Isn't it just another way to waste time better?"

She came around the front of her desk and leaned against it. It came across like a practiced move, like something she rehearsed in her spare time.

"It's not a gaming system. It's a communication tool, and a study tool. That isn't why he needs it, though. It's an *optimizer*. They get more out of their brains. Multi-tasking. The kids that have them have more time to spend with each other and more time to study and more time for extracurriculars – like gaming – because it lets them do it all at once. With upside-down learning they're all listening to me lecture at home anyway, and doing problem sets when they get to class. This way they can do something fun while they listen. They're still using their own brains. They're just using them better."

Ms. Sloan swept her hair back into a knot and cocked her head. A blue LED flashed behind her right ear. She smiled at me. The smile of a zealot, I told myself. At least now I knew where she found the time to practice her desk-sitting.

She tapped the light with her index finger. "Right now I'm going back over David's grades while I talk to you. I could probably be doing three or four more things as well – listening to music and texting and driving. You wouldn't even have known if I hadn't told you."

It was true. I would have sworn I had her full attention.

"How do you, um, access all of that stuff? How do you know you're paying enough attention to everything?"

"Practice, for starters. I've had my Pilot for three years now. I've trained my brain, the same as you train yours. It just helps me use my time better. I know that David got 68 percent on our last quiz, for example. If I graded on a curve that would be a serious problem."

I sighed, defeated. I was willing to be the mother who didn't let her kid get the latest toy, but I couldn't disadvantage him in school too. Maybe Julie was right and he deserved a break. I didn't like it, but I would go along.

I drew the line at attending the procedure, then erased it, then drew it again, then erased it again. In the end we all went, a Saturday morning outing for the modern family. David thrummed the window as we drove, a massive sound in an otherwise silent car. I would normally have told him to knock it off, but I was perversely happy to see that at least he had the sense to be nervous. Sophie dozed in the seat next to him, even though she had only woken up an hour before.

Another side effect to weigh against benefits. No seizures yet today, but a comatose ten year old.

Julie had been the one to meet with the doctor and make the arrangements, so this was my first visit to the Neural Implantation Center. It didn't match my expectations at all. The waiting room was warm and inviting, full of comfortable-looking armchairs and couches rather than the metal and plastic torture devices where we spent so many hours waiting for Sophie's doctors. It didn't even smell like a hospital.

"Why does it smell like fresh-baked cookies? That can't be hygienic," I muttered to my wife.

Sophie broke away from me to investigate a shelf full of children's books. I kept an eye on her as a Piloted nurse explained everything the brochures had already told us. Maybe I needed one of the devices myself, so I could listen and observe and process without losing anything.

I had definitely missed something, because David looked crestfallen.

"It's okay," Julie said to him, putting her arm around his shoulder. "It'll be ready by the time you have to study for exams."

I remembered this from the literature, though I didn't recall pointing it out to David. They would do the installation today, but the device wouldn't be turned on for another month.

"Your head has to get used to having something else in there," I said, pleased to have something else to contribute to the conversation. "Plus you have to attend a couple of orientation sessions to learn how to use it. It’s not too late to change your mind, you know."

I knew I shouldn’t have added those last bits, and I was rewarded with a vicious shake of his head. "I want this, Ma. Moms understands." He looked to Julie for support.

“Your Ma knows," she said. "She’s here, isn’t she? We’ve already paid the deposit. You’re allowed to change your mind, but we’re committed if you are." She shot me a glance that I read as, ‘Back off.’

"Moms is right," I said. "We’re here. Ready when you are."

The nurse had apparently finished her checklist, because she beckoned to David and turned on her heel. I watched our boy disappear with her through an unmarked mahogany door.

"That’s it?" I asked. "Off he goes?"

"Looks like," Julie said, also staring at the closed door. "Feels odd that we aren’t supposed to follow, but I guess they’d tell us if we were. The whole thing is made to seem so easy."

I agreed. "I can’t believe it’s an outpatient procedure."

We sat down in the two chairs nearest the corner where Sophie sat reading in a beanbag chair. I picked up a magazine and was amazed to find it was the current week’s issue. Julie pulled out her tablet and started working on a spreadsheet. Her fingers moved quickly and surely. As always, I was impressed by her ability to put aside the things she couldn’t affect and concentrate on something else. I flipped open the gossip rag to a random article.

I was still on the same page two hours later when they let us into the recovery room. David dozed under mild anesthesia. His boyish face looked even younger than usual, and they had shaved the honey brown curls from the right side of his head. He seemed lop-sided. A bandage behind his ear was the only evidence of the surgeon's trespass. Beneath that bandage was a hole, small and raw and neat. Beneath that, a gross intrusion on his perfect brain. How had they done so much so easily? Such a contrast with Sophie. In order to decide if Sophie was a candidate for epilepsy surgery, the neurologists had removed the top of her skull. Pre-surgery surgery. They had mapped her mind, gridded it with tiny electrodes in a silk-based substrate that settled into the curves of her brain like it belonged there. All that to discover that the focal points of her seizures were too scattered to be removed or safely zapped. Corrective surgery was still impossible.

David's new implant, threaded in through that one tiny hole, would settle into his right parieto-temporal junction, according to the literature. It would relax, get comfortable, put its feet on the coffee table and wait to be activated. In an hour we would be on our way home with the boy with the boosted brain and the girl with the busted one.

I ran dozens of extra miles over the ensuing weeks, trying to assuage my fears. Most of them proved unfounded. No infection, no seizures, no noticeable change. David, whom I had started calling "Ze Brain" in my best Herve Villechaize, did not act any different, except for an endearing little tic where he raised his hand halfway to his head, realized he shouldn't poke at the spot, and transformed the motion into a fake stretch and yawn instead. He did a lot of stretching and yawning. He dutifully attended the follow-up classes, learning to access something that was still only theoretical. As his access date grew nearer, he began drumming his fingers on all available surfaces. One night after dinner, while we all watched a movie together, the tapping got to be too much for me and I threw one of the couch pillows at him to get him to quit. He surprised me by bursting into tears. Sophie crossed the room to him and wrapped her arms around him. He hugged her back.

"What's up?" Julie asked him.

"What if it doesn't work?" He lifted his hand and then forced it down, clutching his sister to him. "What if I don't like it?"

Yes! I wanted to say. It's not too late! Instead, I told him what I thought he needed to hear. "It's what you wanted, kiddo. You'll be able to keep up with your classes, and spend more time doing stuff you like."

"It's natural to be scared, Davey," Julie said. For all the nicknames I came up with, she was the only one he allowed to call him Davey.

"I swear I want this. I really do."

Sophie sat back. "You know what I do when I'm scared? I pretend I'm somebody else who wouldn't be scared. Like a superhero, or Moms."

I glanced over at Julie, and she caught my eye and smiled.

"This is going to be great, David," I said. "You'll see."

At breakfast the next morning, Sophie had two massive tonic-clonic seizures in a row. Heartbreak city after a successful month. David was closest to her and lowered her from her chair to the kitchen floor before she hurt herself. I wasn't sure when he had gotten big enough to do that so easily. He pulled his sweatshirt off and placed it under her head, then turned her on her side. Another piece of me broke off and caught fire and burned out under its own fuel. These were the seizures that still terrified me: that small body, engaged in its own tortured dance. I was proud of David, but I wished his actions hadn't looked quite so routine.

Julie ended up taking David to the activation appointment. I stayed with Sophie while she slept. I updated her seizure log, checked in with her doctor to say that she was still breaking through, read through various parent accounts online to see whether anyone had anything new or different to say. I tried to stay off of the Pilot parent forum, which I had already browsed a dozen times in the past. There hadn't been any negative accounts, which made me all the more suspicious. What doesn't have negative accounts? Peanut butter has negative reviews. Puppies have negative reviews.

They were gone only two hours, arriving back with a clatter of groceries.

"Celebration!" Julie announced, revealing an ice cream cake nestled in one of the bags, the kids' favorite. I wished I had thought of it. "Where's the young 'un?"

"Still sleeping."

"You check on her?"

"Of course. And the monitor is on," I said, indicating the receiver on the countertop, tuned to the sensors in her bed.

I turned to David. He didn't look any different. "So, how does your new improved brain feel? Extra brainy? Are you solving world hunger yet?"

"Not too different."

"Are you doing the exercises now?" I caught his chin with my hand and gently turned his head to see the light marring his perfect skin. He grunted and nodded.

"So you're talking - well, grunting - and unpacking the groceries and doing what?"

"The exercises, Ma. I'm doing times tables, like they told me to. They said it's like rubbing your head and patting your stomach."

"Rubbing your stomach and patting your head. Keep practicing."

I pointed him toward the groceries and turned to Julie.

"Cake now, or cake later?"

She glanced at the clock. "Lunch cake, in an hour, if Sophie's up. Otherwise dinner. Maybe by then the boy will be doing quantum physics."

"I'm not deaf, you know. Soon I'll be paying better attention than ever, and you'll have to be extra careful what you say when you think I'm not listening."

"What have we doooone?" wailed Julie, mock horrified. "Back to the doctor, quick!"

He finished unloading the groceries, tossing a head of purple cabbage between his hands like a basketball. "Do we really have to wait an hour for lunch? I could eat a horse."

Definitely still the same kid.

December exams rolled around, and David aced them. We celebrated with another ice cream cake, season be damned. Sophie ate a small slice. Even though the ketogenic diet had long ago proved ineffective for her, I was still convinced that we might be able to control the seizures better if we controlled her sugar intake. And her stress. And her sleep. And her temperature. Poor kid. Wait until she was a teenager and we broke the news about alcohol and caffeine.

And what if her class was soon full of children with Pilots too? Surely it was only a matter of time. We had managed to keep her just a year below her age level and working well despite the doctors and tests and brain-numbing medications, but there was no way her head could ever host that enhancement. She would fall farther behind. Maybe there would be special classes for all the kids who couldn't get Pilots for one reason or another. I let that train of thought chug into the logical future for a moment. We would deal with that when the time came.

Toward the end of winter, David asked me if he could start running with me before school. I tried to be casual about it, though I was secretly overjoyed. I took him to buy a new pair of running shoes, since he had grown out of his last gym sneakers over the winter break. His feet were like snowshoes now. I teased him that if he walked barefoot across the lawn after a storm, someone would think a Yeti had passed through the neighborhood.

For our first run, I allowed him to set a pace. We set out through the neighborhood, matching stride for stride. I argued with myself over whether to talk or run in silence. I didn't want running with me to become connected with invasive conversations, but it also seemed like a good opportunity. I settled on the topic at hand.

"So, you think you're actually going to try out for cross country?"

"It's not much of a tryout, really. Anybody can join and run with the practices. I think they only have to make decisions when there's a race with limited entries. I'm not all that into racing in any case."

"No?"

"Nah. I want to run with my friends. And..." he paused to navigate some roots pushing up through the sidewalk, then stayed quiet a little longer than I expected "...you know how you always used to tell me you wanted to teach me to run because of the way it helped you think?"

I stayed quiet and he spoke again. "I was hoping it would work for me too. You said it helped you think, and it helped you stop overthinking. That's what I want."

"Is the Pilot bothering you?"

"No! I mean, I know I need it, and I'm doing way better in school. I don't think I could go back to living without it. It's just...loud."

"Is there a way to adjust the volume?" I asked. He gave me a look of disappointment. I shut up again.

"No, not volume loud. Just...what can I use? Busy. My head is always busy."

"Mine feels like that too sometimes, so I can't imagine what yours must be like," I said. He ran with his chin up and his shoulders back, easily, naturally perfect. I wondered what else he was doing in his head while we ran. Math problems? Chinese conjugations?

"Yeah...I was hoping maybe if I ran I could figure out a way to shut somc of it up for a minute."

"I hope so too," I said. I sped up a little, and he matched my stride. We ran in silence, or I did at least.

In April, Sophie's seizures increased in frequency. Most of them were complex partial, knocking her out but not down. We would see her disappear on an almost daily basis, disappear for seconds or minutes to a place that she couldn't find words to describe.

"It doesn't matter where, anyway," she said at dinner one night, "It's not here. I miss here when I'm there."

"So long as you don't miss there while you're here," Julie said, doling out the whole-wheat pasta I had made.

"No, I like here, Moms. I just don't know how to stay." Another piece of me broke off.

That night, after Sophie was in bed and David had locked himself in his room to do homework and play videogames, I bent my own rule about not running after dark. Julie watched me change into shorts and nodded in understanding.

Dinner felt heavy in my stomach. Cool spring air usually energized me but my limbs were like lead. Still, I ran. I ran until I was no longer thinking of our daughter who didn't know how to stay, or our boy who was becoming an adult in a world that demanded so much more from him than I would ever have imagined.

The next day, I picked Sophie up from school and took her to do some grocery shopping. The route home passed close to David's school, and as I pumped my soft brakes, waiting to take my left turn, I noticed a blur of movement out of the corner of my eye.

"I see David!" said Sophie, face pressed to the window. David's cross-country team. I searched for him and found him in the middle of the pack, his face serene. They were all serene, actually, their bodies straining and sweating but their faces showing no sign of exertion. A couple of them joked with each other, sharing relaxed smiles. None seemed entirely present, and I hoped they had the focus to look both ways as they crossed the busy rush hour streets back to the school.

They were a strange collection of animals: a herd of boys, scrawny bare chests thrust forth and heaving, legs churning as they vied with each other for position. They would achieve great things, these boys. Their parents - we - had given them everything we could. They would spend another year or two or three at their excellent school, with their excellent brains doing more than any brains had done before. How could they not succeed?

And yet, even as I watched their healthy young bodies navigate a perfect spring day, I worried. What kind of society were we creating where kids voluntarily changed their brains to keep up with all the input coming at them in a constant stream? Surely there were some who would bow under the immense pressure to succeed, to do more, to do more all the time and never stop doing. I couldn't help imagining the noise in all those Piloted heads.

One of the boys near David stumbled. I saw my son reach out an arm to steady him without breaking stride, but the kid behind him clipped his heel and fell. Two more ran over him before someone at the back of the pack stopped to help. He brushed his bloody knees with his hands, then took off after his friends.

The traffic light changed and we left the boys behind. When we reached the house, I turned off the car but lingered for a moment, key still in the ignition.

I turned to face Sophie. "I have a secret to tell you."

She unbuckled herself and climbed into the passenger seat to hear what I had to say. She was all about secrets.

"I can see the future," I said in a conspiratorial voice. "Not all of it, but a little. In a few years, almost everyone is going to have a Pilot, except you and me."

Her eyes grew wide. "Even Moms?"

I considered. "Yes. She'll have one too. People with Pilots are going to do some very good things, but you and I and a few other people will be the only people without them. And the others are going to make it seem like we need them, but it'll be okay."

"Because it's okay to be different?" She looked skeptical. She had heard that line before.

"Because we're going to be different together. As long as you don't have one, I won’t have one. We’ll both do fine." I was about to add, "I promise," but stopped short.

Sophie nodded like she understood. I kissed her forehead and hoped she’d never have to. I counted the hours until I could run all of this out of my mind.

Trash Talk

by Holly Schofield

I'm not a complainer, not me. I roll with the punches. I'll be just another dead trash collector in about ten minutes but, hey, that's okay. My son won't die and, here's a bonus, my life insurance policy will pay out.

Unless they consider it suicide.

Here we are, hugging in the middle of my living room, me in my robo-assist, my fists locked behind Ricky's head, up high, like a boxer's. Ricky, that's my son, he's pinned right against my chest.

I can't see much now, things are blurry; must be sweat that's in my eyes. Maybe that'll save me 'cause it'll short out the servos sooner or later. That was a joke. I'm hanging tough. By the way, guys, before you do anything down at the cop shop with this voice record, edit out all the emotional crap Ricky and I said earlier at the beginning, like, right when it started recording, okay? Kinda embarrassing.

Lemme tell you about the assists. Us union guys aren't issued fancy ones like the reality stars get—ours don't have hardly any medi-sensors or monitors or nothing—only basics, like the LifeSwitch. And they don't come with no webcams, just a remote link and a voice recorder in the sleeve controls. You velcro a battery pack at the top of your ass and then jam your feet in the boots and ease the assist on like a really,

really stiff coverall. You can't even see the eight servo motors or the carbon fiber rods under the plastic. The memory foam grabs your calves and thighs and arms, and you hit the 'On' button and, uber-quick, it's slaved to your movements. In, like, thirty seconds, you're up and running.

On a good day.

Since the city cut back the maintenance budget, there's all sorts of glitches with the assists. Mine's all battered and scratched and the shoulder hatch is just duct-taped on.

Ricky, that's my son, twenty-eight years old and smart as a chip, he says I should tell management that the assists are a bit wacked. What he don't know is, and I'm being real frank here since it don't matter no more, I tinkered with my assist last week, so I'd be setting myself up if I asked them to run diagnostics on it. See, there's one stop on my route, got these goddamn decorative rocks right in front, I gotta heave the cans up and over each friggin' time, makes the bursitis in my shoulder kick up something terrible. So I ramped up the assist, just a touch, and that meant I had to fiddle with the limit control, tweak the processors a bit, you know? Guys my age got hardware skills, not like today's kids that can't tell firmware from their underwear. Still, now I wish I hadn't done that. Goddamn, do I wish it.

Anyway, I know you cops are busy guys. So I'll get to the point.

First, though, I need to tell you just a bit more about the Lifeswitch so things make more sense. Like, take Johnno last month: his lungs couldn't hack it no more and the asthma meds were too friggin' expensive but what was he gonna do? Twenty-two years he's been chucking cans on the west end route. Nobody's gonna hire him for anything else, not in this Slump. Don't know what the country's coming to. Anyway, Johnno got to the point where heaving a full can into the truck made him cough up a lung for a good three minutes, even with his assist cranked up to max. Poitr, the depot tech, he told me how it went down that day. Johnno was finishing up his route when Poitr's screens blared so loud the depot practically shook. That's what happens when a LifeSwitch goes off. It's a union requirement, see? Been too many cases where a can jockey got hurt on the job and no one knew. Johnno took his last breath and his assist had triggered the alarm. The medics were there in minutes but Johnno was splayed out in the lane, dead, with a full trash can spilled out all over him. They had to cut the assist in pieces to get it off. We had a nice little memorial for him, in the coffee room, and the union even paid for donuts.

Today, I wore my assist home with me. Yeah, I know, against union rules, sure, but Ricky wanted me to move his old piano from my basement here at the farm to his new apartment. It's an upright, one of those old-school pianos that weigh more than a garbage truck. I lowered it into the basement the day we moved to the farm, Mandy and me. Ricky was just a twinkle in our eye. Mandy had all these ambitions for the kid and he hadn't even seen the light of day. I couldn't afford much so I'd got this old piano out of the town dump. That was back when people just trashed stuff. None of this 3-D printer recycling nonsense where you gotta sort the trash components so goddamn carefully these days.

So what I did, I wrapped a wire cable around the piano with Mandy dancing around, chattering and stuffing a blanket at the edges so it wouldn't scratch the finish. Then I backed my old Suburban up slowly over the front lawn–you shoulda heard that woman of mine yelling about her flowerbeds–and hitched it to the other end of the cable. I put my shoulder to the piano, those were the days–before this bursitis–and that wooden beast slid down the first step and hung there while the cable went zing and tightened up. Then I backed the Suburban slowly toward the house. The piano slid the rest of the way down the stairs, easy as pi. Those were the days. I'd give anything for Mandy to still be alive and yelling at me about something. The breast cancer cure came along just five years too late, ya know, or she would be here in the living room right now, yapping away, getting us out of this mess. Goddamn, sweat or something is running in my eyes again. Wish I could wipe them.

He's a good kid, Ricky, but not tall and not muscle-bound, if you know what I mean. He's got his dad for that stuff. So when he said he wanted the piano at his apartment, I was happy to help. But my shoulder's been hurting all week. Bursitis is hell. Not complaining, mind, just telling you why I wore the assist home from work. I don't want the blame put on anyone else but me, see?

What I can't figure is—–let me yap a bit, guys, I got time—–we got that bunch of cancer cures now, right? Well, for the common types. We got that colony on the moon, right? Well, the Chinese do. And we fixed AIDS good. Well, not counting AIDS 2.0, but, at least, there's progress, right, even in this crappy economy. So why haven't they fixed diabetes yet? Like, come on. Ricky's life has been a tough one, all because of the Big D. Giving himself insulin jets every few hours, 24/7, pain in the ass and pricey. Regular joes, like Ricky and me, we can't afford those new patches they got now. And he needs sugary snacks even oftener than the jets, or it's coma-time. Missed out going on friends' camping trips and a school trip to Disneyland when he was a kid. I was too goddamn nervous to let him out of my sight that long. You know us single parents, always a little twitchy.

Ricky's such a good kid. I mean, to be born right when the Slump took down the economy, that's rough. Him choosing music teacher as his profession, that's damn smart. Not gonna get obsolete any time soon. Let's see a bot teach piano, eh? Those upscale parents on the west side are always gonna want the status of a real live teacher watching their kids plink out notes on a keyboard.

Anyhow, Ricky met me at home today. Well, you know that, 'cause you'll have found our bodies in the living room by now. At least I hope someone finds 'em before too long. The heat of the summer, that we wait for all year, it isn't always a good thing, know what I mean? We were gonna move that piano. I'd come in the back door through the mudroom, letting the assist help me up the back steps. Steps are hard on the knees with the weight of the assist, eh. Ricky walked in the front door about ten seconds later, beaming from ear to ear. Staggering a bit, hadn't had time to eat for a few hours but pushing through it. Tough, like his dad. His big news, he couldn't wait to tell me, was he got himself a fancy job teaching music up at the university. That's my boy! He was all dressed up in a fancy suit. Guess that's why he didn't have any insulin jets handy–must've left them in his other pants or something.

I was so proud, I gave him a big hard hug and that's when it happened. The assist jammed. Stuck us both in my living room holding Ricky like a piece of wood in a vise. My wrist controls were right there, centimeters from my nose but I couldn't reach them. Ricky of course never wore a phone or nothin', said it interfered with the music nodes he sometimes patched on his skull. That boy was always playing his tunes.

"Ricky, see if you can hit the controls on my wrist," I said.

He didn't say nothing, which, at the time, I thought was weird. Anyhow, he sucked in a long breath and managed to twist an arm up and around my wrist. Then he let his arm fall, just dropped it like a stone. Well, he'd hit Connect alright, as well as Record. Connect started playing some service message about some goddamn maintenance routine they were running down at the depot. Still no big deal, I thought, Poitr or someone'll answer soon. At least, they'd miss me on tomorrow's shift or a neighbor *might* stop in. Mind you, the nearest neighbor is a good three klicks away. We liked the peace and quiet out here in the country, Mandy and I.

"Ricky," I said next. "Son, see if you can wiggle out of here and get some help. Maybe if you twist a bit in my arms, you might lose some skin or dislocate your shoulder but I bet you can slide out."

"Yeah...," he said all long and drawn-out like and then he sagged down in my arms. Sugar-coma, dammit.

I yelled and prodded but he was too far gone. The service message played over and over.

So here we are. Thanks for listening to me spill all this crap, guys. I got another favor to ask, too.

I know you cops have reports to make and forms to fill out, but if you could keep quiet about how things happened here, about what, God help me, I'm going to do next. Keep it from Ricky, I'm askin' you. If you could do that, it would be a fine thing. I don't want the boy spending the rest of his life having the guilts 'cause dear ol' Dad did this for him, you know?

Anyhow, I think I can bypass some stuff, mash two little contacts together, and get the shoulder motor working. I did it before in the shop when I ramped things up. Just the one shoulder will do it. So far, I've scraped off the duct tape and now I've got a couple of fingers inside the shoulder hatch. So, if I can connect up that servo to trigger a rotating action, see, my arm rises up, my fist pivots toward my head, my neck snaps, and that'll set off the LifeSwitch and call up you guys and the medics. Ricky will be saved and, hey, I gotta save my boy, no matter what. I'm not grumbling about it, just saying it so you cops can figure out stuff when you get here.

No, I'm not complaining...I'm just, you know, rolling with the punches.

A New Man

by William F. Nolan

[Neuro-prom Passcode: REQUIRED (Press Any Key to Enter)

Passcode: ____________

Passcode: ACCEPTED

BEGIN CONFESSION #TEA3170B-X3075 DOWNLOAD..........

Unspooling.................

start transcode;!complete!

checksum.......................

</gmd:linkage>
</gmd:CI OnlineResource>
</geop:mappingFile>
<geop:processingApplication>
<geop:PH_EnvironmentObject>
<geop:documentation>
<gmd:CI_OnlineResource>
<gco:CharacterString>GeoServer WFS</gco:CharacterString>
</geop:name>
<geop:purpose><gco:CharacterString>produce representation of observation datasets in Science Modelling Language - a GHL-based application schema</gco:CharacterString></gmd:purpose>
<geop:type><gco:CharacterString>Software</gco:CharacterString></geop:type>
<geop:version><gco:CharacterString>Complex

RUN #TEA3170B-X3075 TRANSCRIPTION:>

"Happy tenth anniversary!" I said, handing the ribboned jewelry box to Edith.

"What's inside?" she asked, eyes aglow with excitement. She was still beautiful enough to astonish me.

"Open it and see," I said.

With a girlish laugh, she untied the red band and opened the box. She gasped.

"Well? Do you like it?"

"Terry! An emerald necklace! You shouldn't have. It must have cost—"

"I can afford it. Nothing's too good for my girl. . ." I've always called Edith "my girl," ever since we met in college. It was love at first sight for us both; I've never wanted another woman. Edith was my treasure.

She lifted the choker from its velvet nest and slipped it around her neck, allowing afternoon sunlight to turn the jewels to green fire.

"It's absolutely gorgeous!"

We kissed, deeply, with a sexual hunger that was still intense, consuming. After ten years, the excitement had not diminished.

We had our anniversary dinner at *Jimmy's*, our favorite Italian restaurant. It was named after actor James Cagney, and framed photos of the long-dead movie icon adorned the walls. In one photo Cagney was posing with President Franklin Roosevelt in the Oval Office during World War II.

Benny LaGarda, the owner, greeted us warmly, excited about a 1949 Cagney film he'd recently discovered, *White Heat.* He was rail-thin, with a short neck, and displayed an obvious overbite when he smiled.

"The scene at the end is *fabulous*," he told us. "Jimmy gets blown to pieces! He's on this really high platform and he yells to his mother, 'Look, Ma—top of the world!', and that's when he's blown to bits!" He directed us to a table near the kitchen. "Too bad they didn't have our technology a hundred years ago, eh? Jimmy might have been saved."

"Ummmm," Edith murmured as she sat down, "smells delicious!" She had always enjoyed the heady aroma of Italian herbs and spices. She was wearing the necklace, the emeralds flashing green heat against the white of her throat.

"This is our tenth anniversary," I told Benny, squeezing my wife's hand, "so we want a bottle of your best champagne."

"Our treat," nodded Benny." If I'd known about this happy occasion I would have baked a cake."

"The bubbly will do just fine," said Edith, smiling up at him. "Wow. . . I haven't tasted champagne since we had Janette."

"Where *are* the children?" Benny asked.

"Janette loves shuttlefusion," said Edith. "The big game is tonight. . . for the West Coast Championship, so we dropped off Jan and Bobby at the 'drome."

"Yeah." I nodded. "We needed time for just the two of us."

"Jan has a crush on one of the players," declared Edith. "I've forgotten his name. Lance something or other. But I'm sure it'll pass.

She's only nine years old!"

"They grow up fast these days," said Benny, taking our order.

As always, the food was delicious: A sumptuous vegetarian feast prepared by Benny himself; the champagne was a perfect complement.

Later that evening we made passionate love; Edith could be a tiger in bed, especially on an occasion as special as our anniversary. Afterward, we had the car drive us to the Friodrome to pick up Jan and Bobby.

"How was the game?" I asked Bobby. At eight, he was easily bored.

He shrugged. "It was okay. Jannie's the shuttle freak, not me. But it was okay."

"It was *super!*" Jan declared. "Best game *ever!* And our team won, thanks to Lance. He was the star. He scored *three* times!"

"Kid's an air head," I said. "Dumb as a sack of rocks."

In the rear view, I saw Jan's chin quiver as she looked away. The silence was heavy.

"Now see what you've done," admonished Edith after a few moments. "A terrible thing to say when you don't even know the boy."

Janette finally blurted: "Daddy, you just don't understand true love!"

At the breakfast table the next morning, Bobby picked at his food, head down, looking glum.

"What's wrong, soldier?" I asked him.

"Why can't we program the table to make a different breakfast?"

"How different?"

"I'm tired of toast and soy bacon. I want a bowl of cereal."

"Now, you know we've had this discussion before. Those kid's cereals are full of sugar," Edith said, "Very bad for you. That's why we don't buy them."

"Look," I told him, "You are not old enough to dictate a menu yet. Later, when you're older and if you still want cereal we can discuss the matter. For now, *you* eat what *we* eat."

Bobby scowled. "Other kids eat it. . . " His voice trailed off as he stared at the food on his plate. He knew this was a losing battle.

"Well, you're not other kids," his mother replied, her expression stern as she dried her hands on a dishtowel. "Stop sulking, and don't waste your food. Children on Io are starving."

He looked at me. "How come all the *bad* stuff tastes better than the *good* stuff?"

I had no answer to that; I'd never figured it out either.

Everything went wrong after the crash.

I had set the auto-drive at near max; I enjoyed the sensation of sheer speed. The car was probably moving faster over the road slot than was prudent. But the slot was designed to keep all cars separated on the GridWay, so I felt safe, drowsing in my seat, eyes closed, picturing Edith's happy smile when I got back to our house-unit.

That's when the slot malfunctioned: As a heavy med truck moved toward me, it jumped the Grid and slammed head-on into my car. I learned later that the ensuing impact tore my body apart as the two machines merged in a horrific tangle of twisted metal. The man in the truck, amazingly, survived with only minor injuries.

I did not: I died in the hospital shortly after arrival. The minute I expired, they flashed my Neuro-prom and affected the dendritic transfer into my new host. I woke up several weeks after the operation flushed with strength, alert and in no pain.

"Welcome back to the land of the living," declared my white-clad doctor, smiling down at me. "The scan shows you're fit as a fiddle."

I blinked at him. "What happened? I don't understand…"

"You were in an accident. Your old body didn't survive intact, but we were able to replicate your damaged mind and restore it into a new physique."

"Incredible. I feel great," I told him. "When can I… I mean, am I free to leave?"

"In a few more days. . . There is some neuro-finalization to complete now that you've been taken out of induced coma. Mostly hippocampus re-integration and amygdala testing. Once that's done, you may go home." He was quiet, only looking down once to make a notation. "As to expectations once you get back, you might be a little unsteady, and have sporadic memory leaks—even some false ones—for the next few months until the imaging is fully absorbed into your recovered Neuro-prom. The organic/holographic mind interface takes time to fully mesh. Other than that, I think you will mend physically in a few more weeks."

I considered all of this, still overwhelmed. "I feel like a new man."

"In a very real sense, that's exactly what you are. Many of your body parts were replaced. In fact, your syths are superior to the originals. Once you finish healing, I believe you'll be pleased with the final result."

"I owe you, doctor," was the best reply I could manage. "Is my wife here?"

He nodded. "Mrs. Airth is in the waiting room. I'll send for her." He turned to leave, pausing at the door. "Have a good, new life, Mr. Airth."

Settled comfortably in the back seat of the new slot car as it hummed smoothly along the Grid, I asked Edith how the kids had reacted to my accident.

"Let's not talk about the children now," she said, pursing her lips in the familiar pout that I found so erotic. "I've rented a wonderful lux-unit just for the two of us in the New Bahamas — a perfect place to celebrate our tenth anniversary."

"But that was weeks ago," I said.

"Then call it a post-celebration," she murmured, kissing me on the neck. Her lips were warm, and her right leg pressed firmly against mine. I was pleased when my new body responded instantly; Edith was a very passionate woman.

The ride back to our place proved to be a memorable one.

At home, Edith had the Wallbar produce two Vodka Martinis. "Here's to your homecoming, darling!" she said, raising her glass.

The drink was strong, and I felt slightly dizzy. Noticing my flushed appearance, she looked concerned.

"Did the doctor say it was all right for you to drink?"

"Oh, sure," I declared. "No problem. Let's have another."

"No *way*. You need to take it easy after all this trauma. He told me about the memory leaks, the mental re-integration."

I protested, telling her I was fine, but she insisted. Changing the subject, I asked: "Where are the kids?"

"I left them with my sister. They do love their Aunt Laura."

My new mind blanked on the name. "I want to talk to them. Let's call over there."

Edith shook her head as she took a sip of her drink. "You know how eccentric she is. Remember how much she hates vidcalls? She never answers. But don't worry, she's good with the kids."

I regarded her a moment, confused. "Okay, but I miss them. At least we can call and leave a message. Let them know I'm going to be fine."

"I told them you were away on a business trip. I didn't want them to know about your accident until we were sure you were going to be all right. They'll be okay until we get back."

"Back? From where?"

She smiled. "I've rented a wonderful lux-unit in the New Bahamas, remember? Nassau—just for the two of us. You'll love it!"

She was right. I *did* love it in Nassau. It was like a second honeymoon. But I missed Jan and Bobby; something seemed wrong. The night of our return home, I found 'Aunt Laura's' number in Edith's cell and called her as she prepared dinner.

"What are you talking about? I haven't seen those kids in ages. *Aren't they with you?*"

"I need to talk to Edith," and I broke the connection.

I confronted my wife, my face tight. "*Where* are Jan and Bobby?"

She looked at me, surprised at my intensity. "Promise not to be upset if I tell you?"

I stared at her. "Go on."

"The children are in a better place." She took my hand in hers. "This world is *not* for children."

I glared at her. My head was pounding. "My *God*, woman! What have you done with our children?" My fists were balled.

"I… dispatched them. It was quick. . . painless. . . "

I couldn't form words; my throat was locked. Finally: "*You killed our children?*" I was shaking.

"I removed them from a violent, hostile world. They're. . . at peace now. Their bodies are resting in the backyard."

A wave of red rage swept over me and I lost all control, lunging toward her. Fastening my fingers around her throat, I squeezed as hard as I could. She tried to scream, twisting frantically to free herself as my thumbs sank deep into her neck.

It wasn't long before she stopped moving.

". . .and that's why I'm here. . . to confess to the murder of my wife."

The officer behind the high desk blinked at me, dark eyes wide. "Look, mister, I'm only a sergeant. Let me get Lieutenant Forbes."

"Fine," I told him. "I'll wait."

Lieutenant Forbes, serious, thin-faced, and balding appeared in due course. "What's the problem?"

"This guy," the officer said, pointing at me; the cadence of his voice was tense. "Says he offed his old lady. Come in to confess."

"I'm guilty," I told the Lieutenant. "You can put me in cuffs." I extended my wrists.

He waved dismissively. "We don't handcuff people until we have a reason."

"Well, I'm a murderer. Isn't that reason enough?"

"Where's your wife now?"

"She's dead, back at our home-unit. She said the children are buried in the backyard."

The officer put his hand up. "I'll have to check all this out Mister. . ."

". . .Airth. Terence Eugene Airth."

"Just sit down, Mr. Airth, 'til I get a full report."

I took a chair by the window and waited.

They found Edith just as I said they would: My confession was confirmed as completely accurate. They dug up two small bodies in the backyard as well, and DNA samples confirmed that it was Bobby and Jan. The investigation about what had happened to our children would require more time to research.

I was placed into a holding cell.

Two days later, Forbes unlocked my cell door. "You're free to go, Mr. Airth. We have no reason to hold you. Apologies for the delay, but we had to be sure that you hadn't killed the children, and the only way was a complete Neural Recovery of your wife's mind data."

"But. . . what I did to Edith. . ."

"No." The officer shook his head. "You're not guilty of a crime."

"But. . . that's *crazy!*"

"It's very simple, Mr. Airth. The investigation revealed that your wife had undergone a change, a major transformation." He paused. "Look, we checked—it happened while you were in the induced coma."

"*What* happened?" I blinked at him. "What are you talking about?"

"Your wife was a *machine* Mr. Airth; there is no law against the shutdown, however violent, of a machine."

My voice wavered. "Edith was. . ."

"A Simuloid Mark 6. What we pieced together was that after your accident, your wife suffered a massive stroke at the news; they used the Simuloid Procedure to offset the stroke, which had completely paralyzed her and put her into a vegetative state."

My mind was reeling. "But why didn't they opt to give her the Neuro-prom reconfiguration like I had?"

Forbes shook his head. "No way to do it. The stroke had destroyed her brain. She wasn't a candidate for that. The murder of your children was a software failure after her Mindmap was degraded by the data cloning procedure."

"But she was so real, so lifelike." I ran my hand through my hair. "So. . . when I. . . did what I did to her. . . it was a machine killing. . . a *machine?*"

The lieutenant smiled. "The Mark 6 is an excellent product, but it's not perfect. It's still a replicant." Forbes rubbed his face, sensing my confusion. "See, you're not a machine, Mr. Airth. Even though your body parts were largely replaced, because your mind was simulated *perfectly* from your healthy brain to the Neuro-prom, you maintained your. . . *humanity*.

"On the other hand, your wife's body *and* brain were totally robotic; since her Mindbuild was incomplete and damaged by the stroke, the doctors were forced into manual reconstruction Safe Mode from her Historychip backup. Unfortunately, the backup had bad sectors that were missed in the cluster verification process. . . In other words, her NeuralOS was corrupted, which is why she malfunctioned with the children. . . I'm sorry for your loss."

<END CONFESSION #TEA3170B-X3075 TRANSCRIPTION:

Compiling.....................

!complete!

Checksum..........................

</gmd:linkage>

</gmd:CI OnlineResource>

</geop:mappingFile>

<geop:processingApplication>

<geop:PH_EnvironmentObject>

<geop:documentation>

<gmd:CI_OnlineResource>

<gco:CharacterString>GeoServer WFS</gco:CharacterString>

</geop:name>

<geop:purpose><gco:CharacterString>produce representation of observation datasets in Modelling Language - a GHL-based application schema</gco:CharacterString></gmd:purpose>

<geop:type><gco:CharacterString>Software</gco:CharacterString></geop:type>

<geop:version><gco:CharacterString>Complex

Encryption Complete.

CLOSE #TEA3170B-X3075 DOCUMENT UPLINK]

Jobs and Industries

Toca la Guitarra

by Wayne Helge

Rhino Esperza, house guitarist for The Albino Monkey, received three requests for a Thompson Tucker song before he lost his shit. All three requests came from a sauced young couple at a table up front. Rhino rejected the first quietly, and ignored the second. But after the third, he responded using the house mic.

"Tucker's playing *The Black Jack Heart Attack* tomorrow," he said while lowering his guitar in insult. He sipped his water, knowing that he was about to offend ninety percent of his audience but unable to stop. "If you want to hear shitty robot music, Tucker's your man. Not me."

With that, the Albino Monkey's energy dropped from the peak it'd reached during the sing-along chorus of "Sweet Caroline," and Rhino knew it was gone for good. Scattered tables began to clear. He played to those who remained. "What about U2? I know 'The Joshua Tree,' forward and backwards. Best album of the 1980s."

"How about Zevon?" said a guy standing back near the bar.

"I only know one," Rhino said, rolling his eyes.

"Tucker could play them all," announced the woman from the table up front. Rhino let it go.

Minutes later, as the remaining crowd howled along with ripe beer breath over the repeating D-C-G chord progression, Rhino couldn't help but wonder whether Tucker's bio-mech arms ever complained about playing a song for what seemed like the thousandth time.

Rhino had the next night off. After a small dinner alone, he practiced the solo from Pearl Jam's "Alive." There was a finger-slide in it that he wasn't hitting. Each time, his ring finger either got stuck or flew past the fret. Usually he didn't mind practicing and would keep at it, but tonight something else was on his mind.

Thompson Tucker, he thought. Rhino usually described Tucker as a player piano, and he wasn't far off. Tucker's bio-mech arms could download anything, play anything, recreate any style. Chords that exceeded the finger-stretching abilities of mortal players were within his grasp. Bio-mech arms never missed a note. But for Rhino's money, they had the emotional depth of a wet spot on the sheets.

And yet, despite Rhino's arguments for analog performances, the growing robo-player movement had continued unabated. Rhino feared the logical conclusion. Once the musicians replaced the business ends of their bodies with robotic parts, what was to stop club owners from dropping live performance all together?

On his next run through the "Alive" solo, Rhino missed the slide again. Frustrated, he stood and dropped his guitar onto its stand. It was nearly nine o'clock. Tucker was probably on stage at Black Jack's already. And Rhino needed a drink.

Minutes later, he had his coat on and was out his front door.

Thompson Tucker kicked serious ass.

He performed from a stool on the otherwise-empty stage. His wardrobe included a pair of faded blue jeans and a solid grey, long-sleeved t-shirt. Rather than hiding his bio-mech arms, Tucker displayed them like a trophy. His sleeves were rolled up onto mechanical forearms, from which flexible hands and long, dexterous fingers extended. When he wasn't playing guitar, his fingers moved, stretching and waving like the legs of a tarantula taking its next step.

And unlike Rhino, Tucker touched on all sorts of styles. One minute he was nailing Lindsey Buckingham's finger-picking through "Never Going Back Again;" the next he was mimicking Clapton's electric version of "Layla." Rhino closed his eyes, listening for a missed note, truncated phrasing, any sign that Tucker was not perfectly recreating the original music.

He couldn't even find one.

After the show, Rhino sat at the end of the bar, nursing his second beer. When Thompson came off the stage to a standing ovation, guitar case in hand, Rhino motioned him over. Thompson tucked the guitar case between the bar and the foot rail, and ordered a double scotch, neat. When the drink came and the bartender asked for the money, Thompson nodded toward Rhino. "I think it's on him, Dave."

"Yeah, I got this one," Rhino said, digging into his pocket for the cash. Dropping three bills on the bar, he said, “Keep the extra."

"Cheers," Thompson said, holding up the glass in his mechanical arm. "To the living arts."

Rhino hoisted his beer bottle into the air and clinked with Thompson. They both drank, Rhino barely wetting his lips, but Thompson tossed back a healthy mouthful. "You good for one more?" he asked.

Rhino shrugged. "Drink up."

Thompson drained another mouthful and popped the glass onto the bar. Rhino could hear the servos of Thompson's fingers whir as his hand released the glass.

"You like the music?" Thompson said.

"Is that what that was?" Rhino said. "Sounded like a copy-paste job to me."

"So you're one of those people," Thompson said. He finished the rest of his drink and called Dave back over. "One more. This one for the road."

"Ok with you?" Dave said to Rhino, who nodded.

Thompson looked over the bottles behind the bar, seemingly done with this conversation. Rhino turned to face him.

"I'm Rhino Esperza. I play the Albino Monkey, four nights a week, three hours a night. One hundred percent natural. And I don't like what you're doing."

Thompson's drink arrived and he sipped it. "Let's see your calluses, brother."

Rhino presented his hands. Even in the dim light of the bar, thick layers of white skin could be seen covering the fingertips of his left hand. On his right, the picking fingers had long nails like vampire claws. Only the pinky was neatly trimmed.

"Your fingers are too stubby to drive a good walking blues," Thompson said, "but I'd kill for calluses again. You should've seen my natural fingers. I could stretch this pinky nearly five frets from the barre." At this, he held up his left hand and stretched his mechanical pinky out from the index finger. Just when it seemed to bend as far as it would go, the tip extended, lengthening the digit.

"You want to hear about these?" Thompson said, turning his hands over. He pulled up each sleeve beyond the elbow, exposing the joints where metal fastened to flesh. "Your camp thinks there's no skill in what I'm doing. But you'll follow suit, just wait. It's a matter of survival in our business."

"Bullshit."

Thompson downed the rest of his second drink and ran the edge of one hand across the other bicep. "What they do is slice the skin, down near the elbow, and then roll it up like a condom in reverse, toward the shoulder. Then they drill small holes in the bone for the bio-rivets, which expand so they won't twist when you move. Did you know the rivets create micro-cracks in the bone? These cracks need to heal and fuse together with scar tissue to secure the rivets."

"So it hurts," said Rhino.

"Intensely," said Thompson. "For a while."

"Sometimes art hurts," Rhino said.

"Yeah. But what's worse is the itching. I can still feel restless joints and fingers that need to be cracked. It drives me nuts. God, what I wouldn't give to be able to stretch out my arms."

Thompson did so right there in the bar, but then shook his head.

"Just not the same. It's the ultimate in unscratchable itches." He picked up the new drink, which Dave had delivered during the story, and sipped again. Thompson's face now looked like an old washed-out photograph.

"Don't get the wrong impression," Thompson said. "You don't stay in the game as a guitarist unless you go through the surgery. And after that, you don't stay in if you can get out."

Rhino shrugged. "So get out. Another set of robotic arms can step up and do the same job. You won't be missed."

Thompson swished the scotch and swallowed. "There's another piece to that puzzle. Maybe you can help. How about a wager?"

Thompson lifted the guitar case onto his barstool and opened it. Inside sat his Taylor 900-series guitar, with the body cut out so his left hand could reach the higher frets. "It has the pick-up installed on the underside of the bridge. Plug goes into the strap knob. No exposed electronics. This guitar probably costs more than you make in a month at the Monk club."

"Monkey," Rhino said, not acknowledging that Thompson's guitar might actually cost more than he made in six months. "The Albino Monkey."

"Whatever," Thompson said, his attention focused on the guitar. "So I'm putting my guitar on the table. These are not small stakes for a guy like you, a player who could increase his take if he just added a few more styles and arrangements. You need more and you know it. But you don't have the time or the talent to do it on your own. Not an old dog like you."

Rhino just sat, staring at the Taylor guitar. "What do you want from me?"

"Your arms," Thompson said.

Rhino looked up, his eyes narrowing.

Thompson said, "A swap, an arm for an arm. Or in our case, a pair for a pair. I think your toned forearms would look very nice sticking out of my shirts. And I could finally scratch that itch."

"What's the bet?" Rhino said.

"A contest," Thompson said. "We have a whole bar full of aficionados, ready to lend an ear." The guitar was out of the case, the strap around his neck now. "A song each, the crowd votes through applause, winner to be determined by Dave. Pick any song. I'll do the same."

Rhino cracked his fingers and thought about the alcohol. He'd had fewer than two drinks. His usual intake during a nightly gig at the Monkey was at least three. Tucker already drank two doubles and was working on a fifth. The question, Rhino wondered, was how the booze affected Tucker's playing. Sadly, he suspected it had no affect on the arms. The only question: who was better?

Rhino was fifty-fifty on the whole idea, and then he looked at the guitar again. Music had been his life, yet the best guitar he had been able to afford was his Jumbo 1970s Japanese-model Epiphone, with the big body and big sound. It was good, and did its job at the Monkey just fine, yet it was little better than a student's model. More importantly, to Rhino, this was a chance to put the whole debate to rest.

Not realizing that Rhino's mind was nearly made up, Thompson made the hard sell. "You win, you get my guitar. You lose, you get my bio-mech arms. So in a way, you win regardless."

Rhino slapped the bar. "Let's do it."

Thompson led the way onto the stage, with Rhino following a good distance behind. As Thompson tapped at the microphone, the crowd quieted, then applauded at what appeared to be a delayed encore.

Plugging in, Thompson explained that both he and Rhino would be performing one song, with the audience to decide the victor.

Thompson turned to Rhino, standing just outside the spotlight's range. "What's your song?"

Rhino stepped forward to the microphone and didn't hesitate. He had known back at the bar what he would play. "U2, 'With or Without You.' An arrangement of my own." What he didn't say was that he had stolen the arrangement from a virtuoso who had popularized it earlier in the century. It was a tough piece, powerful.

Thompson nodded but retained the guitar. A smirk crept in, and Rhino realized what Thompson planned to do.

"Really amazing. That's exactly what I was thinking," said Thompson. "Beautiful song."

Thompson retuned the guitar to open G. After checking the sound by picking each string in turn, he thumbed the low D string over and over, to set the bass line. And then he was off.

Rhino closed his eyes and listened. Of course, Thompson played the same arrangement that Rhino had intended to play. Better,

Thompson played it exactly as it sounded on the video Rhino had seen of the virtuoso. There were no notes missed, not even a fret buzz from a finger slightly out of position. Simply put, Thompson played it the way it might have sounded had Rhino played it a hundred times, and then spliced only the best parts together into a single performance. And Rhino knew that that was beyond his abilities, tonight or any other night. It was perfection. It was impossible.

As the chorus returned for the second time, Rhino thought of the lyrics, of how he too would be giving a part of himself away.

And then Thompson finished the song. Strings hummed harmoniously for just an instant before he deadened them. Then the sound of applause, of cheering, of whistling and yelping and howling hit the stage like a wave, forcing Rhino to catch his breath.

Amidst it all, Thompson removed the guitar from around his neck and beckoned Rhino forward. He shouted into Rhino's ear as he handed off the instrument, but had to shout again to be heard over the noise. "It should still be in tune."

Donning the instrument, Rhino plucked each string, hearing them each ring true, and waited for the noise to die down. If this was going to be his last performance with these arms, it would be done right.

"Freebird!" somebody yelled from the back, and a few people laughed. But then Thompson held up his hands for quiet, and his subjects abided.

To get ready, Rhino ran his fingers up and over the fretboard, playing scales and then arpeggios. The notes sounded clean, his finger-picking precise.

"Boring," Thompson said from the edge of the stage. Unlike Rhino, he remained inside the spotlight to see this through.

Rhino's deep exhalation was picked up by the mic, sending a rustle into the crowd. Then he inhaled and began.

As with Thompson, Rhino thumbed out the bass line first. If he couldn't keep proper rhythm, he had no chance at defeating Thompson.

But it wasn't rhythm that caused the first gaffe. There was a flourish that had to be done up near the seventh fret, halfway through the first verse, and Rhino went for it. But just like at home, with the "Alive" solo, his ring-finger didn't stick the fret. He adjusted quickly, but not before a missed note and a buzz sounded out over the crowd. And then, while he was wondering whether they had heard it, he missed the stick when he slid his hand back down toward the frets near the neck. Shit.

Right then, barely into the first chorus, he knew it was over. He could stop right now. And after that mess, why keep going? Why not simply admit that at his level of playing the bio-mech arms were, indeed, the best choice? Why not simply admit that he had been wrong all along?

And yet, he didn't stop. The second verse came out solid, if functionally uninspired, and Rhino began to wonder whether he could finish solidly. At least he could lose with some pride remaining.

But then the second chorus gave him hell. One missed note. Another note held too long. His thumb hit three uneven notes in the bass line, sending his rhythm to shit. And when he sped back up, he got going too fast. Now the song was cooking like a jazz trio's hi-hat.

Or a rock song.

Still knocking out the bass line, Rhino walked over to Thompson and yelled for a pick. Thompson handed one over, clearly unsure of what Rhino had in mind.

Hadn't Rhino said it would be an arrangement of his own?

What Rhino had in mind was the end solo of "Alive," the most mind-fucking bad-assery he could muster. And it was fresh enough in his head that he could adjust for the retuning on the fly. Sure, he'd miss notes. Lots of them, maybe. But if he could get the crowd caught up in the emotion of it, he had this wrapped up.

Rhino timed his bass line strum to the right speed. He let the crowd know what was coming with a "yeah! yeah! yeah!" into the mic.

And then he burned that motherfucker down.

When the song ended, he didn't know if he'd won. Frankly, he didn't care.

Three months later, Rhino sat on stage in The Albino Monkey, accepting requests. A voice called out, "Zevon!"

"It's becoming a nightly feature," Rhino said, rolling his eyes and earning a laugh from the crowd. The three-chord structure rang out from his 1970s Epiphone, which sounded as good as it ever had. The Taylor had been a beauty, but Rhino had sold it for just enough to cover the cost of his two new toys.

Confident that the song would be well-taken care of, Rhino closed his eyes, opened his ears, and went on autopilot.

The Bathory Clinic Deal

by Jennifer Brozek

For once, it wasn't scalding hot out. The sun shone down on the cement steps but the cool breeze kept Jackie and Lara from the usual afternoon roast. They watched the people walk by in their bubble of a busy day, cocooned by personal technology feeding them music, news, political reports, and business dealings. Jackie sighed and wished he could afford the most basic education modules so he and Lara could learn online instead of going to the ever underfunded, perennially out-of-touch, state provided school.

"I'm hungry." Lara's voice was small and sad.

Jackie saw that Lara wasn't watching the people passing by. She was watching what they were holding—all of the packages of fast food and cups of fancy coffee. He checked his ever-present, beat up backpack for his water bottle and saw it was mostly full. After taking a swallow, he offered it to Lara. "Here, drink this. The whole thing at once. It'll make you feel full. I can get more at Home."

When he said the word "Home" they both knew they weren't talking about a real home. It was the state run dormitory where they could sleep in relative safety—which meant his little sister slept with him because of the predators among the other kids—and they could get one actual meal a day. It wasn't tasty, despite Cook's attempts otherwise, but it was filling and they both ate as much as they could in that one sitting.

Lara did as she was told, gulping the tepid water down.

"Think of apple juice." Jackie's voice was soft. He watched her close her eyes as she took another swallow, slower this time. "Sweet and tart."

"I can almost…"

"Shhh. Don't talk. Just think of apple juice and drink."

This time Lara did. She sighed with regret as she finished the bottle. "That was good."

Jackie took the bottle back and stuck it in his backpack. For a while the two of them sat in silence. There wasn't much to do and loitering at Home wasn't encouraged. It only led to extra unpaid chores.

"I wish…" Lara stopped. She shook her head, sighed, and slumped back down again.

Jackie grimaced. He hated that his sister was turning out just like him. He knew she was going to say something like, "I wish we had a library connection" or "I wish we could go to the park" but those things, like everything else they wished for, either cost money, was limited in hours, or was reserved for people with private citizen connections. Stuff they didn't have and couldn't afford.

He glanced over at her, didn't like the droop of her mouth or the glassiness of her eyes and decided. "Hey, c'mon. I've got something to tell you."

The return of her bright eyes and curious tilt of her head filled him with love. The two of them began their "we've got to talk" saunter around the block, dodging shoppers, workers, and joggers. Out of habit—a bad one—Jackie's eyes picked out the most expensive things on the people they passed: feathered eyelashes, fiber optic mood hair, a woman with cat's eyes, an older man in a leather jacket with badly done implanted goggles, implanted jewels—not that you could tell if they were real, fake, or implanted citizen connections. One man was waving his Smartie around like a baton.

What Jackie wouldn't give for an all-in-one smart device like that or smart glasses. He'd never have to worry about a connection again. But that kind of thought wasn't getting him anywhere. Neither was the sudden urge to steal the damn thing. Besides, they might soon be able to afford such things, the low end versions, for themselves. He turned his focus to Lara with an effort. She was watching him, waiting for him to speak.

"I wasn't going to tell you..." He stopped at the clouds brewing on her forehead. "Don't look at me like that. We agreed; some things I need to do on my own to help us."

Lara made a brave effort to smooth her face into neutral. "But you're going to tell me now?"

"Yes. I am." Jackie paused, unsure of how to say this. They turned the corner away from the downtown district towards Home. "I. Hmm." He shrugged. "I've been accepted to the Bathory Clinic."

Lara stopped walking and stared at him. Her mouth worked as dozens of questions crowded in her mind. All that came out was, "How?"

Trying to play it off like it was no big deal, Jackie shrugged again. "I went in, got tested, got approved." What he didn't say was that he skipped school to take a two hour extremely personal questionnaire, had one hell of a physical that included a genetic scan, and then had his blood drawn."

"But… Sue?"

His pretend girlfriend from last year. "A lie. To protect her from you-know-who."

Lara frowned, looking far-too-adult. "But… you're only fifteen!"

"And you're ten. What of it?"

"The law…"

"Was changed. They dropped the consent age for cosmetic procedures to fifteen back in February."

Lara's voice dropped into a tone reserved for conspiracies. "But… the *Bathory Clinic*."

And there was the rub. He had no snappy answer for her. Instead he looked away. "They pay well."

The Bathory Clinic was the pinnacle of plastic surgery, if you could call it that. It gave the old their youth back. No one really knew how it worked but everyone knew it was stupidly expensive to get the procedure… and it required the blood of teenagers who met a stringent criteria that included that they be between the ages of fifteen and eighteen and be a virgin. Other than that, the rest was just scuttlebutt on the street.

Of course, no one wanted to admit to being a Bathory Clinic client. The rich wanted to pretend they really were young. And no teenager wanted to admit to being a virgin. At least, not any of the guys he knew. As for the girls, well, it was dangerous to admit either in the dorms. Too many wanted to take something from someone that they could never get back.

"How well?"

Lara's question pulled him back to the here and now. "I don't know yet. I'll know when I go in for my final… everything," he waved his hands to encompass all that he did and did not know, "…on Monday."

"Monday."

"Yeah."

"Wow."

"Yeah."

Lara thought about all this for a long time. Long enough that they were about to take the second turn when she finally asked, "Will you be okay?"

He squeezed her to him in a brief side-hug. "Yeah. I think so. I hope so." When she was quiet again for a long time, Jackie stopped them and turned her to him. "What's up?"

"What's going to happen to me?"

"Nothing we don't want. I won't leave you behind."

Again her brow furrowed. "What if I said I didn't want you to do it?"

"I guess I'd have to ask why not."

"Then I'd have to say that, one time when I was talking with Tanya, we talked about this and Tanya knew a guy who did it and…

she said the Bathory Clinic stole his life."

Jackie sighed. This was one of the more popular rumors on the street. "Then I'd have to say that that was probably just something Tanya heard from people who just wanted to talk."

"But, it was her cousin. They said he looked like a drug addict for months after each treatment, all skinny and yucky and stuff." Lara looked at the ground, her voice soft. "I'm scared for you."

He lifted her face to his. "It's going to be okay. If it was really dangerous, it wouldn't be legal and they wouldn't let kids do it." When she looked unconvinced, he smiled with a lie. "And if it's bad, I won't do it again."

But Jackie knew that even if it was bad, he'd stay with it. Especially with the amount of money he'd heard the clinic paid. It would be enough to get him and Lara out of Home and into their own *real* home. With private bedrooms and everything. Besides, he was no stranger to pain.

He stood and the two of them started walking again. They walked in silence, enjoying each other's company. Also, Jackie knew that Lara needed time to think and make a decision.

They passed a guy in the process of Elfinization. He had the pointed ears and the impossibly platinum hair but his head was bandaged in that way that said he'd just recently undergone the surgical reconstruction to thin and elongate his face. Jackie wondered why the man would be out in public like that. Then he realized that, no matter what kind of mods you had done to you, life went on and a mod like Elfinization wasn't cheap. Most likely, the guy had a job to go to.

"Okay," Lara announced. "You can do it. But if it's bad, you stop after the first treatment."

Jackie smiled and nodded. "Thanks."

* * * *

The Bathory Clinic public waiting room was just like every other medical place Jackie had been in, only nicer. Everything seemed cleaner. The chairs were plush and soft like suede. The front desk receptionist looked calm and poised unlike the receptionist at the State run medical facility all the kids at Home had to see once a year. There were even digital papers around where you could read the news or the latest tabloid.

Jackie swiped through images of movie stars on the red carpet in ridiculous clothing and mods. He stopped at a picture of his favorite actress, !Skylar!. She was almost completely unmodded; just a couple of tasteful gems around her eyes, accenting them and making them seem wider but not weird. Not like anime mods. As he studied her face, her beautiful, unlined eyes, he realized that she had been his favorite actress for as long as he could remember and she hadn't changed at all.

A young man came into the clinic and Jackie gave him a double take as he went up to the receptionist. He was tall and too skinny with a mop of brown hair that was styled to fall over one eye. His clothing screamed money: designer jeans, two toned boots that were all the rage, a silk shirt, and smart glasses. Jackie had seen fake versions of all of these and what this kid was wearing weren't the fakes. The smart glasses were top of the line and embellished with gold. They were amazing. To the point that Jackie almost missed the conversation between him and the receptionist.

"I'm sorry, Chaz, you don't have a session, you're too old."

Chaz shook his head. "Sorry, darlin', I'm not. There's been a mix up in the records. I'm seventeen. It's right on my ID."

Jackie watched as the receptionist's polite smile tightened into a firm line of annoyance. He watched as her eyes flicked around the reception area to himself and another nervous looking girl.

"Mister Daly, not only are you eighteen but you failed your last physical. You are no longer a client of the Bathory Clinic." Her clipped tone could have scarred diamond. "It is time for you to leave before you are removed."

Chaz lowered his voice but Jackie still caught every pleading word. "Please. I gotta have my session. I need it. You don't even have to pay me. I'll do it for free."

It sounded like a junkie pleading for just one hit to get him through until he got the money to pay what he owed.

Jackie swallowed hard as two large uniformed men came in and grabbed Chaz by the arms. One spoke so quietly to the desperate kid that Jackie couldn't hear what was said. Whatever it was, Chaz calmed at once and nodded. "Yes. Shiny. Yes." The guards escorted Chaz to the back and that was that.

Again, it seemed like a junkie being promised that hit he needed but first he had to do something for the dealer.

Both the other girl and Jackie must have looked horrified. The receptionist smiled, "I apologize for that. Sometimes people get in over their heads."

This platitude didn't make Jackie feel any better and he almost ran when the receptionist beckoned for him to come to the back with her. "They're ready for you."

The back hallways of the Bathory Clinic were even more plush and comfortable than the front reception area. Everything was decorated in a motif of burgundy, black, and gold, accented in white. The first time Jackie came back here, while taking the tests to qualify, he was afraid to touch anything. He was still nervous about breaking the artwork but had come to understand that this lush scenery was designed for the people used to it—the real clients of the clinic.

This time, his first time as a prospective client, he was left in a private sitting room filled with comfortable furniture, refreshments, and entertainment. Before the receptionist left, she pointed out the restroom down the hallway and assured him it would not be much longer.

Jackie enjoyed a bit of the snacks, resisting the urge to sweep the whole plateful into his backpack to savor and share with Lara later. After pacing around the room, he poked his head out of the room and looked around. There was no one in the hallway. More out of curiosity than a need to go, Jackie headed towards the restroom.

He stopped when he heard voices coming out of a room between him and his goal.

"You promise, Mannie? You promise I'll have another session

soon? I can see wrinkles around my eyes."

The woman's voice sounded old and young at the same time. Much like what Jackie could remember of his grandmother asking for more soup. He peeked into the room and saw a beautiful woman in a flirty dress that fell to the tops of her knees. In sky high heels, she was taller than the older man she was with. Her wrists and fingers were covered in classic gold jewelry that twinkled as she stroked Mannie's graying hair. Jackie could see thin lines in them indicating they were computer enhanced.

"Your laugh lines are lovely, Joy, but yes, I promise. It's just my turn now."

Mannie, his voice patient, turned enough for Jackie to see what looked to be a man in his late forties, maybe. You could never be sure once you knew someone was a Bathory Clinic client. He could be forty-eight. He could be one hundred and forty-eight. Right now, he had the soft look of a man who sat too much, ate too well, and indulged when the mood took him.

Jackie let out the breath he had not known he'd been holding. Mannie and Joy turned to look at him. Jackie froze, unsure of what to do. Mannie's soft face, the one that loved the woman he was with, turned hard and assessing as he looked Jackie up and down. Suddenly, Jackie knew he was not in the presence of a soft man.

"Is that him?" Joy's voice was awed and barely above a whisper.

Mannie raised a hand to quiet her as he continued to pin Jackie with his unflinching gaze. "Your name?"

"Jackie…"

"Is there a problem?" The voice came from behind Jackie, startling him.

As he whirled around to come face to face with one of the no-name, no-ID security guards who had escorted Chaz into the back hallways, Mannie spoke, his voice unconcerned. "This young man was just asking where the bathroom was."

Jackie nodded, his heart pounding so hard in his chest he thought he'd break a rib.

The guard looked between Jackie and Mannie for a moment. "This way," he said to Jackie. "Sir," he said to Mannie with a deferential nod.

Escorted to the restroom, Jackie found that he did have a sudden need to use the facilities and was thankful that everything seemed to be in the right place and worked in a standard way. Of course, the quality of the sink, the toilet, the towels, even the tiled floor, was so far beyond what he was used to—marble, granite, some stuff he couldn't identify—that if he had put too much thought into it, he wouldn't have been able go. Not to mention it was the all time cleanest bathroom he'd ever used.

Jackie was not surprised to see the guard waiting for him when he was done. Without a word, the large man, not much more than a blur of "big" and "uniformed," escorted Jackie back to his waiting room. The guard left with a nod and was immediately replaced with a familiar face: Technician Costa.

Technician Costa was a hard faced woman with kind gray eyes. The severe bun she wore her hair in did nothing to soften the sharp lines of her patrician nose and thin lips. Jackie liked her anyway. He liked the way she treated him like an adult.

"Sorry about the wait, Jack." She handed him a slim tablet and sat on one of the plush chairs. "There was a bit of a ruckus."

"Chaz?"

Jackie saw Technician Costa's mouth press into that same line of annoyance he saw on the receptionist's face and wondered if that was something that was trained into Bathory Clinic personnel.

"Yes, Chaz. I hope that little scene didn't dissuade you from becoming one of our clients. Erity said you looked unsettled."

"Erity?" Jackie flushed, not knowing who she was talking about.

"Erity Parker, the receptionist."

He nodded. It was good to finally have a name for her. "Um, I was wondering. He said… Chaz… he said he wanted a session enough that the clinic wouldn't have to pay him for it."

"Oh. Oh, that." Technician Costa looked relieved. "Some of our clients find the sessions pleasurable. Most can handle it. A rare few… well… the Bathory Clinic will take care of him. We'll send him for counseling."

Her hushed voice shifted into something more professional and clipped. "But we're here to talk about you. This is the final consent form. I'm required to ask you each question in specific and you must answer each one completely. If you have any questions, we are to discuss each in full until you understand your rights and responsibilities. As before, this interview is being monitored and recorded. Shall we begin?"

Jackie, glancing over the digicontract on the table, nodded. "Yes."

Technician Costa leaned back in her chair and began. “What is your full name?”

“Jack Edward Sullivan.”

Tap. Checkbox marked.

“Are you here at the Bathory Clinic of your own free will?”

Jackie remembered the day he and Lara were dropped off at Home by parents beaten down by a system designed to do just that. He had been ten. Lara five. His father had said, “I’m sorry.” His mother had said, “Be good and protect your sister.” Home had taken them in, fed them, clothed them, and sheltered them to the Federally mandated standards required and nothing more. There was no love, no care, no real desire to help. It was a just a necessary job. If that was not coercion, forcing him to fend for himself and his sister, he didn’t know what was.

Even as the thought raced through his head, Jackie nodded. “Yes.”

Tap. Checkbox marked.

“You will be paid the sum of $20,000 dollars for this first session and every session afterwards. This money may be paid out in $5000 increments for the month of the session and the three off months afterwards or it may be paid out in a single lump sum. Choose one: monthly increments or a single payment at the time of your session.”

Jackie did not speak. He could not wrap his mind around the concept of having that much money. It made him want to leap for joy and flee in terror. So many thoughts crowded in his head.

When Jackie did not answer, Technician Costa leaned forward. “Jack, may I make a suggestion?”

"Yes, Technician Costa."

"Call me Giada."

"Giada." Jackie's brain was numb.

"I'm going to suggest that you take the monthly increments. Most teenagers have parents they can turn to. We know that you're a ward of the State. This makes things more complicated because Home is not going to want to let you or Lara go. They'll lose funding for the two of you. It's a numbers game. If you take the monthly increments, you can manage your lives on a more reasonable level."

Giada tilted her head, looking at him. "Unofficially, since it's not on any of the medical forms you've signed or are going to sign, I will tell you that the Bathory Clinic has a transition specialist for cases like you. You're young but just old enough to legally become your own person and take on the burden of caring for Lara. With the funds from the session, you'll have the means to do both. Our transitions person will help you set up a bank account and move you into one of the Bathory Clinic owned apartments nearby. You'll pay rent but, unlike other places, you won't need to pass the credit check. We know where your money is coming from.

"However, you'll *officially* be on your own and no longer a ward of the State. That's why I'm recommending the monthly increments."

Jackie nodded, his brain still stunned by the amount of money. For a brief instant, he thought about reuniting with his parents and letting them deal with it all. He pushed that thought away. He'd told Lara they were dead. His parents had abandoned them. They could stay dead. "Monthly increments, please."

Tap. Checkbox marked.

"Do you understand that you are required to refrain from all sex?"

"Yes."

Tap.

"Do you understand for a full thirty days leading up to your session you are to refrain from all drugs, including alcohol, unless prescribed by a Bathory Clinic physician, and must pass a Bathory Clinic physical the day before your session?"

Jackie nodded. He never did get into the drug and alcohol scene. Too easy to fall prey to someone who wanted power over you. "Yes."

Tap.

"Do you understand if you break the rules to this contract, or once you turn eighteen, that all Bathory Clinic benefits become null and void and you will no longer be a Bathory Clinic client?"

"Yes." He had seen the results of that already but this was his only chance to get himself and his sister out of Home. To give them a chance at a real future.

Tap.

Giada smiled. "Good. Please sign here."

Jackie used the tip of his finger to sign the contract and stared into the onboard camera until it winked at him, indicating his picture had been taken.

Giada stood up and Jackie followed suit. "So… now what?"

"Now, we get you ready for your first session."

"Okay."

She stopped him. "May I suggest that we have our transition

specialist, Alicia, go pick up Lara from school so they can gather all of your things from Home? We've picked out a nice two bedroom apartment for you guys."

Jackie stared at her and then realized that he wouldn't be in any condition to get Lara from school. All of the literature he'd read said that he'd be very weak for the couple of days following the session. If all this was to happen now, that needed to be done first. "Oh. Right. Can I record a message for her for your specialist, for Alicia, to play? Lara won't come otherwise."

Giada smiled, "Smart kid. Of course. And don't worry, we're going to take good care of you both. You're important to us."

Jackie nodded, wondering just how much the super rich paid to stay young… and how much he was going to wind up paying in the end.

* * * *

Jackie looked around the surgical center. There were computer stations surrounding a comfortable looking recliner chair. Everything was in muted beiges and whites. The only oddity was the fact that Giada's chair was on rails in the floor. Those rails circled the recliner.

"It doesn't look so… medical-ly."

"Medical-ly?" She did not look at him as she typed on the computer.

"You know. All of this?" He gestured to the room and the recliner.

Giada turned and smiled, "The less you see, the less you worry. We try to make the whole experience as pleasant as possible." She patted the recliner. "C'mon. In you go."

Jackie climbed into the chair and settled down. After a moment's stiffness, the recliner warmed and softened, conforming to Jackie's shape. It made him feel like he was floating.

"Good?" Giada tapped something on her tablet.

"Good."

"Okay, Jackie. The first thing we're going to do is immobilize your head…"

Panic welled. "Wait! Aren't you going to put me to sleep or numb me or anything?"

She tilted her head. "No. You're going to be awake. You won't really feel time passing and you won't be in pain. Believe me, no one has ever hated this experience. It's okay to be nervous but it's time to get this done."

Jackie knew she was telling him to get himself together and earn that $20,000. His mouth was too dry to speak. He nodded and tried to relax.

Giada resumed her practiced setup. "First, we're going to immobilize your head. This is vital to the process. It's going to tickle."

Something came out of the chair behind Jackie's head and cold lines of metal slid down the sides of his head and neck, molding itself to every curve and bump. It did tickle and threw a pleasant shiver down his spine.

"This is for the visual stimulation. You can keep your eyes open or closed."

A strip of metal about two inches high wrapped itself around his face at eye level. Jackie guessed it to be about an inch out from his nose. Right now, it was just a shimmery piece of metal. He could see Giada moving around him in a fluid motion and realized she must be riding the chair on rails.

"Keep your breathing relaxed. This is for audio stimulation."

As she spoke, part of the head of the chair cupped itself around his head; again, not touching. Jackie remembered something in the literature about the music being pumped directly into his ears.

"This is the VIT collar. It's going to be a touch cold at first."

VIT. Vitae Infusion and Transfer. The cold metal sliding around his throat made him tense up again. The panic welled even as he tried to keep control.

"Wiggle your toes."

Jackie obeyed, wiggling his toes as hard as he could. Distantly, he felt Giada's hand on his arm and something pressed to his mouth. Something. A straw?

"Here's some water. You okay?"

He drank, sucking down deep swallows of the ice cold water. The delicious sensation of cold traveled down his throat and chest to pool in his stomach. As the chill warmed, Jackie realized he was still wiggling his toes and stopped.

"Better?"

Jackie tried to nod and failed. "Yes. Thanks."

"No problem. Now, here's where the fun comes."

Feeling like his head was floating and his arms tingled, Jackie smiled, realizing Giada had pulled a fast one on him. The water had been drugged in some way. It was the only explanation for the sensation.

"Now, I want you to start counting out loud, backwards from ten to zero."

"Okay." He took a breath. "Ten… nine… eight…"

"Begin visual and auditory harmonization."

The metal band in front of his eyes began to glow and pulse with multiple colors as one of his favorite songs blossomed in the middle of his head.

"Seven… six… five…"

"Begin glandular stimulation."

Jackie felt the hair on the back of his neck rise and shivered again.

"Three… two..."

"Begin magnetic alteration of the subject's cerebral field."

Different emotions washed over him: fear, love, hate, desire, apathy, contentment, and a myriad of everything in-between. He clenched his fists in an effort to control what was happening and to relax into it, not sure if this was how it was supposed to be.

"One… zero…"

"Begin the VIT process."

There was momentary pain on both sides of his neck that exploded into the best wet dream Jackie had ever had. Falling into light, everything he once thought 'felt good' paled into comparison of this… whatever this was.

"And there you go. Enjoy."

Giada's words were a whisper of silk amidst the light, sound, and sensation of everything. For the next thirty seconds or three thousand hours, he couldn't be sure, Jackie was lost in the best waking dream he had never had. His heart raced, his muscles clenched, and he gasped for air. It was like the best runner's high mixed with the shock of his first orgasm. There was nothing but the light and the music and the tingle of pleasure all over his body.

* * * *

"Wake up, Jack. Wake up. Your session is done."

"Don't worry about that, Jack. All boys do that during their session."

"One leg at a time. Good. Now the other one."

"I'm Alicia."

"Just hold onto me. Slow steps."

"Let me have the bag. It's okay. Everyone's always woozy."

"Alicia, your transition specialist."

"Apartment 215. See? That's your apartment… okay, let's just get you inside."

"I've put your aftercare instructions on your smart glasses."

"No, you want to sleep now. Lara's fine."

"I'm Alicia. I'm going to be helping you."

"Just remember to put on your smart glasses and follow the instructions. All of them. Then call me when you're better."

* * * *

Waking was a combination of half confused memory and pain. Jackie refused to open his eyes until he sorted out some of what he remembered. The one thing he could fasten on was "smart glasses." Apparently, he had smart glasses now. Something he'd lusted after for ages.

Opening his eyes wasn't as bad as he thought it would be. Everything seemed dim and slightly out of focus. He blinked a couple of times and cleared his head. Looking around, wincing at the pain in his neck, he saw he was in a plain but comfortable room: bed, desk, entertainment system, computer, end table. Smart glasses on the end table.

Sitting up in a sudden motion because it was real, everything was real, Jackie gasped in pain as bolts of agony went shooting throughout his body. He felt like he'd run a marathon and then was beaten as a reward. Every single muscle hurt in that way that said "you overdid it in a bad way, man."

Trembling in the pain, Jackie sat there until he was able to think again. Then, with a slow, careful motion, he reached for the smart glasses. They were almost too heavy to pick up. Only his desire for the thing kept him from dropping the smart glasses before he could put them on.

A brunette woman's face popped up. "Hello, I'm Alicia Stanton. I'm your transition specialist. I hope you aren't feeling too bad. Though, I've been told by other clients that you should feel like you've been run over by a truck. In any case, welcome to your new home. I have Lara situated and I've hooked her up with an education module and a curriculum but we can go over that later. Right now, the most important thing is for you to take care of yourself."

She gestured to the right and a list popped up. "These are your aftercare instructions. They include mandatory supplements which, I'm told, taste awful but will make you feel better almost immediately. Since you are now awake, I've been notified and will schedule an appointment to see you tomorrow. Don't worry, I'll meet you in your apartment."

There was a blip and the calendar appointment popped up. That was when Jackie realized that he'd been non-functional for almost a day and a half. Fear for Lara surged and he stood, staggering. He grabbed the cane that had been left helpfully nearby.

Moving as fast as he could in the baby steps his body could manage, he left the bedroom and was struck by the most delicious scent. Jackie stood, stupefied, trying to identify it. Unable to, but swearing it smelled like bread, he stumbled down the hallway onto a scene he thought he could only dream of.

The hallway opened up on a single room broken out into several areas: the kitchen area with a bar separating it from dining area, and an entertainment area that was separated from the rest by a long, curving couch. Lara sat at the dining room table, working on something on her digipaper. From where he stood, Jackie thought it was a math problem. Lara had her "concentration face" on as she used her stylus to work the problem out.

Something in the kitchen binged. Lara looked up and smiled. She didn't even see him as she hurried into the kitchen to pull a loaf of bread out of the oven. An oven. A real one. Jackie saw that Lara felt safe and carefree for the first time in her life and he knew the pain he felt right now was worth it.

"Careful," he said when she touched the loaf and gasped at the pain.

Lara looked up and grinned. "Jackie!" She crashed into him for a tight hug. He couldn't stop his cry of pain and Lara pulled back, looking him over. She gave him the kind of once over only a ten year old can give. "You look awful. Are you okay?"

Not willing to take away her joy, he smiled and nodded. "Just sore. You've got to be careful with me for the next couple of days." Months, maybe, he did not say. He knew that the average recovery time was four to eight weeks. Sometimes as much as twelve. That was why sessions were allowed only three times a year, four months apart. "How you doing?"

"I've got an education module. Math and science. Real math, not that stupid baby math. And books. Real books, look!" She pointed to a shelf of real paper books. "And bread. I baked bread. Well, I took it out of the freezer and put it in the oven and baked it. But… we have food. Good food, and books, and I have my own bedroom!"

Jackie stared at the small shelf of real books, surprised beyond expectation. He had expected the basics: a nice, small place with a few things to make it comfortable. Instead, they had a palace, their own bedrooms, a real kitchen, and… paper books, a luxury that he had never even dreamed of.

While he was looking at their good fortune, his smart glasses binged, indicating he had a call. It was from Technician Costa. "Hello."

"Hello Jack. I've got some wonderful news. But first, how are you feeling?"

He glanced at Lara, who was puttering in the kitchen, getting out stuff for the bread. "Oh, you know. Sore."

"That's normal. Just make sure you take your supplements with food. It may be tiring but you have to do it."

"Yeah." He sat down at the dining room table and saw the digital paper with a news subscription. "What's this good news?"

"You're almost a perfect genetic match for one of our platinum level clients and their session with you went so well they'd like to sign you to an exclusive contract for a year."

He frowned, idly swiping through the news pages. "What's that mean?"

"Well, it means several things. You'll get paid $25,000 a session. You'll have four sessions a year. You need to abstain from all drugs and alcohol for the year. Also, you'll need to have monthly exams here at the Bathory Clinic."

"Four sessions. But…"

"Yes, I know. In the case of the VIP contract, you'll essentially be an employee of the clinic. We'll give you menus and keep you healthy."

"How much time do I have to think about this?" Jackie's eyes fell on an article in the paper and he zoomed in on it, reading the first paragraph. Then he zoomed in on the candid picture of the dead body.

"You need to give me a verbal contract on this call. Our platinum client is most eager. We'll get the necessary documents in a day or two."

Lara came over and plopped a plate with a piece of warm bread slathered in butter on the low table in front of him. She had her own large hunk of bread, bit into it messily, and grinned a butter smeared smile at him.

Too afraid to say no and lose what he saw in front of him, the decision was already made. "Yes. I'll do it."

"I'm so glad to hear that. We'll talk soon. Now, I've got some paperwork to set up and give Alicia when she comes to see you. Talk to you later."

"Yeah. Bye."

Lara pointed to the zoomed-in photo in the newspaper. "Who's this?"

"Just a guy I met once." Jackie swiped the picture of the dead body and article about the tragic drug overdose death of Chaz Daly out of view and promised himself, *he* would keep control. *He* would do better. But even as Jackie bit into that piece of heaven known as fresh baked bread, the taste of it was like ashes compared to the feeling of a Bathory Clinic session.

Zipperback

by K. H. Vaughan

The walls at *Les Écorchés Humaine* were white and red composite, marbled with pink and blue veins, and the fixtures cold surgical steel. Hard surfaces reflected the buzz and hum of the crowd, mostly models and fashion industry people with the requisite sprinkle of celebrities. There was skin everywhere in the trendiest styles. Jazz, young and beautiful, sliced his way through it all. He looked around, new eyes registering the work of the top designers in the business: *Agata Wie, Takakura, Agennix Verpflanzung, A. G.* He barely noticed the sensation as the lenses adjusted, zooming in and as he changed magnification, scanning for evidence of seams, rejection, and decay. Appraising and sending the data feed back to his eyes' owners in the Syndicate.

A thin Fraunhofer model with a designer skin secured over her own passed by him languidly and smiled. Old technology, the skin was nothing special, and was poorly fit at the waist. Not hardcore like the Katsura girls, original skins completely replaced with new models attached to a nanotech matrix embedded in the hypodermis. He scanned the crowd around her. All the perfect skins in shades from alabaster to mocha, everything lighter than a retro paper shopping bag. A gap in the spectrum from that light brown until you hit deep purple blacks and pure monochrome onyx marketed under names like *Soul of*

Abyssinia and *Zulu Chic*. He smiled back and stroked her arm with feigned admiration as she passed, so the samplers in his fingertips could capture the skin's DNA. Probably worthless. If the sequence was cutting edge she'd be up on a pedestal out of reach. This was off the rack.

Jazz came up through the Syndicate as a runner and spotter on the street. He was disposable and worked hard to change that, took years to work his way up to a cutting crew and actual money. Now he spent his nights cruising galleries and openings at the fringe of legitimacy when he wasn't running his crew. The Syndicate was giving him the chance to push higher, move off the street into real management, but he didn't get any slack in his other job. Hungry kids were coming up behind him, pushing from below. Just last week one made a play to muscle him out, but his lieutenants stayed loyal and put the kid on ice. When Jazz got to the chop shop they fixed a neural inhibitor on the base of his neck, ran a scope down his mouth and opened the carotid so it would pump right into his throat just above the larynx. They forced the rookie runners make bets on whether he'd bleed out or drown first.

His node rang and he activated it on audio mode only. The gallery went silent.

"Hey baby," the voice rang through his skull. Juan/ita. "How's the reception?"

"Typical fashion week. I don’t like the new lines. The *couture* is all animal prints and cubism. Who the fuck wants to look like a Picasso?"

"Did you see the Charon show?"

"Yeah. It keeps getting worse." House of Charon's new line of detachable epidermises was engineered to die and slough off with a controlled decay rate. It was perverse given how much it cost to keep them alive at all. They had models wearing skins with Stevens-Johnson Syndrome and Harlequin Ichthyosis on the runway. The designer hadn't been right since protesters burned her with acid. They'd repaired her face, replaced her eyes, but something inside had died.

"Worse? That's wonderful," Juan/ita purred. "I should warn you, I'll want cock later."

"Mine or someone else's?"

"I don't care as long as it's attached to you."

"Alright, pick one. What about you?"

"Do you have a preference?"

"Surprise me. Hey, that reminds me. I saw Dorcus Q."

"That one? Straight female to male convert. Made the change and called it quits. Pussy." Jazz could see Juan/ita's eyes rolling.

"It's what he wanted. You have to be who you are. That's the whole point."

"No. You don't," Juan/ita said. "*That's* the whole point."

"Alright. Hey, I got to go back to work. I love you."

"Of course," Juan/ita said and hung up.

Jazz's eyes settled briefly on a rep from Falkson 1889, a beautiful young black man with a corset in Scandinavian white skin laced up the back with scarlet ribbons. He picked a bite-sized roasted turkey from an appetizer tray floating past and bit down on the morsel, tiny bones crunching in his mouth.

*   *   *   *

Khatak closed the précis as the car pulled off the Parkway by the Brooklyn shoreline. The door opened in front of a small garage that was listed as unoccupied and under a tax lien with the city. It was in bad shape on the outside. Brown goo was leaking from the worn-out Chinese photovoltaic array on the roof, and the three-foot flood barrier on the doors appeared to be rusted open. Detective Brant from Homicide was waiting outside. Khatak checked his hair and makeup in the glass before he got out. It was one-way; she couldn't see him.

"Oh look: it's the fashion police," Brant said.

"Fuck you," Khatak said. "You want this case? I'll ride back to Manhattan right now."

"You saw the pictures. This is a Biologicals case and you know it."

Khatak nodded and slipped a fresh pair of crime scene booties over his shoes. "Yeah, you're right about that," he said.

"Come around back," Brant said. "CSU entry is through the loading dock."

*   *   *   *

The cement floor and white tile walls inside had been steam-cleaned, fumed, and blasted with UV before the cutting crew brought in the product. They left the waste stacked neatly in the corner, but the CSUs had already sorted them onto tarps. Six corpses dressed and drained, eyes and organs removed, and the skin taken intact.

"Well, you sure know how to get a boy's attention, don't you Brant?"

"I hate this shit," Brant said. "Harvesters."

"I don't care for it much myself."

"They left one set of kidneys and a liver."

"Then they've got high-end clients."

"Yeah?"

"They don't try to move poor quality product, not even for the export market." Organs for transplant used to be an import business, but decades of the third world trying to climb out of poverty had poisoned those sources. The food and water supplies were so filled with toxins and mutagens that everyone who could afford organs wanted either manufactured product or European and North American donors. A lot of people wouldn't touch a manufactured part for religious reasons. Even a shitty American liver could sell at a premium in Indonesia.

"Well," Brant said. "Enjoy your freak show. I'll confirm the hand-off and let the patrol coordinator know to route the canvas and any neighborhood incidents to you."

"Thanks. Don't let the door hit you where the Good Lord split you."

"Didn't know that was in the Quran."

Khatak gazed at the flayed corpses on the tarps. "I've got relatives in Bible country."

*   *   *   *

By the time Khatak left the scene, the techs had sequenced the bodies and identified them from the DNA registry. The kidneys were positive for Autosomal Dominant Polycystic Kidney Disease that somehow didn't get fixed in the womb. They found three sets of usable prints from the harvesters. Two were from identical Emiemi Pavan *prêt-à-porter* skins from last season, both in new condition. The biomechanical analysis suggested two different people wearing the same model. The third came back as a Kazakhstani rug dealer who went missing in Newark eighteen months ago. No body was ever found. Khatak looked at the file pictures as the car drove him back downtown. He'd been a good-looking kid and now someone was leaving his prints on a room like the one he died in.

*   *   *   *

Jazz woke late, Juan/ita tangled in the bedclothes beside him. He'd returned well past midnight and they'd played late into the morning. He cleaned up and drank tea, checked the info feed and his messages. He had a noon lunch meeting with a black market medical supplies dealer and then a Tyler Golden Surgical runway show before meeting with his Syndicate boss, Mako Blanc.

Jazz went to the closet to dress, selected a vagina from the rack and left the penis he finished with last night in the cleaning unit. He put on tight jeans, a designer t-shirt with prosthetic breasts built in, boots, and a unisex leather jacket. Mako seemed more at ease if you dressed casual and skewed female. The chop had gone well last night, so he should be in a good mood, but it was impossible to know. His node rang and he clicked his sensorium over. With a quick flip, the closet vanished and his lieutenant appeared on the virtual screen behind his eyes. Lin looked agitated, but then he usually did. He had an amphetamine pump installed in his side, giving him a permanent edge one drip at a time.

"Bad news, boss. Cops found last night's jobsite."

"How clean did we leave it?"

"Pretty, but all the trash wasn't taken out. Not sure what happened yet."

"Find out. The higher-ups know?"

"Probably. I mean, how could they not?"

"Yeah. I'll call it in. Better I call them than the other way. Find out who fucked up. We'll talk about this later."

Jazz hung up, flipped back to his closet. It was so late when they finished packing the new merchandise and he'd been on no sleep. The slow-acting stimulant mix was wearing off, leaving him jittery and stupid. He trusted Chow and Nico to finish the cleanup so he could go home to Juan/ita. Shouldn't have been a problem.

"Shit," he hissed aloud.

"You O.K., baby?" Juan/ita murmured sleepily from the bed. "Did you check your serotonin this morning?"

"Yeah, I'm good."

"Don't be out too late tonight, alright? Be careful, I love you."

"Me too."

*　　*　　*　　*

Khatak entered the Surveillance Monitoring and Utilization Department, identified himself and made a formal statement documenting the case he was investigating. Access was strictly controlled. The door wouldn't even unlock until he was verified, logged, and the investigation approved. Sometimes the desk sergeant out front would just shrug and advise you that you needed a warrant to even go inside. The sergeant was near retirement. Liked to talk while you waited.

"I don't know how you deal with all that biological shit. Stolen kidneys I get, but the fake skins and all of that post-gender stuff? It's too weird for me." Khatak could see the gears turning in the old man's head. Literally. There were cutouts in his temples filled with clockworks that responded to neural activity. Some days Khatak was surprised he could get them to move at all.

"I'm just saying, I go to the public bath and I don't even know what I'm looking at anymore," the sergeant continued. "Are they boys? Girls? Who knows? They're tying their boobs down, stuffing their pants and sticking hormone strips on the face to grow hair. The boys are walking around in bikini tops full of gel."

"You're wearing eye-makeup," Khatak said.

"A little shade and liner for definition," the sergeant protested. "It's right out of the training manual. Helps intimidate suspects."

"Right. I'm intimidated just looking at you. You hear about the new socket sets? Only been around about five years now."

"Socket sets?"

"Genital swapping. Your genitals get replaced with a socket and installed on a plug. As long as the models are compatible with someone else-"

"Wait a minute, wait a minute," he shook his head, gears spinning madly. "As long as the hookups are right, we could swap our junk and you could fuck me with my own dick? That's pretty messed up."

"I had this case last year, big society party. These people, they get zoned on Savage, Erosynthene, and Endorphine analogs and go nuts on each other. The next day they gotta figure out who's got who's crank, who went home with the wrong vagina in their pants. So this one morning they all woke up and someone has stolen all their units. Turned out to be a Prince in the Emirates. They caught him in the Riyadh airport with a suitcase full of other people's plug and plays. True story."

The sergeant was still laughing when the doors clicked and the system let Khatak inside.

* * * *

Khatak's A. I. Liaison Officer, Detective Johnson, was in her cube, bathed in the crisp light of monitors. They could talk informally for a while, but once the inquiry began it would all be on the record. Johnson would monitor and assist while Khatak talked to the Eye of

Providence, the police A.I. that would search for his perpetrators.

"So, here's my problem," Khatak said. "I've got six bodies in a chop shop in a dark zone. No surveillance, and the physical evidence is going nowhere so far. Uniforms are canvasing the neighborhood and people are going to try and give them stills and footage but that will all be firewalled from the investigation while it gets vetted for admissibility."

"Brooklyn?"

"Yeah."

Johnson shook her head. The citizens of Brooklyn voted to be a surveillance haven in the last election. No public drones or cameras controlled by the state except for selected high security sites. Private security cameras in non-public areas only. By the day of the vote, the predators had already researched every target, asset, alleyway, and route in and out of the Borough. When the cameras went dark, crime jumped 800% in twenty-four hours and leveled off around 100 times baseline. Vaginal counter-rape implant sales went through the roof. Vigilantes came crawling out of the woodwork patrolling the streets with their own cameras but unless they could prove the footage was incidental a defense attorney could get it tossed. Judges had already dismissed a dozen attempts to over-ride the referendum and turn the cameras back on.

"We tried to tell them this would happen," Johnson shrugged. "Serves the assholes right. Next election's two years away."

"In the meantime, if anyone saw anything I can only get verbal reports and so far there's nothing."

"So, how do you want to build an inquiry for the Eye?"

*　　*　　*　　*

Jazz tried to maintain her composure as she waited in Lucia Bartholomew's waiting room. Mako Blanc had brusquely ordered her to call back later when she tried to tell him about the police investigation. Could be nothing. Could be death. No way to tell yet. Bartholomew moved counterfeit pharmaceuticals and dubious stem-cells in and out of the eastern seaboard like a ghost. No one knew how she did it. She was ninety but looked half the age, spending fortunes in rejuv clinics. She had a first-generation subcutaneous nano matrix but developed a hypersensitivity to foreign epidermises which resulted in necrotic rejections, the decaying tissue putrefying and sloughing off in sheets. Now, the only skin she could attach was her own, cloned in a lab. She never wore backless because the seam down her spine was too visible. When she swept into the room is was in an ambiguous mix of grandmotherly fussing and coquettish flirtation that Jazz had trouble reading.

"Jazz, darling! Oh, look at you, that's gorgeous. Is that... yours? Can I touch you? Your skin is so beautiful, I wish I could see what you look like with it off."

"Well, anything you buy is yours, my dear."

"Then perhaps you are for sale?"

"Sadly, I'm under contract."

"Ah yes, Mr. Blanc. How is that predatory old copraphage?"

They negotiated for twenty minutes, working to offset their accounts in trade. No one bought anything legal with cash anymore and hard currency was tough to dispose. She did accept a case of Mako's hundreds that she would fence at 30 cents on the dollar off the network in South America. They kissed goodbye and Jazz promised to visit soon, as if it had been a purely social call.

The car drove her past a veterans' home on the way back, where amputees with ancient prosthetics argued and played dominos with worn plastic fingers. It reminded Jazz of the residents in the subsidized housing block she lived in as a child. All those senior citizens with their faded, wrinkled tattoos and blown out wide-gage piercings dangling like strips of gristle. It had been sad and ugly. She watched as an old man with a supplementary exoskeleton, the kind they used for unrepaired spinal injuries and Acquired Myasthenic Syndrome, swept the walk in front of the home. The left arm of the carbon fiber frame caught and stuttered on every backstroke. He appeared resigned, closing his eyes and waiting calmly until the servos caught and moved his arm into position for the next motion. He passed out of sight as the car drove on. Jazz turned on her node, switched her sensorium to virtual, and called Mako.

"Sir, I'm sure you're aware…"

"Yes. Don't worry about it. I know you'll make it right." Mako was paranoid about taps, even with the secure encryption systems in place. Jazz thought communication on a secured link was safer than talking in person because anything said aloud could be intercepted. Any place and anything could be bugged. The standards for implanted communications node encryption were so high only the NSA could crack them, and it would be expensive. No one was going to authorize a tap on Jazz and Mako's conversations. But Mako always assumed someone put a back door into every system and encouraged his people to say nothing unless it was face to face. He looked calm and sounded relaxed, but Jazz wasn't certain.

"Of course, Sir. I saw our friend this morning."

"Excellent," he grinned, transplanted shark teeth gleaming. "What did that zipper-backed old hag have to say for herself?"

* * * *

The room was soundproofed, secured, and quiet. Khatak and Johnson sat in the conference room with the Eye of Providence interface, checked the recording and verified identification and authorization with Central Control. The Eye could connect to every system, but there was only one way to access it. You had to talk to it in person. Cool air drifted through the vents. They were alone with the Intelligence, at least in this room. It could be discussing dozens of other investigations at the same time. Johnson activated the case recorder.

"On the record," Johnson said. "Preliminary inquiry on case file 2090/611672. Present are principle investigator Detective Khatak, R. T., and A. I. Liaison Officer Detective Johnson, N. B."

"Authenticated and authorized. Eye of Providence sworn and on the record. How may I help you?"

Johnson had assisted Khatak in developing his parameters to stay within the guidelines for probably cause and admissibility. The Eye wouldn't release anything it found that it estimated would not pass those tests or violate the various laws restraining its powers, but they didn't want to say anything that might create the wrong impression in court. The law prohibited the Eye from running analysis without a specific inquiry from an authorized user and could only answer questions, not make suggestions. It was smart enough to let you know it had something without breaking the law but no capacity to lie if it tried. It was always under oath and on the record.

"Hi Eye," Khatak said. "For the specific case referenced, we have a crime scene within the Brooklyn Surveillance Dark Zone. The nature of the crime requires the transport of unwilling individuals, medical equipment with components that cannot be reduced below an estimated nine cubic feet storage space, and illegally obtained biological products back and forth across the surveillance barrier. Accessing only legally permissible surveillance data, within a one block radius of all border and crossing points from the Brooklyn Surveillance Dark Zone, please generate a list of individuals and vehicles with sufficient transport capacity."

"Completed."

"O.K. exclude all individuals with confirmed activity outside the Dark Zone within one hour of the medical examiner's estimated time of death for the victims."

"Completed."

"Beginning with the victim records, cross reference all victim activities and records for evidence of any legally discoverable possible connection."

"Completed."

"Run a geospatial and behavioral probability map using all legally permissible data points for the victims and the individuals identified so far. Are there any patterns that exceed minimum improbability threshold to establish probable cause?

"I can identify five-hundred-sixty-three individuals meeting your parameters. This search does not include the use of information deemed discriminatory or illegal by applicable law. The probability of a judge finding any evidence obtained from the release of these identities to you inadmissible is estimated at .35. This exceeds department guidelines."

"Off record," Khatak said. When the Eye winked off, he looked at Johnson. "What do you think? Do we have probable cause to get a warrant?"

"You can establish opportunity but no direct connection. I don't think it's enough. Try the next tier."

"On the record," Khatak said. "Eye, in the file materials for the current case, I've flagged six additional open cases with a similar M.O. Run the same inquiry on those cases. Cross-reference all individuals for common elements. For all individuals identified across two or more inquiries, create a subset with publically identifiable connections to the medical and fashion industries, and a subset for those with a criminal record."

"Complete."

It took several more rounds of questions before they got down to a manageable list with a predicted admissibility of .95. Khatak had the Eye release the records, then he and Johnson left to sit in her office and review. They sat by her monitors, each looking at the files in their internal sensorium feed, hands sliding across the virtual touchscreens in unseen duet.

* * * *

Jazz pulled the counter-surveillance hood away from her face as she walked into the dark hall holding the Tyler Golden Surgical runway. Bright cheerful music washed over the murmuring of the crowd. Models strutted and turned. Tyler Golden didn't do removable epidermises but held patents on a variety of procedures for implantable chromatophores, subcutaneous electric arrays, and safety devices. Jazz saw a lot of people with safety tattoos and tracking implants. No one would chop and strip someone for skin like that unless it was special order. There were some strange fetishists out there though, so she maintained a catalogue of people she had seen that might appeal to collectors. You only needed a face to locate someone later on if you could match a buyer for a custom snatch and slice. There was an executive in Westchester who spent a lot of money on custom-ordered skins but nothing you could wear in public or show anyone. The worst tattoos, birthmarks, C-sections, burns. He kept the skins alive but never wore them himself that anybody had heard of. Wasn't even rigged for it. Just a freak.

The show didn't look promising, although the mood-reactive and digital advertising arrays were interesting. Perhaps the subcutaneous camouflage and skin tone adjustments might be useful, but it was out of her area. She slipped away to the bathroom and activated her node. Juan/ita had been calling her for an hour. Jazz tensed, returned the call

"Jazz, I've been trying to reach you," Juan/ita cried on the line.

"What's wrong? What happened?"

"It's my Armin Kerlec. It's dying."

"Juan/ita, I can't deal with this now—"

"It's going gangrenous at the edges. I can't afford to replace it Jazz, I can't."

"O.K., O.K. Look, I've got to take care of some business. We can fix it. Alright, baby? We can fix it."

When she got off the call with Juan/ita she changed shirts, reversed the jacket and swapped the vagina for a penis. Mako said to find out why the crew screwed up and there was a meeting later in a safe house in the Dark Zone. He checked his face in the mirror, pulled a hat over his head and made his way for a rear exit.

* * * *

"Khatak, I've got something for you," Johnson said. "You want to switch off retinal display and join me out here?" They'd been researching the persons of interest and cross-referencing the interviews coming in from around the scene all afternoon. Khatak switched, blinked a few times and re-oriented.

"Watch your boy, here. Jazz Kincaid. He's in the biological fashion industry. Sealed juvenile record. This is all archival footage near Brooklyn."

Johnson ran him through a series of smart camera feeds, the computer handing him off from camera to camera as he moved in and out of range.

"He's wearing counter-surveillance clothing. Hoods, glasses, hats. Presents as different genders. All fashionable but it's cloaking," Khatak said.

"And he avoids face traps."

"Damn, you're right. He's not looking directly at signage or signals, clocks, monitors. Anything you would normally look at out of habit that could have a camera built in. You have to train that. That's not an accident."

"So, he's trying not to be seen. Could be a government operative, could be a paranoid civil libertarian, could be in witness protection. Evidence of active efforts to avoid surveillance is not probable cause."

"No, but he's a party boy – fashion industry types aren't usually camera shy."

"Unless he's on the shadow economy side."

"Bingo. Why's a Manhattan fashion industry boy in and out of Brooklyn so frequently?

"No record of business or personal relationships within the Dark Zone. No transactions of any kind when he's in there."

Khatak nodded. "Let's get a warrant so we can locate him right now."

*　　*　　*　　*

Jazz slipped through Manhattan, changing cars and appearance, working to avoid cameras and slip tails. He'd always been careful, but with the police investigating the crime scene he took extra steps. Not much longer. He just had to make a little more bank and he could buy his way out of the Syndicate. He and Juan/ita could start their own collection. She already had the designs sketched. He had the connections. They were so close, now. Juan/ita called several times but he did not answer.

*　　*　　*　　*

"There he is," Khatak said. Johnson locked his face, ordering the camera system to hand him off as he moved. He was moving steadily toward the Dark Zone.

"Not sure 'he' is right," Johnson said. "Looks like that one's a post-gender transsexual with a socket."

"That one can't afford that kind of surgery."

"You know a lot about socket culture, Khatak?"

"Some. Primarily from theft investigations. Pretty select crowd. They don't talk much to cops."

"Yeah, plus it's embarrassing when someone steals your genitals. They don't even have laws to cover this stuff."

It was true. Just a month ago Khatak arrested a freak with a case filled with prepubescent vagina plugs that he could install in partners of legal age. Turned out they were all manufactured tissue. Perfectly legal. They had to give it all back. Asshole even wanted an apology.

"Post-gender is different from Trans," he said. "And the socket stuff? Near as I can tell, it's more about kink than identity, at least for debutant crowd. I can't speak for everyone."

"Yeah," Johnson said. "My wife used to be a man. This isn't the same vibe."

"Didn't know you were married."

"Twelve years."

Jazz slipped out of a cab and into a building out of camera range. Johnson pulled back and scanned to pick him up at the exits. When he came out he was wearing a completely different outfit.

"That's another counter-surveillance move," Khatak said. "Does he know we're onto him?"

Johnson shrugged. Crime syndicates still had dirty cops. They watched as Jazz slipped into a car and the vehicle headed for the Parkway.

"He's almost in Brooklyn. You want to wait and see if we pick him up coming out?"

Khatak nodded.

"Not much choice. If we send a unit to pick him up we don't have enough to hold him and his crew will be in the wind."

* * * *

"Shit. I just got an alert," Khatak said. "Internal communications surveillance picked up a call to Mako Blanc right after we got the warrant on Jazz. I think someone dimed our boy out to his boss."

"Your case. What do you want to do?"

*   *   *   *

The car pulled up behind the restaurant and Jazz slipped out into the dark parking lot by the service entrance. He looked around. High fence around the lot, no buildings with a clear view close by. He could see the lights of the Metropolitan Storm Barrier out over the water. The Barrier Authority was Federal, and crawling with fixed cameras and drones, but they weren't allowed to train them on the shore. It was quiet. He keyed a quick text message to Juan/ita to say he'd arrived, but he wasn't ready to talk directly yet. Not until after he'd had a long talk with Lin, Chow, and Nico. He went to the door and stopped with his hand on the knob. His node had an incoming message. Unknown contact. Only verified contacts could reach him on his node. Everyone else was screened out. He opened it.

We issued a surveillance warrant on you this afternoon and know you have entered Brooklyn. Mako Blanc knows you are under investigation. Go to nearest police station and request Detective Khatak, Biological Trafficking and Enforcement Division. We can protect you.

Jazz stood frozen while the text scrolled across his vision, tiny glowing characters floating in space. No. There was no way that was legit. Impossible. Organ cops were just trying to flush him out. He closed the message, took a deep breath and opened the door.

He could hear voices as he came down the stairs, the runners laughing and horsing around, Nico barking at them to settle down. He stepped inside the door and smiled.

"Chow. Nico," he called. "You find out who fucked up?"

There was a sharp sting on his neck and his body went stiff and numb. He heard Chow's voice in his ear.

"Yeah."

He could see Mako's teeth glitter in the light, and the shine of surgical steel. He tried to speak but couldn't move his diaphragm enough to get any air behind it. He mouthed the word, "Juan/ita," but could make no sound.

*   *   *   *

There was a detective he did not know standing in the rain outside the restaurant when Khatak pulled up. He hadn't bothered to pull a précis to see who he was dealing with.

"Hey, the Meat Cops have arrived," the man said affably. "I'm Kim. Come around the back. You won't believe this shit."

Inside, the body was laid out on a steel table, cleaned and dressed. The eyes were gone and the skin lay loosely on the floor in tatters. It had been taken off in strips.

"You see anything like this before?" Kim said.

"'Punitive flensing,' they call it. Harvesters keep them awake through the whole thing. Start down the back and cut it all away."

"No shit?"

"No shit."

Khatak kneeled down on the floor, and looked carefully at the skin, once delicate and fine, now empty. It was already starting to rot.

Protean

by Ree Soesbee

"...case file US-zero-six-four-three-four-seven, subject Dr. Roland Izaks. This will be an incarnate memory deposition for the US branch of the Allied World Authority. Resonant Agent is Tamara Deice, identification number five-three-nine-seven-Beta-Tau-Tau. Interrogative Agent is Ren Videk, identification number seven-six-five-two-Sigma-Sigma..." My partner's voice droned on, readying the preliminary holorecording as our vehicle landed outside the house.

He's Videk. I'm Deice.

I slid out with a cautious glance toward the building. "You sure we can't skip this one?" I asked wryly. Videk shrugged ever so faintly, giving me a raw smile as he flipped away the lens of his holorecorder. He got out of the car and strode up the gravel drive without a word, trusting that I would follow. I did.

Videk's clearly a Chance. He can't hide it; at a lanky six foot four, he's easy to spot in a crowd. Dull brown hair, murky eyes, wide mouth tugged tight over asymmetrical teeth, my partner's not what anyone would call handsome. Some agents might complain that he's not genetically optimized for our job, but I don't mind. Videk's interrogatives are sharp, and he's damn handy with a gun. He's solid, and that's all that matters.

My genetics are of a higher quality, but I wasn't templated to be an agent, either. That's another reason I give Videk the benefit of the doubt. Petite, white-blonde, with a perfect pixie-like tilt to my nose, I'm no Chance, that's for sure. My DNA's a mod on the artisan template, which means I can recognize twenty three shades outside the standard color spectrum, and both my concentration and manual dexterity are significantly enhanced. I was given a few special options, too, like the randomized freckles across my nose. My purple-blue eye color was one of those; an 'extra' my mother chose from a bionetics list. She wanted me to be a painter, but that tiny little chromosome ruined the plan.

Even with a genetic system as advanced as ours, there are accidents. Scientists don't know everything. There's this story about a group of mice during early laboratory trials; two out of a genetic batch unexpectedly went psycho and killed the other ninety-eight. See, the scientists had been testing mods on the eye-color genome, and unknown to them, they'd just discovered the genetic link between that purplish hue and psychic aptitude. Those two mice were the first known Resonants. For them, it was a matter of survival. Smashed in tight quarters, constantly touching the others, their little minds assaulted by memory after memory...

I guess my life could have been worse. The minute they discovered that I was a Resonant, my original template became irrelevant. I was assigned to government service from the time I was five. Still, I've never enjoyed being an agent; I don't have the right internal geometry. You could say I'm squeamish. That's why I tried to avoid this particular case assignment. It's a cold case, and old memories are thicker than new ones. They're cloying. They linger, like the smell of rotting food days after you've taken out the trash.

Videk clomped up the stairs leading to the massive brick mansion at the end of the drive. He rang the bell, and without hesitation, we were buzzed in. From the moment we stepped inside, I was overwhelmed. The foyer was immaculate. Everywhere I looked, I saw antique furniture, soaring architecture, masterful paintings in gilded frames – an artist's heaven. My heart leapt, but my brain got down to business. The gold frames were covered in dust. The furniture brocade was pristine, with only a few narrow paths crushed into the carpets. No one lived in these beautiful rooms. They were just for show.

"Take us to Dr. Izaks," my partner requested, flashing his badge as a young man came to greet us. The servant's eyes widened and he nodded, backing away. Our footsteps echoed in hallways as silent as the grave.

At the center of the mansion we found a rumpled little den. The room seemed out of place, a squalid cave hidden within the mansion's golden walls. Paper littered every flat surface; notebooks, science journals, reference books and scrap newspaper articles. As we entered, an old man rose from behind a desk half-buried in crumpled files. He was a Chance, but then again, he'd have to be. Chicken… egg.

The doctor was heavyset, with a bristling beard, and eyebrows knotted into a bottle-brush over the bridge of his nose. Worn denims and a faded flannel shirt spoke of a man ill at ease with his opulent surroundings. The rigid tilt of his shoulders and the push of stiff fingers against the desk said even more: he was prepared for conflict, though his smooth voice and clear eyes betrayed no sign of emotion.

"Tzohora'im tovim, Agents. Please, have a seat. I've been waiting for you."

His casual greeting made me pause. Typically, a suspect wasn't supposed to know we were coming. "Dr. Izaks?" I ventured, frowning.

"That would be me."

"An honor to meet you, sir. My name is Tamara Deice. This is my partner, Ren Videk. We..."

"Of course."' Izaks waved his hand negligently, cutting me off. "And to anticipate your question: yes, I'll comply with a deposition." Rather than arguing guilt or innocence, Izaks simply radiated a studied nonchalance. I suppose I should have been relieved. Instead, I felt off-balance. Even though we hadn't charged him as a suspect, Izaks was too at ease. A pair of AWA agents intruding on your home usually made people bristle — if not worse.

Videk's eyes narrowed, but he managed a polite, if curt, nod of thanks.

Izaks gestured toward a pair of thickly cushioned chairs. My partner sat down and flipped the pale blue holorecorder lens over his eye, wasting no time in getting to our purpose. "Very well. We are on the record. Dr. Izaks, by the authority vested in me as an agent of the AWA, you are hereby compelled to tell the truth in this inquisition. If you fail to do so, your possessions, freedom, and life may be forfeit. Do you understand this obligation?" The doctor murmured in assent, shuffling through the drawers of his desk for a bottle and a glass.

Ignoring them both, I made a circuit of the room, letting my fingers trail over books and shelves. Memories slithered through my mind like rivulets of rain. Cold. Stale. Nothing unexpected. No signs of danger, no echo of panic about our arrival. I drew myself together, hand falling to my side, and gave Videk an approving nod.

The thin glass of the lens shimmered. My partner asked, "Dr. Izaks, when was the last time you saw your wife?"

Izaks uncorked a carafe of bourbon and smoothly poured an inch into a beveled glass. "Two days after my son's tenth birthday. Toby'd just been diagnosed with Amelier's Disease, and Rachel was very upset. After he was in bed, she went for a drive. The police found her car a week later. Abandoned." Izaks's words were clipped and rote, as though he'd told the story a hundred times. He waved the bottle in our general direction, offering, but Videk shook his head.

"Amelier's?" Videk pressed. "That's a hereditary condition, isn't it? Passed down on the mother's side?"

"Quite so, Agent. Rachel was devastated. The diagnosis was terribly hard on both of us. I always assumed that was why she left. She simply couldn't bear to watch our son waste away. Toby died six months later." The portly doctor lifted his glass of bourbon and took a swallow. "Forty years," he said softly. "Has it really been that long?...

"Ah, well. Eventually, the case was archived."

I sat down in the chair opposite Videk. My partner chose his words carefully. "Two weeks ago, sir, a body was found in a shallow grave outside of Casper, Wyoming. It was badly decomposed, but a DNA scan has identified the remains as Rachel Deanne Izaks."

The doctor's eyes widened, and his studied nonchalance cracked. "She...her body? How... how did she..."

So Izaks didn't know everything, after all. "The cause of death was multiple stab wounds from an unknown weapon," Videk supplied. The doctor's eyes flicked from my partner to me and back again, shadows moving in their depths. Fear? Anger? Abandonment? Izaks refilled his bourbon, and this time, the liquid splashed. Videk continued, "After Rachel's disappearance, you established Protean Bionetics. Your company's work with genetics and gene-splicing has eliminated hundreds of chromosomal disorders. You've been very successful, doctor. You've also accrued a significant fortune."

"Nearly eliminated," the doctor muttered, recovering. "Some defects still circulate in 'chance' chromosomes carried by people with randomized, non-engineered genes. In time, though, I'm sure we'll eliminate them. Cancer, autism, sickle cell – things of the past." Dr. Izaks cleared his throat aggressively. "You'll see."

Videk ignored the interruption. His interrogation style was smooth, authoritative, but reassuring. "Would you like to add anything to your earlier testimonies, Dr. Izaks? Something else you remember, or any reason to believe she'd come to harm?"

The doctor shrugged."As I've said in the past, Rachel seemed happy. Except for... well, Toby." Izaks looked away, eyes focusing on me. Before Videk could continue, Izaks asked, "You're a Resonant, aren't you, Agent Deice? One of the earliest, I'd guess, given your age. Spontaneous? Not by design?"

"You know I can't answer that, sir…" I said awkwardly. I wasn't supposed to speak, other than to provide testimony. What was he playing at?

"An accidental masterpiece, like Da Vinci's sketches, or Siquieros's paintings. Interesting." Dismissing me with a shrug, Izaks turned to consider Videk. "Though if she's an oil painting, son, you're spray-paint on a brick wall. Fucking genetic graffiti."

"I'm sorry?" Videk blinked, the old man's vulgarity taking him by surprise.

Izaks looked my partner up and down, from his scruffy brown hair to his gangly limbs. "You're not engineered, son. I'd bet you're one hundred percent random, as haphazard and muddled as God made you, carrying around tens of thousands of genetic flaws. You're like a kazoo in an orchestra. Why?" The question wasn't rhetorical. "Why?" Izaks pressed, narrowing his eyes.

"I wasn't a planned conception. Doctor, did—"

"Alterations could have been done in utero. Were your parents hippies? Poor? Unwilling to indenture you to a government subsidy?" As an afterthought, Izaks muttered, "You don't look African."

Videk sat up more stiffly, the glow of the lens shimmering between them. "Does it matter?"

The doctor pressed on, talking as much to himself as to my partner. "Even if you were, Africa's covered under the UN plan. Good investment, that. The more embryos they clear, the safer we all are from hereditary diseases. Planet-wide inoculation, you might say." He tilted his head inquisitively. "So why leave you out in the cold?"

"My parents didn't want me altered."

"Ah." Izaks nodded sagely. "The religious sort, I suppose." Shaking his head in disapproval, the grey-haired scientist crossed his arms and tugged his flannel shirt. "I've heard that argument a thousand times. 'What God has shaped, we've no right to alter.' Is that about right?" He sipped his bourbon with a considered sigh.

"Could we get back to the deposition, sir?" There was a trace of annoyance in Videk's tone. "Did you have any reason to believe Rachel had been killed?"

With a faintly amused smile, Izaks answered, "No. Rachel never gave me any reason to think she had enemies. She just… disappeared." He rubbed the bridge of his nose between calloused fingers. "I stayed in Wyoming for a year after Toby died, and then I sold the house. Too many memories."

Videk pressed, "Did your wife keep a journal? A diary? Is there any chance –"

"Chance." Izaks swirled the alcohol in his bevelled glass. Deep lines creased his face, half-hidden behind the bramble of eyebrows and beard. "It's my life's work to eliminate chance, agent. As is yours. We both want to find the flaw and remove it before it harms society, isn't that right?" He finished his drink in a rapid swallow and set the glass down on the desk. "No. She left no journal, no note. Nothing."

Videk sat back in his chair, glancing toward me.

Leaning forward, I addressed Dr. Izaks in a gentle tone. "In accordance with the law, I'll need to verify your testimony before we proceed." I extended my hand toward the doctor without explanation.

Izaks didn't need to be babied through the process; he'd helped write the Resonant protocols. Indeed, the old man gave me a knowing smile as he clasped my fingers. With the touch of his hand, warmth flooded my senses; I saw flashes of light and felt the draw of a long breath of air—

In front of me stood a little boy, his body frozen in mid-run. He had sandy hair, soft brown eyes and even features. Handsome, but not template, with a slender bone structure and a fox-like, narrow smile.

This was an old memory, half-forgotten but much loved, the edges blurred and softened by time. The boy moved past me, waving a blue, metallic toy, its details unclear. Before he could escape, a dark-haired woman scooped him up, lifting the child high into the air. "Toby, didn't you hear me calling?" she scolded gently. "Toby!" Her eyes shone with love as she spun him around.

"Time to go inside..."

Slowly, the resonance faded. I felt Dr. Izaks's other hand beneath my elbow, steadying me. Some people recoil when they feel the transfer of a Resonant. The sudden drain of energy causes nausea, weakness, and puts a heavy strain on the subject. Sometimes they even get violent – after all, I'm literally sapping their life away. Dr. Izaks simply frowned with compassion.

Once again, the man managed to surprise me.

I let go of his hand and closed my eyes, trying to stifle the rush of adrenalin humming in my veins. Every Resonant experiences the energy transfer differently. Mine is somewhere between a sexual release and the awe of a million unnamed colors. It's beautiful, and distinctly sensual. I'm an artist, after all.

Resonance is a bit of a crap-shoot, drawing out images and feelings of importance to the subject. It works in legal cases because the guilty tend to linger on their crimes, giving those memories weight. I can't just tug out anything; the memory has to be near the forefront of the subject's mind. That's why I need a good Interrogative like Videk. His questions bring the relevant memories forward, so I can find them. Still, resonance isn't perfect. I experience the details only as the subject knew them. I live through someone else's memory… and memory isn't the same as truth. Memories can betray you.

Nevertheless, it's my job to make sense of the memory I experienced, and get it on record. "Resonance confirms a happy family association, with no signs of trauma or abuse. He remembers his wife fondly, even lovingly. The memory was circa..." I estimated, based on fading and slippage. "Forty-five years ago."

My partner nodded appreciatively and resumed his questions. "You never remarried, did you, Dr. Izaks?" Videk's lens made a little halo in the air each time his head moved.

"There are more than twenty thousand gene pairs in the human DNA strand, Agent Videk," Izaks answered. "More than 2.85 billion nucleotides in a single genome. The possible combinations—the copy variation, alone—is nearly infinite. Even with bionetic enhancement, every individual is unique. Remarry? No. I loved my family. They were utterly irreplaceable.

"Ah, you think I'm a hypocrite?" Izaks chuckled at my partner's unguarded expression. "First, I say want to re-engineer humans, and then I say each one is unique? There's no conflict in my mind. A template is not a clone. Look at your partner. Have you ever met anyone exactly like her? Of course not. Even if two individuals are built on the same template, the raw materials of each composition are different, and therefore, so are they.

"There are a billion potentials in a strand of DNA. It is a roadmap of physical and racial qualities, innate mental capacity, and overall genetic makeup. Bionetics can ensure potential. It can remove flaws, but you must understand this fundamental fact: we see only the pieces. We can eliminate some of the variables, but we can only guess at the infinite combinations. Scientists input the numbers, but we cannot control the reckoning of the sum. That is the province of God."

"You believe in God?" My partner raised an eyebrow.

"Of course. God, the soul, and most things written in the Torah. I simply don't believe He's infallible. Tell that to your parents."

Videk frowned in irritation. "So you know, doctor, my parents weren't particularly religious." He shrugged. "It was more... well, the genetics program had already failed them once."

"Failed?" I asked curiously.

My partner glanced at me, and his crooked smile was wry. "Something like point-ought-five percent of modified embryos don't survive the process. My parents decided they'd rather have an imperfect baby than another perfect funeral."

"Ah, yes..." Izaks refilled his glass. "I know how they felt. My wife and I struggled for years to conceive a child. That was the reason I went into bionetics. I began my career as a research scientist, working on methods of invitro fertilization." He rolled the heavy glass back and forth between his hands appraisingly. "Agent Deice, you seem to have recovered. Shall we look again?"

I nodded, and he set down the glass. Once again the grizzled old scientist reached for my hand, and once again, he showed no sign of fear. His eyes met mine as our palms touched, fingers interlacing–

His young wife, her brown hair shining. Sunlight through a kitchen window. Fear and joy warred on the beautiful canvas of her face, widening her brown eyes. "You're sure?" Rachel asked. "It worked?" There was a depth to this memory, as if years of waiting, of trying and failing, added thick layers of guilt to its weight.

He pulled her close. "Even if this is my only success as a doctor, I'll be content." Warmth radiated through the image like a summer breeze. "Now, tell me, darling...

"What are we going to name him?"

The second transfer was more powerful, its resonance stronger and the pull of transference deeper. This time, the loss of vital energy showed. Doctor Izaks paled, and his skin grew cool beneath my fingers. Nevertheless, the old man managed a wan smile as his palm slipped free of mine.

"Subject memory confirms. Dr. Izaks," my question came out in a rush, "you performed the invitro procedure. Did you alter the child's genetics? Did you engineer your son?" Shivers ran along my spine and the skin of my arms. I could feel every brush of fabric, hear every whisper of sound. The feeling was joyous. Videk frowned at my impertinence; it was against protocol for me to ask questions. I bit my lip, forcing myself to fall silent, and breathe.

Izaks nodded heavily. "Minor encoding, for increased intelligence and physical capacity. The technology was in its earliest stages, purely rudimentary. Today, such modifications would be considered superficial."

Videk spoke quickly, cutting off my next barrage before it began. "Did Rachel agree to those changes?"

Izaks nodded, face as grey as the brushy tangle of his hair. He reached for the bourbon, but the dark, caramel liquid threatened to splash out of the glass when he tried to lift it. Instead, the old man merely rested his hand around the cool crystal, staring mournfully down at his drink.

"Do you need a break, Doctor?" Videk asked.

"No… no, not yet, thank you, Agent." Izaks looked up. "Rachel was part of the process from beginning to end. We both believed that bionetics would help us conceive, but we hoped that it would also eliminate the flaws that caused her miscarriages. In that, we were correct."

Videk started talking again, asking more questions, but I barely heard the words. My thoughts were arcing with electricity, darting from one conclusion to the next. Like a painting in which the shadow tilted toward the light, Izaks's entire tale was strangely askew. The resonance was too universally pleasant, his memories too perfectly appropriate. He'd been ready for our questions. Ready, somehow, for my resonant pull. It shouldn't be possible, but he was feeding me memories. How?

Izaks was hiding something. Did he kill his wife, perhaps because of her genetic flaw? Did he blame her for passing Amelier's to Toby? Did he blame himself? But, no, I hadn't felt hostility beneath the memories I'd experienced. He couldn't have killed her. That was why he'd been so open to our questioning. He wasn't guilty of Rachel's death.

I thought of the metaphorical painting again, its shadow tilting toward the light. My artist's eye broke it apart, separating shape from meaning. Not an apple, just a circle. Not a bowl, a concave plane. Not a light source, but patterns, streaks of color on canvas. The same technique could divide Izaks's information into its simplest parts.

Izaks helped his wife conceive. He modified his son's DNA, with her permission. He removed the flaws… But, no.

"Doctor," I broke in, not caring if I interrupted Videk. "You specifically eliminated hereditary flaws in the embryo that might have caused a miscarriage. How did you miss Amelier's Disease?"

"I… suppose I made an error… overlooked it. " the doctor stammered. "We wanted to carry a child to term., and Amelier's doesn't cause miscarriages. I wasn't paying attention to that portion of the strand."

Anger flashed through me, quick and sharp. "You're a world-class bionetics researcher. You don't make that kind of mistake." The doctor didn't reply.

"Give me your hand." I demanded. I gave him no time to prepare or collect his thoughts. This time, Izaks wasn't going to hide behind prepared memories. I wanted to know what he was thinking, and I would take the truth from him by force, if necessary. Forgoing the usual courtesies, I dove into his thoughts–

"Now, Toby. It's time for bed."

Rachel's voice was weary and filled with frustration. Toby was having another tantrum, the child's argument rising and falling with indefatigable stubbornness. Izaks sat in the office, reading his mail, only half-listening. It was unimportant. A common household disturbance.

This memory was different from the others. It was cold, like a serpent, and it trickled through me slowly, as though rising from deep waters within his soul. Beneath it, I could smell turned earth. The iron tang of blood.

Down the hallway, the bedroom light snapped off with an angry, resolute click, but the child's voice grew louder. "No. I won't!"

There was a thump-thump-thump of tiny feet pattering on the floor. A ssshshrnick, not unlike the smooth tearing of scissors through fabric – the sound of a knife through flesh. Like a striking snake, over and over, in quick succession. There was a gurgled, half-choked whisper of scream. Izaks looked up from his mail to see that the bedroom light was on again, and there was a child's shadow in the hallway. I saw blood pooling on the floor.

"Why are you looking at me like that, Daddy?" Toby asked as he lowered the kitchen knife. The child's voice was eerily calm and trusting. "I haven't done anything wrong."

Rachel's body lay crumpled on the Chinese rug, clothing bloodied, her face locked in an expression of horror and fear...

I shuddered, my heart racing with stolen emotions. "You knew Rachel was dead." I forced the words out between tingling lips. I opened my eyes, wider than before, and saw every detail of the room in sharp, crystal focus. "Toby..." I swallowed, trying to hear past the blood pounding in my veins. His horror was still too strong inside me. "He..." I couldn't say the words.

"Agent Deice," Videk said sharply, rebuking me. "Remember your duty."

I am the Resonant. Videk is the Interrogative. I don't ask questions; I simply confirm or deny what my partner unearths. This is exactly why that rule exists. My control was as thin as the edge of a razor. I wanted to demand answers from Izaks. I wanted to shake him until the truth came out, and with this much adrenaline in my system, it felt as if I could shatter bones.

"Deice!" Videk said again.

I am the Resonant. Videk is the Interrogative. I confirm or deny. Nothing more.

"Apologies, Agent Videk." I managed. Keenly aware of the holorecorder, I reported, "Memory indicates that the subject was aware of his wife's death. She was... she was murdered by their child. Toby."

Videk's eyes flashed over the digital record, double-checking the index within the glowing blue fragment of glass. "How did you hide this?" he whispered, taken aback. "Our interrogatives – the other Resonant depositions..."

The doctor was breathing shallowly, face white as a sheet, and his eyes had taken on a sunken quality. The resonance was withering him.

Shuddering, Izaks pulled up another of the room's overstuffed chairs and sat down. "Resonance draws more than memory, Ren Videk. It collects empathy, as well. A transference of the mind and the soul." He wheezed and paused for breath. "Government Resonants are genetically enhanced according to a template I designed. A template built on the precepts of an investigative agent: logic, rational thought, intellectual dissection. The engineered Resonants were only looking into the mind. Your partner, on the other hand, is an artist. Like all artists, she can see into the soul."

Always the professional, Videk stayed on-topic. "Was Toby's genetic flaw a factor in Rachel's death?" His face was grim beneath the cowlicks of his rumpled brown hair.

Izaks chuckled grimly, a low, dark sound. "Yes, Agent Videk. Toby's 'genetic flaw' was very much a factor. But the flaw wasn't that Toby had Amelier's Disease. The flaw, you see, was in something Toby didn't have."

Almost to himself, the aged scientist murmured, "Scientists can manipulate flesh–choose eye color, eliminate physical deficiencies, increase physical potential. We can enhance the capacity for intelligence, ignite the spark of psychic ability, remove the flaws that cause sociopathy and other mental weaknesses. But that's not all." The doctor looked up wearily. "Everything we are is encoded in our DNA. Everything. Do you understand?

"Come here, Tamara. I want to show you something more." I heard Videk protesting the doctor's condition, reminding me that each resonance depleted the subject further, and Izaks was not a young man. Still, unable to restrain myself, I gripped the doctor's hand–

The forest smelled of cold earth and damp leaves. Izaks scraped a shovel over pine needles, trying to cover the darker earth below. Nearby, Toby played quietly with a toy police car.

"We can't tell anyone, Toby. We have to say your mother left us, and we don't know where she's gone. Can you do that?"

Toby gave his father a careless smile. "Sure," he said without any sign of concern. The child looked back down at his toy, running the wheels over a fallen branch along the ground. Vrooming at the car, Toby added, "Hey, dad? I'm going to bed at eleven from now on.

"You don't mind, right?"

I struggled to concentrate, filled with an ocean of churning energy that threatened to overwhelm me. Myriad unnamable colors swam before my eyes. As I gasped for breath, I heard the doctor's sorrowful voice.

"I didn't wield the knife, but I am as much to blame as my poor son. The capacity for evil is simply another facet of our biology, as is the capacity for kindness or compassion. The 'roadmap' of our DNA contains both potentials. My son's evil was innate. With all the benefit of loving parents, positive heredity, education and moderate wealth, he was still capable of remorseless murder. The flaw was in his design, and I did not see it until it was too late.

"Were we made in God's image?" Izaks challenged. "If so, as we are imperfect creatures, He must be an imperfect god. Religious folk claim the flaws are deliberate. I have seen the horrors mankind inflicts on one another, from Auschwitz to the Somali atrocities, and I cannot believe any sentient, caring God would purposefully allow such things. No, there is a flaw in our roadmap, a deficient genome. An error in our DNA.

"Look at the other genetic mistakes He made in our construction – all of which science can correct. This is no different. The human spirit has the erroneous capacity to delight in suffering. Evil is a tragic flaw, but like other genetic malfunctions, it can be eliminated." He sighed softly, sinking further into his chair.

We stared at the doctor wordlessly. In my color-blurred vision, Izaks reclined amid a haze of yellows and reds, hovering in an aura of shades impossible to describe. Despite his pale skin and sunken eyes, the doctor seemed almost to glow with a chaotic, fire-like shimmer. I could only stare, overcome by awe.

"After Toby died," Izaks murmured, "I studied his DNA obsessively. I also researched the genomes of murderers and warlords, gathering genetic material from individuals whose spiritual aberrations could be quantified, categorized, compared and contrasted. I also studied those exceptional people who show ultimate compassion; paragons of human morality. In so doing, I discovered discreet differences. I identified the gene sequence which allows evil to enter the human soul… and I discovered how to remove it."

Videk blanched. "That's not possible..."

"Ah, but I have proof. Look at the world around you, Agent Videk. War is a memory. Humanity is finally attuned to the needs of the less fortunate. Within a generation, we have constructed a multi-national moon base, established a worldwide system of legal regulations, and taken huge strides to end starvation and poverty. Mankind has become gentler, more altruistic. More at peace."

"A generation?" Videk's eyes flashed behind his holorecording lens. "You're talking about the UN genetic program."

"Yes. Creating the template for that program spread my modifications much farther than Protean's bionetic designs ever could." Dr. Izaks breathed heavily, seemingly relieved. "A fortunate opportunity to share my cure with the world."

Aghast, Videk whispered, "You're trying to create a human without evil. A 'perfect mankind.' But in so doing, you're removed their free will, taken away their ability to choose for themselves. How could you do that?"

"How could I not?" Izaks choked angrily. The sound was a shadow of his earlier stentorian proclamations. "Leave the children flawed, diseased, when I could offer succor? No, Agent. In this, I've been a far better maker than the original. I've shaped mankind into an image superior, even, than myself. The creation should be greater than the creator. A student should outdo the master. A son…" his thoughts trailed off darkly.

I looked at him, and the last piece of the painting became clear in my mind. At last, I understood the shadow, and I knew why it was pointing the wrong way. "Toby didn't have Amelier's Disease, did he, Dr. Izaks?

"He died of it," Izaks confessed softly. "He just wasn't born with it. After I buried Rachel, I gave Toby the disease by injection. While he was asleep..."

I slipped forward and placed my hand on the doctor's wrist. His pulse was barely more than a flutter. "Doctor," I asked impulsively, hoping he could still hear me. "I never told you I was designed to be an artist. How did you know?"

Izaks smiled a weary little smile and closed his eyes. "Ah, my dear," his voice was almost too light to make out, "Who do you think fashioned your template? Who put you into the agency, and brought you here when the time came? Yasher koach, Tamara Deice..."

With that, the pulse faded into nothing, and he was gone.

I don't know if the doctor was right, or if the death of his wife had driven him to madness. But as I knelt beside him, mind swirling with his memories and heart pounding with the raw energy of his life, the agent in me condemned Izaks for daring to consider himself equal to God.

The artist could not help but understand.

"Baruch dayan emet," I whispered, closing my eyes. I'd known, somehow, that I shouldn't have taken this case. Turns out my instincts were right.

My partner tapped his holoimaging lens one final time. "File US-zero-six–four–three–four–seven, subject Dr. Roland Izaks, incarnate memory deposition.

"This case file is now closed."

Autoimmune

by Katrina Nicholson

For the first time in almost three decades, the United States needed doctors. The rumor had been circulating among the MSF staffers in Cambodia all day, but I didn't believe it until I got the letter.

It was lying on my cot, the white paper dappled by the late afternoon sun shining through the mesh windows of my tent. The office in Sisophon had printed it out on the same letterhead as all the other emails I'd gotten from the regional Doctors Without Borders headquarters in Kuala Lumpur. It had the NGO's logo on it: a stick person inside a red scribble. I snatched it up, staining the paper with the reddish brown road dust that coated my freckled hands.

SUBJECT: USA PROJECT OPPORTUNITY
From: Dr. Amran Sanggomitra [projectcoordinator@msfmalaysia.org]
Sent: Wednesday, March 12, 2138 1:37 P.M.
To: Dr. Jennifer Harper [msfoutreacharanh@msfmalaysia.org]

Dear Dr. Harper,

We have been hearing many good things about you from the supervising physicians on the Cambodia project. Instances of malaria, dengue fever, and typhus in Banteay Meanchey province are all down since you began your program of tracking disease vectors in rural areas.

However, we are writing to you today to let you know that your home country may have more need of a doctor with your particular skills in epidemiology and infectious diseases. In the last three days, 41 cases of an as yet unidentified infection have appeared in Atlanta, Georgia. Immunoprogrammers from all major automated immune system providers have thus far failed to engineer antibodies to combat the disease. The government has quarantined the city and asked for our assistance.

Please let us know by the end of the day if you are interested in heading an emergency mission to the United States. The government there has offered to provide funding for any and all needs your team may have.

Dr. Amran Sanggomitra
Project Coordinator
Médecins Sans Frontières Malaysia

As I read the letter, my exhaustion evaporated. So the rumors were true. Chanthou, my Cambodian guide/translator/LPN, was watching me from the doorway of the tent, a look of curiosity on her wide, open face.

"Have they found something for you, Jenni?" She asked me in French.

I nodded, feeling my short brown curls bob against my cheeks. This was what I'd been waiting my whole career for.

The team I settled on was small, partly because the deadline was tight and partly because I was too excited to wait. After a decade and a half in the field chasing the usual suspects, here, finally, was something new.

In the day and a half it took me to track down Naman, Matheus, Abioye, and Phuong, the MSF doctors I knew from working in various villages in Banteay Meanchey, there were 63 more reported cases of the mystery illness in greater Atlanta. Our first team meeting was on the plane the US government had chartered for us out of Phnom Penh. It was a corporate-looking jet, furnished with carpets and real wood. Waiting for us on the conference table were brand new tablets configured to receive real-time updates from the immunoprogrammers who were still attempting to figure out how people who couldn't get sick were suddenly being struck down by disease.

“I don't understand,” Naman said as he paged through patient reports with brown fingers weathered by age and exposure. “These people all have automated immune systems. This shouldn't be possible.”

Naman was Indian, born in 2068 to a wealthy family in Bangalore. At the time, immunosystems were still new enough that they couldn't be bought in India at any price. Within a few years they started to become available, but by then it was too late. The window for successful immunosystem implantation is short – between the fetus leaving the protection of its mother's immune system and its exposure to its first bacterium. Any longer and the implanted immunosystem battles for control against the infant's natural immune system, with catastrophic results.

I got my immunosystem for free from the US government, and I think Naman resented me for it, because even though he had a quarter century more experience, people tended to see me as the better doctor. I could be the friendly 'Doctor Jenni,' a round, motherly forty-something waltzing into a disease ward without so much as a surgical mask, smiling my freckled smile and making everyone feel better while Naman had to shuffle around in a full space suit scaring the wits out of the patients.

Most people didn't realize 'Doctor Jenni' had an unfair advantage. My immunosystem could fight off everything from influenza to the Ebola virus, usually before I even developed much of a fever. It also helped my cells regenerate when I was injured. It did malfunction occasionally, of course. All computers do. But a quick virtual scan forwarded to the iProtect Online Troubleshooting Clinic in San Francisco and it was good as new.

In the century or so since they were invented, immunosystems had spread throughout the developed world, making doctors obsolete. My profession now mostly consisted of elite students from developing countries that couldn't afford the thousands of taxpayer dollars per person needed to outfit a nation with permanent disease protection. Then there were the do-gooders and the people like me, whose curiosity overrode their need to be clean and comfortable. When I told my parents I wanted to be a doctor, they cried. But I was determined to get out – living in a country where it was almost impossible to die made for more crowding than I could handle.

"Perhaps your immunity is not so all-encompassing after all, Jenni," Abioye mused as he stared at a chart with a long list of symptoms. "Back home in the Congo, new diseases are still being discovered. Perhaps the immunosystems have run across something they are not able to repel."

"But the point of computerized immunity," Matheus argued, tapping his fingers under his chin in one of his characteristic Brazilian gestures, "is that the system will keep trying new antibody formulations until it finds something that works."

"And with 328 people now infected, it's hard to believe not one of their systems has found anything that works and passed it on to the rest via their automated packet data transmissions," Phuong put in. She had studied immunoprogramming in Toronto before returning to Vietnam for her medical degree, so she knew more than the rest of us about how immunosystems worked.

"Are we sure it's not just another software glitch?" Naman asked.

Phuong shook her head. "Glitches are always confined to a single model year. But with this we're seeing cross platform compatibility - people with ImmunoBoost models installed in 2087 are affected alongside babies with this year's GermStops."

"But surely the source code–"

I waved my hands to forestall a descent into computerese. "That's not what we're here for. Let the programmers handle the computer end. We're going to handle this thing the same way we would deal with an outbreak of cholera or dengue. Diagnose the condition, track its spread, and identify its transmission methods and origin. For that we need facts, not guesses."

Because the cases were spread over the greater Atlanta area, we had to split up. But this time everything was backwards. As head of mission, I, who had immunosystem protection, was stuck back at headquarters while my colleagues, none of whom had anything beyond what their natural immune systems provided, dispersed to take samples and do interviews at the various Atlanta area immunosystem troubleshooting clinics.

In an act of supreme irony, the government representatives who picked us up at the airport took us to the old Centers for Disease Control and Prevention building in Druid Hills to set up shop. Stories of the CDC and their legendary battle with AIDS were what prompted me to move to Lebanon to study epidemiology and medicine. Now the CDC was a crumbling hulk of concrete and glass. The only reason it hadn't been torn down and replaced by more condo towers was that it had been designated a national historic site. Wandering through the echoing, dust-shrouded halls where one of my heroes, Dr. Don Francis, had once walked was creepier than I expected.

I chose a conference room on the first floor that was so old it actually had a chalkboard and ordered my government support staff, most of whom were computer experts, to fire up the equipment left to molder in the lab next door - centrifuges, scanning electron microscopes, mass spectrometers, electrophoresis, gas chromatography... we were going to need it all.

There were now almost 2,000 cases. Naman and the others were working frantically, interviewing the patients who had developed symptoms earliest and sending back blood and fluids for testing. I had to do all the lab tests myself because there were no lab techs closer than Port-Au-Prince. By the time of our end-of-day teleconference I felt like there was sand under my eyelids. At this point I'd been awake for more than 36 hours. 15,744 people were ill. The troubleshooting clinics were overflowing and people were starting to panic. The government had flooded the internet with exhortations for people to stay at home and avoid contact with one another, but there was only so much people could do. There were 14 million people living in less than 140 square miles. Even if they wanted to leave, they couldn't. The government had shut down the intercity trains and planes when they put the city under quarantine.

I rubbed my eyes and tried to focus on the chalkboard, where my list of symptoms taunted us as we attempted to make a diagnosis.

Fever
Headache
Fatigue
Loss of Appetite
Muscle Aches
Inflammation
Photosensitivity
Trouble Breathing
Anemia
Rash

They could be the early stages of dozens of different diseases.

Influenza, mononucleosis, pneumonia, gastroenteritis, typhus, hepatitis, tuberculosis, dengue, Legionnaire's disease... the list went on and on and the argument over which it was likely to be raged back and forth over the teleconferencing screens. But it didn't make any sense, because all of these diseases were known, which meant the immunosystems should be able to take care of them no problem.

If we were going to crack this thing, the answers lay in the end stages of the disease. So far only 18 of those infected had succumbed, but their end stage symptoms were maddeningly general as well - kidney failure, respiratory distress, ulcers, seizures, cognitive dysfunction, and liver failure. Autopsies seemed to indicate that it was even odds as to which would be the one that ultimately killed the patient. The only clue we had was that the disease seemed to progress more quickly in young people. All of the dead so far had been infants and small children.

I'd been working in rural infectious disease clinics for fifteen years, and my gut was telling me that there was something in two of the symptoms. The swelling and the rash. They meant something - something that was on the tip of my brain. But it wasn't until I saw the autopsy photos of a three-year-old boy who had died this morning that it jumped from my brain and out my open mouth.

"Lupus!" I blurted, staring at the butterfly shaped rash on the dead patient's face. It was almost identical to the rash I'd seen on an eight-year-old Cambodian girl who'd been brought to one of my malaria clinics. Her blood test had come back negative for malaria, but positive for lupus.

The diagnostic debate suddenly stopped and all the faces on the screens turned to look at me. I almost wished I hadn't spoken, because of course the idea was absurd. But all the same I was sure I was right.

"Lupus? Really, Jenni?" Naman scoffed, staring at me with that superior look I hated.

"The butterfly rash, the joint pain, the swelling... light sensitivity and ulcers... the systemic involvement... it's got to be lupus. It's the only thing that fits."

"But that's preposterous," Matheus insisted. "Lupus isn't a communicable disease."

"I know."

"Lupus is gradual... the symptoms come and go... this thing is killing people within days," Abioye added.

"I know. I still think it's lupus."

There was a silence. I could tell what they were thinking - that I was losing it. Too many hours without sleep. Too much stress from a mounting death toll. It had pushed me over the edge. But for me, outbreaks were energizing. They were a treasure map to follow, a puzzle to solve. When normal people were at their worst, I was at my best. Jovial Doctor Jenni lived on the surface, but underneath there was a stone cold disease hunter.

"Well, there's a quick way to find out," Phuong said, breaking the long silence. "You've got the blood samples there. It'll only take a minute."

I could feel their eyes watching me as I separated the serum from one of the blood samples and prepared it for ANA testing. I added the immunofluorescence and put the slide under the microscope. When I saw what I had, I looked for a way to share the images over the teleconferencing feed.

The image of bright green antinuclear antibodies - so many that there was barely any black space between them - appeared on the screen. There was a stunned silence. And then:

"It's not possible. How is this possible?" Naman exclaimed.

"Lupus is an autoimmune disorder, not an infectious disease. It occurs when a patient's antibodies mistakenly attack the body's own cells," said Matheus. "In order for it to occur in someone with an automated immune system..."

Phuong said what we were all thinking: "The immunosystems aren't fighting the infection. They're causing it."

The immunosystem companies were not impressed by our discovery. We invited their programmers to the table to help us figure out why a system designed to protect was now attacking its host - and more importantly, how to stop it - but we got the same responses we'd all seen from people in leadership positions all over the world: "We disagree with your results," "We question your methods," and "That's not possible." In other words - it's not our fault. Go blame someone else.

In the end only one programmer put himself at our disposal. His name was Bran and he was a skinny, green-haired, 24-year-old immunoprogrammer from the GermStop Troubleshooting Clinic in Kirkwood. His had been the first clinic to see patients of this new, more aggressive form of lupus which Abioye had named systemic lupus digitalus. Bran had come here on his own time, and his reasons for doing so were immediately obvious. An angry red rash spread across his cheeks and the pain in his joints had curled his fingers into claws. Bran was dying.

I quickly helped him into a bed and sent my minions to Hatfield-Jackson airport to retrieve the supplies that MSF had forwarded to us from a medical warehouse in Cameroon. Luckily, my personal medical kit contained a syringe of morphine for poor Bran, whose face was contorted in agony as every joint in his body swelled up like a balloon. He flinched away from the needle at first – most Americans his age had never even seen one – but offered up his buttock eagerly once I explained what it was for.

“I need you to cut it out,” Bran wheezed through his constricted lungs after his body had relaxed enough to allow him to think straight.

“Lupus isn’t like cancer,” I told him, my voice muffled through the surgical mask I wore as a precaution while I took his pulse with my gloved hands. “It’s everywhere. You can’t just cut it out.”

“No, you don’t understand,” Bran insisted. “Automated immune systems aren’t like natural ones. They’re controlled by a central processor that designs and produces antibodies. Taking out the processor can stop the spread.”

“That's like trading lupus for AIDS,” I argued. “You have no natural immune system. Without your processor you'll be vulnerable to everything from sepsis to the common cold. Plus, the antibodies already in your system won’t just disappear. You’ll still be sick.”

"Better sick then dead," Bran wheezed.

He was right. Not one person who'd contracted lupus digitalus had recovered on their own, making the fatality rate for the disease closer to 100% than even the most pessimistic epidemiologist would normally go.

"I don't have any anesthetic," I warned Bran.

"I don't care. I want to live."

I wouldn't recommend unanesthetized, unassisted surgery to even the most experienced field doctor, but Bran's immunoprocessor was just below his skin between his shoulder blades. I was able to dig it out with a minimum of bleeding. The morphine took care of most of the pain, but it wouldn't help Bran if his wound got infected. Without his processor, his body couldn't even repair the two inch rectangular hole I had left. I filled it with antibacterial gel, replaced the flap of skin, and covered the whole thing with sterile dressings and medical tape.

"That's it," I told Bran. "Now we wait."

"No, now we work," Bran insisted. "Removing the processor can't be anything other than a temporary measure. Without an immune system, I won't survive long. We have to find a cure."

"First we need to find out how it's transmitted," I countered.

Bran was my first patient interview, and the results were disturbing. Bran had not touched any of the patients he had treated. His diagnostic tools were wi-fi based and noninvasive, so he hadn't even handled any of their bodily fluids. Secondary contact through surfaces such as doorknobs and light switches also seemed to be out - everything in the troubleshooting clinic was voice activated. We reviewed the files on his patients and found that they had almost nothing in common - not genetics, environmental factors, or lifestyle. Yet there was a clear progression.

When a patient came down with the disease, the next people to report feeling ill were family members, work colleagues, and friends. Matheus had even traced a cluster of cases back to a coffee shop, where an early patient had infected the rest of the patrons - even those she hadn't talked to.

Proximity was key. But eliminating all of the most common transmission methods left us with only two options - that it was airborne or that it was transmitting itself in a way I'd never seen before.

"I don't get it," I fumed, resisting the urge to scatter the timeline I'd carefully crafted on several sheets of paper. I hated it when the disease got the upper hand. "The only thing these people have in common is the fact that they were in the same room at the same time. It's like this new lupus is an invisible flea, hopping from person to person."

My words froze Bran as he fiddled with the paper printer I'd unearthed from the basement.

"It is hopping," he said in his raspy voice, which as I predicted, hadn't gotten any better.

"What do you mean?"

"Automated immune systems send out data packets to other immune systems within range. It's a method of sharing cures that's based on the way viruses spread."

"Viral immunity."

"Right, but if your processor's data is corrupted, it could be telling everyone else's processors to produce antibodies that are going to try and kill you."

I swept the timeline aside and pulled my tablet across the table. "What's the range on the transmitter?"

"It's powered by bioelectricity so it's not very strong. It's about 80% effective within three feet, 40% within four feet, and beyond that the effectiveness drops drastically. By seven feet it's less than 5%.

I called up images of the interior of the coffee shop. It was small. The way the tables were positioned, a person moving from the door to the counter would be within four feet of every person in the shop. Even those who weren't immediately infected could pass it on to the people they were sitting next to.

"That's it. We've got it."

Now it was a race against time. The government sent a warning out over the net advising people to stay seven or more feet away from other people, especially if those people had recently visited any of the hot spots we'd identified. Naman and the others were surgically removing immunoprocessors from patients, which would keep the disease from progressing, but without a way to reverse it, it was only a matter of time before something else got them. Immunoprogrammers were combing through millions of lines of code in the infected processors, trying to identify the source of the disease, but even working in concert it could take them months to get results. We had to track down the source of the infection.

I was eager to get started, but my departure from the CDC was delayed by my realization that in treating Bran, I'd exposed myself and my entire staff to lupus digitalus. I fancied I could already feel my joints starting to swell. Rather than calling one of the other doctors away from their work, I trusted my surgery to my most steady handed government assistant. It wasn't pretty. They balked when I told them they'd have to go under the knife too, so I ordered them to quarantine themselves here at the CDC while Bran and I hit the streets. I had to dig up an old wheelchair from the basement for Bran. His joints were too swollen for him to walk unassisted for more than a few minutes. Had I not needed his expertise, I might have left him behind.

We started at the GermStop clinic in Kirkwood. It was only a short ride away on MARTA, the city-wide light rail system, but Bran being in a wheelchair made things difficult. It had been years since there'd been a disabled American, so there were a lot of stairs to negotiate. As Bran and I wrestled with his chair, I wished for a car, but of course there were none of those left either. The instant we were past the threshold, the doors whooshed shut automatically and the train sped along its pre-programmed route.

Atlanta trains were always crowded, but the few people who weren't smart enough to stay at home saw the protective masks, goggles, and gloves Bran and I were wearing and spilled out at the next stop.

The GermStop Clinic was a madhouse. There were people lying on cots or on the floor, largely unattended because the staff were overwhelmed. Bran dug up the records for his first reported patient - Marcus Peter Gallant, a 19-year-old software salesman. I would've liked to speak to Marcus himself, but he was unconscious. His intracranial pressure was so high it was pushing his eyes out of their sockets.

The elder Mrs. Gallant, who was over 90 years old, was still lucid despite having fallen ill shortly after her grandson. She sat by his bedside clutching his limp, puffy hand with fingers that were swollen painfully at the joints.

She tried to turn her head and look at us when we arrived, but her neck muscles were too stiff. "Why Marcus?" she asked. "Why Marcus and not me?"

I gave her my reassuring Doctor Jenni smile.

"His immunosystem is newer and more efficient than yours," Bran explained as I surgically removed Marcus' processor. "So it's killing him faster. This should help."

Mrs. Gallant wasn't able to answer many of our questions about where Marcus had been before getting sick, but she did give us his phone, which allowed Bran to back-trace his movements using the geotags in his online updates.

We had no idea how much time had passed between infection and Marcus showing up at the clinic, so we followed his path backward in time, stopping to compare the names of the people who were tagged in the background of Marcus' life with my list of infected people. Anywhere he had interacted with someone who later fell ill was out as a disease vector. Marcus had already been infected when he met them.

That eliminated his apartment, the Chinese takeout counter nearby, his workplace, and the park where he liked to eat his lunch. The last two days of his life before going to the clinic took us on a loop between these same places until, on the evening of the third day, Marcus visited an unmarked location on the other side of the city for almost two hours.

My gut was back in full force. I could feel that we were getting close. I wanted to run out there and start knocking on doors, but I wasn't invincible this time. I forced myself to call the clinic and talk to Mrs. Gallant first.

"Mrs. Gallant, Marcus' phone is telling us he visited an address in Bankhead a few days before he got sick. Do you know anything about that?"

"Mark's cousin Jonathan lives in Bankhead," Mrs. Gallant wheezed. I'd removed her processor but it hadn't helped the swelling in her throat. "Jonathan's a shut in. Mark brings over his groceries once a week."

"What does Jonathan do, Mrs. Gallant?"

"Computers," came the wheezed response.

Bran and I looked at each other. It wasn't a damning response - most jobs in modern America involved computers in one way or another - but my gut was telling me this guy was involved.

We caught another mostly empty train across town and my tension levels climbed as the number of miles between us and the mysterious Jonathan dwindled.

"I've got a bad feeling," Bran admitted.

"Me too, though I couldn't tell you why."

"I think on some level you've realized the same thing I have: that this looks like a virus."

"Lupus isn't a virus, it–"

"Not a virus virus, a computer virus," Bran interrupted. "I think this kid Jonathan wrote lupus digitalus. It's too fast acting, too deadly, and too easily transmittable to be an accident."

"The question is: why?"

We had let the government and the immunosystem companies know our suspicions and where we were going, but we couldn't take them with us - not even the cops - because they could all be exposed. So, armed with nothing but a taser and a nightstick offered to us by a sympathetic member of the Atlanta P.D., we approached the home of Jonathan Gallant.

Bankhead was an industrial district and Jonathan's home was a run-down 21st Century warehouse squashed between a recycling factory and the huge filters that cleaned the sluggish waters of the Chattahoochee River. It was accessible only by a set of rusted metal stairs that rose three stories to a heavy door with no window that probably led to an office. Bran had to leave his wheelchair and lean heavily on me as we climbed.

"Can I?" Bran asked me. "I've never used a knob door before."

It took Bran a couple seconds to figure out that he had to turn the knob. The door swung open with a squeal, revealing a messy, stinking room lit only by the blue glow of a computer monitor.

"Hello? Jonathan?" Bran called.

I didn't bother calling out. I'd smelled that smell many times before. I felt along the wall and found two switches which activated the lights. Flickering fluorescents illuminated the carnage. Several bags of groceries bearing rotting fruit, vegetables, and meat sat on the desk near the computer. On the floor next to a rolling desk chair was a thin man in his twenties with the bluish grey skin common in people with severe dehydration. He was lying in pool of diarrhea and vomit that looked like rice water.

Bran put a hand over his surgical mask in an attempt to block out the cloying smell. It was a combination of fish and decay. He hobbled over to the computer as I moved to examine Jonathan. From the smell and the condition of his body, I estimated Jonathan had been dead for about a week.

"Look at this," Bran said.

On the computer screen was a typed message.

By now you are sick and dying and you wonder - why is this happening? It's happening because I made it happen. There is too much immunity in this country. Nobody gets sick, nobody dies. The people just keep piling up and up and there's nowhere we can go to be alone with our thoughts. All we can do is carve out a tiny corner of this overpopulated anthill to hide in. Well I'm sick of hiding, so I have sent a plague to thin the herd. Someday our descendants, who have inherited a nation with actual personal space, will thank me.

The message had never been sent. By sifting through Jonathan's files, Bran also found the source code for lupus digitalus along with the code for the immunoprocessor he had hacked.

Bran copied the lupus code and sent it to his colleagues in the troubleshooting clinics. I forwarded a copy to Phuong - she would know what to do with it. Bran also found a digital plane ticket in Jonathan's name. He'd been booked on a flight to Ecuador that had left eight days ago.

"I don't get it." Bran said, looking down at the body.

With my gloved hands, I gingerly rolled the body over to show Bran the bloody hole between Jonathan's shoulder blades. His was a lot more slapdash than Bran's. I suspected Jonathan had done it himself with a kitchen knife and a mirror. The processor itself sat on the desk under a laser scanner.

"Jonathan removed his processor," Bran guessed. "He probably hacked it and gave it lupus digitalus so when Marcus came over to deliver the groceries, the infection jumped to his cousin. But Jonathan didn't have a processor. Why is he dead?"

I fished a plastic bottle of Tropical Monsoon spring water out of the recycling bin next to the desk. The label read: 'product of Thailand.'

"After automated immune systems became widespread, the FDA removed a lot of the purity regulations for food and water, assuming that the immunosystems could handle any contaminants. When Jonathan removed his processor, he left himself with no capacity for immune response. He probably contracted cholera from bacteria in the water and was dead in a matter of hours."

Bran looked at the body with some sympathy. "Sounds like a

horrible way to die."

"It is. Don't touch anything unless you want to join him. His feces are all over the place and we've got no immune systems either."

After that, Bran couldn't get out of there fast enough. I have to admit that despite all my training in infectious diseases and my desire to look under every rock, I wasn't far behind him. You don't realize how much you rely on immunity until it's gone.

Once they had access to the source code for the lupus digitalus virus, the immunoprogrammers were able to come up with a patch that cured the disease in just a few hours. We were able to replace the immunoprocessors we'd removed and patients started to get better. Hands uncurled, joint swelling abated, seizures stopped.

Word went out about the cure on the net and people turned out in droves to hang around in the personal space of friends who had it. The immunosystem companies declared the crisis over and went back to business as usual. But I got another letter. This one was from the government, asking me to stay on in Atlanta and reopen the CDC. They were smart enough to recognize that Jonathan had opened a Pandora's box - if one disgruntled hacker could create a lupus computer virus, what's to stop the next one from creating diphtheria? Or measles? Or Ebola? They needed someone around who could tell one from the other if the immunoprogrammers were going to have a hope of fighting it.

Naman, Abioye, Matheus, and Phuong left for projects in Haiti, Bolivia, Sierra Leone, and Laos. There were still real diseases to track out there, but I let them go without me. I had always dreamed of running the CDC.

Bran agreed to be my first employee. I arranged for him to start medical training through the outreach department of the University of Health Sciences in Phnom Penh immediately. Several other immunoprogrammers who had also come down with lupus digitalus expressed interest in doing the same, so I estimate that within a few months we'll have enough trained staff to respond to a crisis without having to call MSF for help.

They all dread the possibility of a new outbreak, but me? If I'm being honest... I'm kind of looking forward to it.

Communication and Travel

Tezt Messages

by Alexandra Grunberg

"Pencils down!"

Several students groaned as they dropped their pencils onto their desks. Kelsey felt pretty good about the test itself, but Mr. McKenzie had given them twenty-five minutes to complete it. That was a long time, even for a midterm.

"You couldn't have made it a little shorter?" whined Cameron as he handed Mr. McKenzie his test. "Fifteen minutes would have been long enough. It's long enough for all the other teachers."

"It's not my fault that you guys are so plugged in these days," said Mr. McKenzie, carrying the stack of papers back to his desk. "And I won't have you tezting in class. When I first started teaching, I thought texting was a problem, but this tezting is getting ridiculous."

"Come on, stop ranting," Kelsey said, shoving her pencil and calculator into her backpack. There were five minutes left of class, but Mr. McKenzie would probably let them out early. "The test is officially over right? Can we turn back on now?"

Mr. McKenzie sighed, but nodded. Almost in unison, the class reached to the back of their necks to turn on their Tezting Devices. The room was filled with a soft hum and the students began to receive their messages.

Cameron flinched once in front of her, and sighed at whatever he saw. Diana flinched two or three times. She had just gotten her Tezting Device installed and still cringed whenever she got a message. At least she had stopped tearing up.

Kelsey also flinched with each electric shock that ran down her spine. Only three so far today, not too bad. She closed her eyes and words flashed in the darkness. A message from Mary, "Oh my God this test is ridiculosis, Mr. Mc didn't even teach us half this stuff, I'm flipping ooouuut!" Kelsey glared back at Mary who stuck her tongue out at her. Kelsey had no idea how she could tezt in class without Mr. McKenzie knowing it. He was very paranoid about tezting and would not hesitate to hand out a detention slip.

Second message from Hayden, "Hey, the 'Habitat for the Homeless' meeting is gonna have to be pushed back to 4:30, Rubin has band practice." No problem, she could go down to the coffee shop and grab a drink, maybe do a little homework. Third message from mom, "I need you to pick up some milk on the way home."

Kelsey held her left hand out in front of her and tapped rapidly on her palm, sending back her own message, "No problem."

She flinched again as a new tezt came in. Mary, "R we gonna hang in class all day? Im STAAARVING!"

Kelsey glared at Mary as she hoisted up her backpack.

"You could have just told me that in person," she said.

"God Kelsey, this isn't the twentieth century," said Mary, pulling Kelsey towards the door.

In the front row, Daniel was still receiving tezts. His girlfriend, Nina, was very attached and paranoid, and he seemed to receive tezts almost constantly. Even when he was not receiving tezts, he still flinched and jerked involuntarily, like he was in a continual state of electrocution. Kelsey had once seen him get fifty messages at once after a pep rally. They had to call in the paramedics. But that was unusual. All the other students knew it was stupid to keep your Tezting Device off for more than an hour.

Kelsey waved at him as Mary swept her out the door. He waved back, weakly, his fingers twitching.

There were some drawbacks to tezting. Receiving messages would always be painful, but eventually you got used to it. Sometimes the Tezting Devices would malfunction, and random words would flash every time you closed your eyes, but all problems could be fixed in a day or two. The surgery was probably the most annoying part. The hair at the base of your neck took time to grow back, though many tezters used the new haircut as a fashion statement. Most people spent the next few days dizzy and nauseous, but the side effects subsided eventually. Kesley had thrown up every night for a week after her surgery, but that was considered a long recovery period.

Now it was just a part of her life, and she could not imagine her life without it. Tezting was so convenient, and everyone agreed that the pros outweighed the cons.

"If I don't eat something right now, I am literally going to die," said Mary as she continued to pull Kelsey to the cafeteria.

Kelsey guessed that Mary was dieting again. She wondered what diet Mary was following now. No dairy? Only brown food? Ten servings of whole grain a day? She had a feeling that when Mary turned eighteen she would get the weight-regulating app for her Tezting Device.

The cafeteria was already full of students eating, chatting, doing homework, and messaging each other. The noise was overwhelming, and Kelsey already had a headache from receiving three tezts at once. She was more used to getting one or two, but she expected a little more after turning off the Tezting Device for twenty-five minutes.

Rubin and Hayden were sitting at the end of a table. They already had their food; they must have run to avoid the line. Rubin waved at Kelsey and Mary.

"Come on, get in line with me," said Mary, her grip too tight on Kelsey's arm.

"Sorry, I packed my lunch." Kelsey broke free of Mary's hand, and started walking towards her friends.

"But what do I do if I can't pick what I want?" Mary called after her.

"Tezt me!"

Kelsey passed groups of friends, all happy to have this midday break. She skimmed the faces in the crowd, trying to catch a wink or a smile, going out of her way to avoid eye contact with others. She wandered over toward a table, but stopped suddenly. She was not sure at first what brought her attention to him, he was out of her direct path and almost appeared to be actively hiding himself, but Kelsey could not just walk by the one unhappy face in the crowd.

Liam sat by himself at a small table in the corner. He was not unpopular; he had friends he could have been sitting with. He did not have any food or books in front of him. He just was sitting, absolutely still, staring at the blank table in front of him. His stillness was unnerving.

Kelsey flinched as a tezt came in.

"I don't know what I want to driiiiinnnnnk :(!"

Kelsey tapped into her palm.

"You want chocolate milk. You always want chocolate milk. Stop pretending you're on a diet and get chocolate milk."

She walked over to Liam and sat down across from him. He did not even look up at her.

"Hey Liam, are you ok?"

Liam looked up at the sound of Kelsey's voice, but his eyes wandered around the room. He was always a little spacey, but Kelsey could tell he was more in the clouds than usual.

"Oh hey Kelsey," he said. "Yeah, I'm fine, totally fine. Totally."

"You sure about that?"

Liam looked like he was about to cry. Kelsey shifted, uncomfortable. If she'd realized he was this upset she might have just walked right on by. She barely knew how to talk to people in person, let alone comfort someone. But there was no way to gracefully leave, so this was her problem now.

"Liam, what's wrong? It's ok, you can tell me."

"I forgot to turn on my Tezting Device this morning."

Kelsey felt her stomach drop. So that was why Liam looked so still. No flinches. No received messages.

"Well, that's not a big deal," she lied, hoping he could not see through her smile. "I mean, it's only noon. When did you turn it off? One a.m.? Two?"

"I turned it off at eight last night."

"What?"

Liam was trying very hard to hold back tears.

"I wasn't feeling well," he croaked. "I thought I would just take a nap, but then I never got up. When I did get up I was already late for school so I just ran here as fast as I could. I wasn't thinking."

"So it's been –"

"Sixteen hours," said Liam.

"Oh my God!"

Kelsey turned around. Mary was standing behind them, carrying a tray with a slice of pizza, a carton of chocolate milk, and a slice of chocolate cake. Apparently, her diet was not going very well. Mary stared at Liam, her mouth wide open. She flinched as she received a tezt, but her gaze stayed locked on him.

"You haven't read your messages for sixteen hours?"

She set her tray on the table and began tapping furiously into her hand. Soon the whole school would know. Kelsey did not know what good that would do Liam, but there was no stopping Mary once she was on a roll.

"Please don't," said Liam. "I don't want this to become a thing."

"It's already a thing," said Mary, still tapping. At the speed she was tezting, Kelsey did not doubt her.

"You haven't read your messages for sixteen hours?"

Rubin slid in next to Liam, followed by Hayden. They balanced trays covered in pizza slices and cookies, coke and cartons of milk, dumping their bags on the floor as they scooted in. Other kids, who had observed their hasty abandonment of their usual lunch spot, peered over at the growing gathering, whispering to their friends in earshot and tezting others. Both Rubin and Hayden were staring at Liam like he was some kind of monster. It was like they were afraid of him, but could not look away, even as they shoved greasy slices of pizza into their gaping mouths. Rubin and Hayden both starting tezting, leaving shiny smudges in the center of their palms, but kept their attention on Liam.

"Everyone just calm down," said Kelsey. "We're probably overreacting. Liam, maybe you haven't gotten that many messages. I usually don't get more than ten in a morning on a busy day. You should still be fine with up to fifteen."

"But it's been sixteen hours," said Hayden. Kelsey glared at him.

"Well it's true!" insisted Hayden. "This is more than a morning. This is a night and a morning. This is basically an evening before, then the night, then a morning."

Mary coughed and pointed discreetly at Liam.

"But you never know," said Hayden, giving Liam a horribly forced smile and throwing his arm around his shoulder. It looked like it hurt Hayden to touch him.

"You don't understand," said Liam, pushing Hayden off, much to the other boy's relief. "It's my mom's birthday. I didn't wish her a happy birthday. Clearly, I didn't even send her a tezt."

For a moment, the group was silent. The only sound was the quiet electric zings as they received messages.

"People forget birthdays sometimes," Kelsey reassured him, shifting uneasily in her seat.

"I know," groaned Liam. "I forgot it last year too. I got a tezt every five minutes until I reached her."

Rubin, Hayden, and Mary began tapping their palms furiously. Soon the little table was surrounded by students, all concerned, mesmerized, and horrified. Liam was slumped on the table. He had not cried yet, but Kelsey could tell that the reality of his situation was getting to him.

"What if you turned it on and off again really fast?" asked Cameron. "You know, so you get like, one message at a time."

"You can't turn it off until all the messages are read," countered Mary. "It's a safety feature, to make sure you don't lose any of your messages."

"Some safety feature," mumbled Hayden.

"Is there a way to delete your messages without turning on the Tezting Device?" asked Daniel, twitching next to Nina, who might have been tezting him right there.

"Yeah," said Kelsey. "Maybe you could call your service provider and have them delete the messages."

"I can't do that," said Liam, his voice muffled. "I accidentally deleted some of my messages last year, so my mom added a block. I can't delete anything until I hear it."

"Why don't you have the office call her so she can remove the block and stop tezting you?" asked Rubin.

"All changes take at least a day to start working," said Mary, still continuously tapping even as she received messages.

"Well you can't just keep receiving messages forever," said Kelsey.

"You're right," said Liam, sitting up. "When the inbox reaches full capacity, the Tezting Device will turn on by itself and start playing the messages."

"When does it reach full capacity?" asked Kelsey.

"One thousand messages," said Liam, and he burst into tears.

"I think we should call 911," said Kelsey.

Liam fainted. All the students held their palms out towards him, scanning a picture message to send to anyone who was not there.

The paramedics arrived within a few minutes. By now the image of the fainted and doomed Liam had gone viral. Students were blinking furiously as they followed the story online. Teachers were blocking the doors from local news stations that were trying to cover the story.

The paramedics had all the students backed up against the wall as they tried to console Liam, who had recovered only to burst into tears again. They had been trying for over an hour to convince him to turn on the Tezting Device, but no one blamed him for being afraid.

"Come on son," said a paramedic, giving Liam's shoulder a reassuring squeeze. "The longer you wait, the harder it's going to be."

Liam winced, but nodded his head. The paramedics backed up to where the students stood, giving him room as he reached around to the back of his neck. Everyone watched, completely still, neither sending nor receiving tezts, as the room filled with a soft hum.

Resonance

by Lauren C. Teffeau

Implants might have transformed society, but they couldn't get the stink of humanity out of Kyoto's public transportation.

Karida breathed through her mouth as she made a path through the thronging commuters to avoid the uncomfortable odors people carried on their clothes and hair. But the disinfectant the maglev station's air scrubbers used still lodged in the back of her throat, prickly and vaguely citrus.

As soon as she entered the station, the disconnecteds swarmed around her. In other countries they had different names, but here they were known as simply *setsudan.*

Strangers spilled out of the cars hovering over the tracks. A glassy-eyed man careened past her. Karida pulled up short, her stomach quavering. He didn't even see her, too preoccupied with his implant to pay attention to where he was going. Another woman—*setsudan*—glared up from her handheld as Karida passed.

Karida forced her shoulders back. She'd have to toughen up if she was going to find Damek in all of this.

The sour taste of scrubbed air lodged in the back of her throat. She swallowed it back. He should have been there by now—she had tracked the train's progress with her implant as she crossed the distance from her apartment to the station, dodging bikes and small processions of school children too young for the subdermal implants. Two girls had pointed at her *gaijin* hair and the tattoo on her upper arm—usually she could ignore the curiosity she garnered as a foreigner even though she'd lived in Japan for almost ten years, but today she was hyperaware of everything. And she wanted everything to be perfect.

She gritted her teeth as another wave of *setsudan* pushed past her. Of course, this was all Damek's fault. Lately he'd been preoccupied with all sorts of existential questions that hummed in the background whenever he and Karida synched. She shouldn't have been surprised he wanted their first meeting to be unmediated by the implants that made their relationship possible in the first place. It would be just another one of his games.

/We'll find each other, don't worry./ His voice had rushed through her, smoothing the knots that had sprung up in her mind at his suggestion weeks ago. He always knew how to comfort her, an expert at untangling her brambly thoughts. And so she had agreed.

But as she stood on the train platform and resisted the press of bodies, a small sliver of doubt wormed through her. She was probably just cranky, being around so many people and without her connection to Damek to anchor her in all the chaos.

Despite being confidants for years, she had never seen Damek in person. Just his blinking avatar whenever they synched. Another one of Damek's idiosyncrasies. He thought the strength of their friendship shouldn't depend on physical trivialities when it was their minds that connected them. In the past, when she asked to see photos of him, as a joke he'd transmit images of vidactors or people he saw on the street. Never the real him.

When she pressed him as to why, he just said, "We share so much of ourselves already. Let this be a surprise."

Eventually, she stopped asking. But that hadn't stopped her from imagining what he looked like, given their virtual conversations and the imagined tells in the discussion archives, scattered throughout like bugs in old code.

How could she find a feeling—one comprised of thousands of digital interactions and sensory impressions that only existed in her head? Karida was unbalanced enough already when Damek severed their connection that morning so they couldn't cheat. She was too accustomed to feeling his presence, always in the back of her mind. All she felt now was emptiness.

Maybe that was what she had to do—find someone just as empty.

Her eyes tripped over the people still cluttering the platform. She had a couple inches on the predominantly Japanese crowd, smattered with taller *gaijin*. But the majority were *setsudan*, often immigrants from less modernized countries hurrying off to their menial jobs.

Damek would be looking for her too. Maybe… She glanced over at a man with dark brown hair—maybe late twenties, a couple of years older than her—assessing the crowd with similar determination. He wasn't Japanese or *setsudan*, she knew that much.

She took a cautious step toward him, and his dark eyes lanced into hers. Then he smiled, barely an upturn of the lips, and something in her recognized it—him—even though she had no prior knowledge of this version of Damek.

He carefully worked his way toward her. He was tall, lanky, with a slight snub nose and prominent cheekbones. Just knowing he was there helped the knot in her stomach unwind, but a new one coiled into place as he stood before her and just looked.

Her hand went to her hair. She'd taken the trouble to tame the tight curls that hung to her jawline at the salon that morning, suffering through a disconnected's touch and later the whispers of the schoolgirls. She did it all so she'd be the best possible version of herself. So he'd envision her this way when they returned to their separate lives.

Damek bowed, his movements precise and formal as befitting the occasion. Karida returned the gesture, partly thankful for the few seconds it gave her to gather her thoughts, partly amused he'd picked up so much of the etiquette over the course of his business trip. Show off. He could never ignore an opportunity to make a statement.

She led him out of the station, eager to escape escaping the processed air and the smothering crowds. The slap of heels against concrete and the whisper of fabric against skin did little to drown out the sudden thumping of her heart.

When they reached the street, Damek swung toward her, another half-smile tugging at his lips. "Well, are you going to say something?"

His voice was richer than the digital version Karida's implant constructed when they synched. But there was an edge to it as well. Was the indomitable Damek nervous too? The thought made her steps a bit lighter.

"*Gomen.* I'm still taking it all in. You're actually here."

Damek shrugged, an elegant lift of his shoulders. "Didn't believe me when I said I'd be visiting?"

"Not exactly." Until she laid eyes on him, she hadn't realized some part of her was expecting this to be another one of his elaborate hoaxes. No matter how much they had endeared him to her over the years.

With fewer competing odors, she could make out the slight tang of incense that lingered on his wool sports coat. When Damek told her he'd be coming to Japan for business, she thought it silly he would come all this way just to pray in a Shinto shrine. He lived in Italy, worked from there, but his latest promotion required a face-to-face meeting with his Japanese employers. The founder of his company still believed in the sacred places, their connection to the land, and required employees of a certain status to visit the Shinto shrine at the headquarters in Tokyo.

Karida, a military brat, didn't understand all the nuances of the religion, having moved here in her early teens with her parents. But Damek must be important for his employer to issue such an invitation. And given the opportunity, it only made sense to find a way for them to meet up at some point while he was visiting the country.

She gestured between them. "It's just that this is so different."

Damek's steps slowed, and foot traffic eddied around them. "In a bad way?"

"No. I… I'm just not sure what to say." She struggled with the words. Speaking was far more onerous than synching. "You already know everything about me."

"I didn't know about the curls. Or the tattoo." He pointed to the ink whorls on her upper right arm exposed by her sleeveless tank. "Or the soft burr to your voice. You can still surprise me." He smiled again, and it was almost as pleasant as whenever Damek shared his emotions with her directly. Almost, because it was still so new.

Crowds buffeted them down the sidewalk, some people giving them strange looks since they were actually talking out loud. Tension knotted her shoulders, but Karida fought for calm. They had passed Damek's test. Surely they could now go back to their normal mode of communication. But he denied her synch request almost instantly.

"Just indulge me a bit longer, okay? So I can imagine you the next time we synch."

She wanted to protest, but she recalled his excitement over their arrangement to see how well their digital friendship would translate to the physical world—awkwardness and all. Their connection had practically vibrated with his enthusiasm, a low thrum that filled her with warmth.

Karida remembered to smile. "For a little bit longer then. What would you like to do?"

Damek chuckled. "What's this, no plan?"

"Well, I have some ideas, of course, but since you're visiting, you should have a say…" She trailed off with a frown. "You're still laughing."

He moved closer, and she resisted the urge to take a step back. This was Damek—her Damek—after all. "I want you to show me the city through your eyes. Show me what your life is like here. Can you do that?"

Karida nodded.

She took him to the sculpture gardens where she liked to sit after her curation classes and synch. She had a special place on a bench tucked underneath the sakura trees. There, a jagged metal and glass installation surrounded her. It was supposed to be a representation of the cliffs of Tōjinbō off the Sea of Japan. Designed to interface with implants, the sculpture created soundscapes that fit her mood while lights danced along the panes in perfect counterpoint. A simple trick, but one she never tired of. Especially after a stressful day of class.

The university was old-fashioned enough to require one in-person session a week so as to not discriminate against *setsudan.* Not that they had any business being in a curation class. But the university didn't want to a risk a lawsuit—*setsudan* were increasingly litigious of late—so she and her classmates suffered through the indignity every Wednesday.

"Have you thought any more about what you'll do when your rotation is up?" Damek's rich voice startled a handful of crows that had gathered around a kitsune statue.

Karida shook her head. She had only one more semester to go, then the mandatory two-year rotation in digital curation. Plenty of time to settle on a real career.

She caught the tail end of Damek's frown. "What?"

He shrugged. "You've always been so organized. I'm just surprised you don't know what to do."

"You sound like my mother."

He held up his hands in mock-horror. "You wound me."

A giggle escaped her—she couldn't help it. "Don't worry about it. When I decide, you'll be the first one I tell."

Damek seemed to enjoy the rest of their meandering walk, past the perfectly manicured garden beds. He even stopped every so often to interface with some of the sculpture's embedded media.

Next, she took him to a café a few blocks away that had amazing gelato. Maybe it would remind him of home. He had to be missing it after such a long business trip.

They used their implants to order and watched in silence as a robotic arm prepared their servings behind a wall of glass. A disconnected was stationed next to the apparatus, looking on under lowered lids. He was supposed to make sure everything ran smoothly—no wonder he was half-asleep.

In a secluded corner booth, Karida sucked down her serving of ginger wasabi while Damek took a few bites of his salted caramel, then pushed the rest around in his bowl with the back of his spoon until it melted. He said he liked it, but he just didn't have much of an appetite. She didn't know what to say to that, so she only smiled—it was getting easier now—but noticed the slight hesitation before he responded in kind.

Maybe he just wasn't hungry. She hated the fact that she couldn't know for sure.

But then he smiled, his teeth flashing out, and he asked, "Where to next?"

While they walked, her eyes kept sliding towards him. She could just make out the coppery bruise of his implant lurking under his skin before it disappeared into the curls at the base of his neck. Was he as unbalanced as she by their meeting? She'd probably ask him in a future conversation, when they were once again safely separated by thousands of miles with only their implants connecting them.

Damek seemed cheerful enough, but by mid-afternoon, a weariness about his eyes began to worry her. More than once, she wished they hadn't disconnected from one another. It would have been no trouble at all to figure out whether he was enjoying himself or determine if was bored by her unpracticed prattle. She knew him that well.

They had been confidants for years after finding each other in the digital ether. A privileged relationship, allowing for prioritized interactions and the sharing of emotions and sensory impressions to heighten their connection.

Though Karida had been more willing than Damek of late. She had no proof, not really, but she couldn't bury the suspicion that for the last six months he'd been shutting her out. Just short periods at a time, hardly detectable if she hadn't been looking for them. It could be as simple as Damek taking a lover and wanting to shield Karida from their more intimate moments. But if that was the case, he would have told her as much, not just pretend it didn't happen.

Confidants could set the limits of the connection—clipping the strands that fed into parts of their mind they didn't want to share. It was polite to accept those boundaries. Especially since they had already pushed past them once by accident. She would just have to wait until Damek was ready to tell her why he closed off their connection from time to time. Besides, she didn't think it could be too serious. He did come all this way to spend time with her.

The next stop was the museum where she had interned last summer. The basics of curating and cataloguing physical objects was a prerequisite of her program and provided a good foundation before moving on to digital curation techniques. Implants had exploded the proliferation of digital content that had been massing for decades, and someone had to sort through the mess, salvage what they could, contextualize and preserve various bits for posterity. The two-year rotation required of all connecteds was a small price to pay if they could enjoy their implants for the rest of their lives, no strings attached.

The cramped museum was in need of renovations, but she had loved cataloguing the old pieces of bone, pottery, and vellum. They were as fragile as eggshells through her glove-tipped fingers.

Damek lingered over the collection, his brow slightly furrowed as he moved from case to case. "I remember how you felt when you came here," he said, his voice bouncing off the walls and glass. "It was always soothing for me."

The security guard glared at them as two other patrons scurried into the next room at Damek's outburst. The guard had always been cranky, barely acknowledging her whenever she came in for her twenty hours a week.

"What's wrong?" Damek asked.

"Nothing," she whispered.

"Something is bothering you." His voice was still too loud.

She inclined her head toward the guard with his furrowed gray brows and mulish jaw.

Damek's eyes narrowed. "I can't talk to you in here?"

She winced. "It's just—"

"What, not customary?"

Speech marked the domain of *setsudan*. Those with implants refrained from speaking out loud whenever possible—not only because synch chatting was easier and more immediate, but also because no one wanted to be mistaken for a disconnected.

Damek glared at the guard. "I won't restrict my behavior to please him. This day is for us. Sometimes I wonder what it would be like to not have this embedded in me." He pointed to the discolored skin on his neck sheltering his implant.

She crossed her arms and stared into a case of splayed out scrolls, the kanji wavering before her eyes. "I hate it when you say things like that."

"Haven't you wondered what it would be like?"

She whirled towards him. "No! Because I'd lose too much without it." His face tightened, but she didn't care as she stalked past the guard and retreated outside. The increase in humidity was a shock, but then it always had been when she came to the museum on a regular basis.

Stupid Damek and his principles. This wasn't how their meeting was supposed to go. She rubbed her forehead as an ache threaded its way through her temples, drawing tighter each moment. Damek had always been the one to ease the knots in her mind. But not today.

"I'm sorry," he said from behind her in a more moderate voice. She nearly jumped. "It's been a long day. I know that's not an excuse but…"

Karida took a deep breath. "It's okay. We've been going strong for the last couple of hours. Why don't we go back to my place? We can relax for a bit and figure out what we want to do tonight before you have to leave."

"That sounds lovely." Damek smiled, though something about it seemed forced. Maybe it wasn't—she had to remind herself she didn't have any frame of reference for him.

The closer they got to the apartment she shared with her mother, the tighter the vise around her head became. Part of her was glad Damek had come, glad they indulged in the novelty of meeting in person, but she still felt empty, even with him standing right beside her.

And the lack of connection just amplified her anxiety. What if, after today, he didn't want to be confidants anymore?

There were always stories, of course, of people meeting face-to-face for the first time and not being able to reconcile the person from the deeper recesses of their mind with the one of flesh and blood standing before them.

She didn't think things had gone that wrong. At least on her end.

"It's a little small," Karida said in a soft voice when they entered the elevator.

"It'll be fine." Damek gave her a pointed look. "You're worrying again. Stop it."

The elevator crawled to the sixteenth floor. The sharp ding reverberated in Karida's chest as she led the way to the apartment.

They slipped off their shoes just inside the front door. Karida had to nudge Damek's dress shoes so the toes pointed to the door.

They padded down the hall. Her mother sat in a western chair in the spare six-tatami mat living room, eyes glassy as she stared into nothingness. She was probably synching or otherwise engaged with her implant's info stream. Karida knew better than to expect her to acknowledge them.

Her mother was still furious after their fight two months ago. Even though her mother was perfectly capable of tracking Karida's signal, her mother claimed her comings and goings were too erratic, interrupting the apartment's serenity. Karida had just one more semester in her program, and then she'd get her own place. When she pointed that out, their fight devolved into a mental shouting match over what Karida was going to do with the rest of her life since she'd made no plans beyond her upcoming curation rotation.

Damek had sensed her emotional spike and was there when she finally retreated into her bedroom and pulled their connection to the foreground.

/Here. What can I do?/

She flooded him with her anger and injustice. That was followed by her guilt over making her mother cry when Karida had said, "Dad would have supported me in whatever I decide if he were here."

Damek took it all, his voice and presence soothing, comforting, until something between them stretched and snapped and everything was good, but different in a way they both knew went beyond being confidants.

She could almost hear Damek's gasp as he darted away from the threads tying them together more tightly than ever before. */Sorry. I didn't—/*

/Don't go./ She reached for him, plucking at the threads vibrating between them. She wove her awareness through his to ease his discomfort and tried to show him just how much he had made her feel. Resonance, wonderful and terrifying, leaving them both more open to one another than ever before when the strands snapped and their minds unfurled into one another.

When she could breathe again, she had glided through his mind in thanks, but already she could feel him retreating into himself. They'd stayed connected, of course, but they had both been careful not to repeat that moment. She'd kept the sensory impressions in her implant's active memory though.

And she and her mother had largely succeeded at ignoring one another since the fight.

Damek cleared his throat, but her mother only angled her chair away from them. The light from the windows fell onto the back of her neck and the thin white scars that interrupted the shadow of her implant.

Karida forced herself to look away. She just shook her head at

Damek's questioning look—it wasn't as though he could fix her fraught relationship with her mother—and gestured for him to follow her down the hall to her room.

She should make tea, but instead she watched Damek as he pivoted in place, studying the walls where her knickknacks and belongings were arrayed. Replicas of Noh masks and Buddha statuary along with a few woodblock prints from the museum she'd gotten with her employee discount, souvenirs from her father's tours of duty so long ago, and a porcelain doll in a brilliant red kimono her mother had given her on her ninth birthday before they even knew her father would be stationed in Japan. Before they'd known they'd end up staying there without him.

Damek closed his eyes and breathed deep, making her suddenly paranoid over what smells he could detect—despite what her mother thought, she did spend a lot of her time here. "It feels like you." His eyes opened and found Karida. "Thank you."

"For what?"

"For sharing this with me."

She scrunched up her nose. "Why wouldn't I?"

Damek lifted a shoulder and settled into the lone armchair in the corner of the room next to her futon. "I didn't realize how tired I was getting."

"Oh. I'm sorry."

He traced the armrest's patterned silk with a short thumbnail. "Karida, it's not your fault. It's just been a long week, that's all."

But it was. She should have kept the tour short. She should have known it was too much to pack into one day, especially since he'd come straight from an early morning business meeting.

Her hands fisted. She was desperate for a brush of Damek's consciousness, telling her everything was okay. But he remained seated, his eyes closed, his face the color of weak tea.

Her headache ratcheted tighter. "What's wrong?" she demanded just as Damek said, "This is nice."

She shook her head. "What did I do?"

"Karida, everything is fine. We're just feeling the effects of being disconnected from each other. I feel it too. That's why I was so relieved when you brought me here. You aren't in my head, but you're around me," he said, gesturing to the room.

"Then why…" Her voice cracked, and she swallowed. "Why have you been shutting me out?"

"I haven't. Today was just—"

"You have! For months. Have I done something wrong?" She spread her hands helplessly at her sides. "Do you…" She could barely get the words out. "Do you want to stop being confidants?"

He rubbed his temples. "Karida, that's not it at all."

"Then what? What are you not telling me?"

Damek rose to his feet. At the same time, he reopened their connection. Karida swayed as Damek's presence swept through her. She sagged with relief. Her mind snagged against the threads, darting along them, eager to restore—

"Easy," he said in a rough voice.

She stopped. The tension shuddered between them like an over-tightened bowstring. "Why? Why are you holding back?"

He squeezed his eyes shut, his knuckles white on the back of the chair. /*Because if I don't, this.*/

A torrent of emotion zipped between them. She gasped as her brain struggled to comprehend all the sensations that crackled through her as the strings stretched tighter.

/*See? This. Every time. Since that day.*/ The day they hadn't spoken of since.

Her eyes drifted shut. She fought to understand the sensory impressions, seeking a pattern in all the noise. /*Didn't know. Didn't mean to.*/

He clamped down on the flow, but their connection still thrummed in the back of her mind, warm, alive.

"That's…that's why I've been reluctant." His voice grew stronger. "That's partly why I wanted to meet. To see if we were the same if we strip the artifice away."

She unclenched her hands and took deep breath. She looked up at him, committing his face at this moment to her implant's cache. "And?"

/*What do you think?*/ He cleared his throat. And suddenly he looked very young. "If we do this…"

"I know."

Bonding was often permanent, allowing for near constant connectivity and unfiltered emotional bleed. If they grew apart, found a way to filter out their bond, times of stress could still trigger it.

Her parents had been bonded. Damek's were too, though it was just as common between platonic confidants who wanted to prove their complete trust in each other and acknowledge the necessity of their connection. From a technical standpoint, bonding was a form of brain damage, as each participant's unique brain patterns were shaped for perfect integration with their pair, usually facilitated by a licensed implant specialist.

But sometimes minds were made to fit together without medical intervention, and the benefits… She shivered as Damek's awareness trilled through her. They had already established the compatibility of their thoughts.

/*Karida…*/ He started slow. He gave her time enough to disengage if she wanted to as the strands drew taut.

But they both knew she wouldn't.

Damek held her hand as they retraced their steps to the maglev station. They got looks, of course, but Karida couldn't bring herself to care. She was still reveling in the depths of their bond. Hyperaware of the heat of his fingers and the smooth press of his palm, she could understand why *setsudan* still expressed themselves in such ways. Implants heightened physical sensations, replaced them with superior, more intense ones, so connecteds didn't need to resort to physicalities to express themselves. But with Damek there beside her, it seemed silly not to after sharing so much.

The lights of the maglev train flashed closer as it reached the turn into the station. Sadness flared across their bond but Damek battled it back, giving her a small smile. "Thank you for today, Karida," he said softly.

"No need to be so glum. You'll have me with you all the time," she said, broadcasting her awe and pleasure at their new level of intimacy.

He opened his mouth to speak, but closed it as the maglev, whisper soft, came to a stop on the track.

/*Thank you, again. For everything.*/ His hand disengaged from hers. She watched him board, watched the train pull away, content with the fact that he never really left her.

Four months later, Karida woke, suddenly uncomfortable, but not sure why. She used her implant and scrolled through her contacts and alerts. She sat up when she realized it was Damek's absence that made everything feel so wrong.

Another one of his jokes? She plucked at the familiar channels, felt her way across the bond that had joined them. But the strands had been rent as easily as spider's silk.

The dull ache behind her eyes flared to life as she tried and tried again to reconnect with him, sending synch requests that would not complete. But only silence. Silence and an emptiness that curled into her gut.

Karida bolted off her futon and was thrusting on her clothes when the priority message arrived and set her heart to racing. She opened it, and a hollow approximation of Damek's spirit flooded through her. Buoyant and bittersweet at the same time.

/I'm sorry, Karida, but I thought it would be better this way. If you've received this, I can no longer sustain our connection. When I found out I was dying, I could not imagine leaving without knowing you, all of you./

The out-of-the-blue suggestion to meet in person, his exhaustion that day—he must have been sick even then. The intermittent moments of silence that had continued despite everything else they had shared…

Damek explained how his trip to Japan was to transfer his expertise to another employee who would be taking over for him. An experimental procedure doctors here had developed. He had taken the opportunity to hide the parts of his mind related to his illness from her, even if they bonded.

Bile crawled up her throat. She never suspected and now—

/I wanted you to remember me as I lived. It was selfish of me, but you have given me a gift. Our bond has been my only comfort these past weeks. And I am only sorry for the burden I place on you now. Yours, always./

She reached for him, but the strings stayed achingly silent.

Her fingernails dug into her neck.

The Memory of Water

by Tom Brennan

Donna dragged her body behind a desert boulder and watched her broken leg morph: clean white bone slid beneath torn skin as the wound's edges closed over, sucking in droplets of blood. Muscles churned like water caught in the artificial tides of Ciudad Madre's inner pool.

Instead of Madre's polling heartbeat, she heard atmospheric static. She winced at snapshot memories of the crash: Seb at the controls, laughing; ocher rubble strewn across the hardtop; their coche spinning through the air. Then starbursts of pain brighter than any Donna had known in the previous two centuries. And relief as her somanet sluiced endorphins.

Now sand scoured Donna's face as cold rock dug into her back but she stared, fascinated, as the molecular nanites reformatted her flesh. She looked up only when her friends began arguing.

"We were going too damn fast," Jorge said, kicking the upturned vehicle.

Seb blushed. "I didn't expect a landslide."

Ailse, perched on a rock, flexed her broken arm. "If you have to switch to manual, so you can show off—"

"Madre's loop doesn't reach here, remember?"

Donna said, “Stop complaining. We’re on vacation.”

From where she sat, Donna could see their intended destination, *El Diablo Rosa.* The setting sun turned the three-hundred meter slab to blood. Donna flexed her leg, testing the nanites’ progress; she’d climb that route in a day or so.

The car lay nearby like a wounded animal flailing its six balloon tires in the air. Black liquid trickled down its exposed belly. Baggage spilled from the trunk: plasmatents, parakites, climbing gear.

“We could push it over,” said Jorge, putting his shoulder to the car.

Donna laughed. “Why? Madre will send out a chaperone when she catches our beacon.”

“That might be difficult since the transmitter is in the roof, the power’s gone and the mountains block—”

“Please,” Ailse said. “I want to go home.”

Seb said, “Someone’s coming.”

A sound drifted closer, a regular thudding like a Pelota ball. Lights on the hardtop grew, became mismatched eyes. Jorge ran over, waving, and for a moment Donna thought the vehicle would run him down. Instead it stopped with a screech and skidded across the road.

Dark smoke pulsed from a dented pipe jutting from the cabin roof. An angular, tanned old man climbed out of the truck like a crab from its shell. He spoke English, then switched to Spanish. “What the hell you doing?”

Jorge pointed at their car. “We crashed—”

“Rocks everywhere,” Seb said. “We couldn’t avoid them.”

The old man reached inside the truck’s cab and the thudding

stopped, replaced by the moaning wind and distant animal or bird cries. "Show me."

The old man knelt down at the car. "What's she use, boys? Gas or water?"

Jorge and Seb looked at each other.

"Water, I reckon, probably a fusion unit. Either way she's sealed tight. Not much I can do with her."

As the old man walked back to his truck, Donna started to unpack a tent but paused when she saw Jorge and Ailse run up to the old man.

Jorge said, "You can't just leave us—"

"Not out here all alone."

The man stared at the wreck. "Guess not. Climb aboard, then."

"What about our equipment?"

"Take what you need and leave the rest," he said. "I got just enough room for the four of you, never mind all your crap."

Jorge, Ailse and Seb climbed up into the truck. Donna hesitated, then climbed onto the seat next to the old man. The truck started with a belch of black smoke.

The man shouted above the engine. "You from the city, right?"

"Ciudad Madre, yes. She will arrange everything."

"You reckon?" The old man spat through the window's flapping plastic sheet. "Gotta be careful out here. You're far from home."

As the truck built up speed, a sharp wind drilled through the starred windscreen and made Donna shiver. She thought about floating in Madre's warm pools, secure and safe. "Where are you taking us?"

The man didn't lift his eyes from the road. "Town."

"What town?"

He shrugged. "Just town."

Donna turned to her friends. Ailse, Jorge and Seb slumped against each other, sleeping like children.

"Orrett."

Donna looked back to the old man. "What?"

"My name: Orrett. Yours?"

"Donna Barca Veinte-cinqo de Ciudad Madre."

"Pretty name."

"Thank you." She stared out at the desert. A yellow glow to the south, beyond the mountains, warmed the night sky and marked the site of Ciudad Madre. At that moment it looked as far away as the stars.

Miles passed before a necklace of lights appeared on the left. Orrett peeled off the fused hardtop and hit a dirt road hard enough to wake his passengers. Soon Donna could make out illuminated globes on wooden poles, with cables sagging between them.

Orrett parked inside a circle of adobe houses. Donna's heart raced, just like the start of a climb, or that moment before she launched herself into the air clutching a parakite. She got out and stretched like a cat, then reached down and rubbed her leg.

Ailse yawned. "Where are we?"

"Town," Donna said.

"What town?"

Donna echoed Orrett's shrug. "Just town."

People emerged from the houses. Some of the men carried metallic objects. Orrett called out, "No need for firepower. Some Madre hitchhikers rolled their jeep out near Soldiers' Bluff."

The town's inhabitants surrounded the four. Donna stared back at them; wrinkled and dusty, grained like old wood, they wore patched clothes in leather and thick cotton. Not all of them wore shoes.

A stocky man stepped forward. "You collecting strays now, Orrett?"

"Couldn't leave'em out there, could I, Frank?"

The man folded his thick arms. "Don't see why not. Madre's never been much use to us."

As some of the people muttered in agreement, Donna said, "Just let us use your comm pod and we'll have Madre pick us up."

Frank spat into the sand. "Nothing like that here."

A small seed of doubt opened inside Donna. She heard her net's background static. "No comms?"

Orrett touched her arm. "Don't you worry about it."

"Hear that?" Frank turned to his audience. "A week to lift the crops and he's telling freeloaders not to worry."

"Now that's enough," Orrett said. "We could use extra hands and these are good as any. The boys can bunk with me, but the girls need a billet."

A woman called out, "I'll take one of them."

"Thanks, Mary. Anyone else? Come on, now. In times of need and all..."

Another woman's voice, this one deep and strong: "I'll take the other."

"You're a credit, Louise." Orrett turned to Seb and Jorge. "You follow me, boys."

Donna shook her head. Crops. Billet. Freeloaders. The words Orrett used meant nothing to her. She pulled her jacket tight around her body and looked toward the horizon and Madre's glow.

As the townspeople returned to their houses, a thin woman spoke to Ailse and took her arm. Ailse looked over her shoulder at Donna, her face a blur.

A squat woman nodded to Donna. "I'm Louise."

The woman walked away, but stopped when she realized Donna hadn't moved. "What?"

Donna didn't answer.

"Your choice, honey, but it gets cold out here."

Donna hesitated, then hurried after her. As she stooped to enter Louise's house she coughed at the smells of cooked meat and some earthy, sharp tang. A glass globe gave off yellow light and oil smoke; a young woman sat reading by its light.

"This is my daughter Sally," Louise said. "Say hello to Donna, sweetheart. Orrett brought her in."

"Hey." Sally smiled up at Donna. "You're a long way from home."

Donna said. "Madre will come for us."

"Surely." When Sally stood up she braced her back with one hand and rested the other on her swollen stomach. "I'll turn in, mom. I'm beat."

Donna watched Sally shuffle through a patterned curtain. She remembered pictures of pregnant women from the old discs but she'd never expected to see one in the flesh. Ciudad Madre delivered its rare newborn to the communidad fully formed.

How could someone still function with their body so...changed?

"Sally's husband is up north, trading," Louise said as she moved cushions and blankets. "If he's not back soon he'll miss the big day. Here, you can take the couch. There's water in the pitcher and the pot's under that chair."

Donna sat on the couch and listened to the whispers from behind the curtain. Everything seemed so different. She looked forward to replaying her net's stored images over the next few decades; back in Madre, she could afford to remember the strange town and hovel, and laugh.

With dusty ocher fingers, Donna traced the raised pattern in the blanket. She'd found what she'd wanted: adventure, change from routine, excitement. But right then she could picture Madre's warm waters so clearly it hurt.

She woke with sunlight on her face.

"Coffee's ready." Louise held a cracked mug out to Donna. "You'd better appreciate it: the beans came all the way from Canada."

The dark liquid in the mug made Donna's heart race until her net cut in. She took another gulp.

Light poured through the windows and open door; the inside of the house blazed with reds, greens, gold. Tapestries and carpets. Blankets and throws. Donna looked through the door, blinking until her eyes polarized and let her see distant sawtooth mountains and desert plains already rippling with heat.

"Where are all the people?"

"Down in the fields, pulling crops. We got some good ground beside the old river." Louise clanged pots on the stove. "Orrett's taken your boys to pick up your jeep. You hungry?"

As Donna devoured her third batch of black-pepper corn mush and eggs, she heard the thud of an approaching engine. She ran outside and saw Orrett at the wheel of a bulbous red and yellow vehicle. A thick rope stretched between it and the battered coche.

"Your jeep was one bitch to turn over, let me tell you." Orrett jumped down from the cab and patted the dusty side of the car. "Heavier than she looks. But we got her. Right boys?"

Donna saw Seb and Jorge grinning from the back of Orrett's vehicle. "Where's Ailse?"

"Still asleep when we left." Seb jumped down and joined Orrett as the old man examined the car. Small children appeared from the houses and yards and swarmed over the new arrival until Orrett shooed them away.

"Can you repair it?" Donna asked.

Orrett's voice emerged from deep inside an open panel. "Doubt it."

Jorge's smile slipped. "How will we get back..."

Orrett looked over his shoulder. "Can't get this drive to work, so we'll put one of ours in. But it'll cost you."

Donna looked at Seb and Jorge but they seemed as puzzled as her.

"Cost?"

"Sure," Orrett said, scratching his crooked nose. "We help you, you help us. That's the way it works. You never heard of barter? Trade?"

Donna hadn't. Madre supplied everything. If the car had broken down in range of the city's net, disassemblers would have stripped it down to raw compounds after another vehicle had appeared.

Orrett shook his head. "We'll think of something."

The men set to work on the damaged coche. First they rigged up a framework of metal bars. Then ropes hoisted the car into the air, with flat rocks packing the gap between sand and chassis. Seb and Jorge passed Orrett strange metal implements and followed his every move.

Donna sat on a low wall and watched, swinging her legs and twisting her dusty hair around her fingers.

Ailse sat beside her. "We'll get back, won't we?"

Donna couldn't help looking up into the sky. "Of course we will. Soon."

Ailse hugged her knees. Her arm showed no sign of injury. "It's like a dream."

"What is?"

"The town. It's so...different." Ailse shivered. "So dirty."

Every surface in Ciudad Madre gleamed; cleaners slithered everywhere, polishing, disinfecting, recompiling waste. Here, everything wore layers of dust and dirt. People, buildings, cars: all tainted.

"We'll get home."

Ailse smiled. “I’m not sure Seb and Jorge want to leave.”

“They’ll have to.”

But one day became two, then three. Donna listened for the whine of turbojets or the squeal of treads on the fused hardtop. But no chaperones arrived. No flyers crossed the sky.

“What are you looking for?” Louise asked, straightening up from the furrowed dark soil.

Donna shrugged, a habit she’d picked up from Orrett. Ankle-deep in the riverside’s fertile swatch, she turned from the empty blue sky and concentrated instead on tugging the slimy stalks from their beds.

Twist, pull, lift. Twist, pull, lift.

Madre would come. Madre would come.

On the morning of the fifth day, Donna woke before Louise and left the house. She ran her hand along the side of the car; her trailing fingers left an uneven pattern in the dust and dew, five parallel cosine waves.

The sun’s rim peered above the horizon. Donna could just make out the fresh calluses on her hand; the nanites seemed to be slowing down, not repairing her body’s damage as quickly as they should. She rubbed at the thickened skin and tried to remember what she could have done to make Madre forget her.

“The novelty’s worn off, eh?” Orrett said.

Donna turned and tried to smile. “I suppose.”

Orrett patted the car. “We’ll get her going soon enough. You’re in no hurry, are you?”

Before Donna could answer, a shout tore through the still

morning.

Louise burst from her house. "Her waters broke a week early. I need clean blankets and extra hands."

As Louise disappeared into another house, Ailse ran up, rubbing her eyes. "Have the chaperones come for us?"

"No, it's Sally."

Orrett pointed an oil-stained finger at Donna and Ailse. "You heard Louise, girls."

They stared at him.

"Get on inside," Orrett said. "Everyone else is already down in the fields."

Donna and Ailse shuffled toward Louise's house. A new viscous odor canceled out all other smells. It hit the back of Donna's throat and made her gag.

"Don't just stand there." Louise pushed between Donna and Ailse with blankets slung across her arms.

Donna followed her into the dark, warm bedroom. Sally lay on her back on the bed, hands clutching her stomach. Her legs made a tent of the white sheet. A shaft of early sunlight picked out her face.

Louise knelt down. "Hey sweetheart."

Sally didn't reply or open her eyes. Donna saw beads of sweat on the girl's forehead.

Louise barked out orders to Ailse and Donna. "You. Blankets there. Water there. No, over there. We're staying for a while, so settle in."

She used a softer voice for her daughter. "There we go, honey.

You just take your time."

"Where's Karl?" Sally panted.

"On his way, honey, on his—"

Sally grimaced and gripped her mother's hand.

"Whoa, that was a bad one," Louise said. "Now, slow deep breaths between each contraction. That's it..."

Donna saw Ailse staring, open-mouthed, at Sally.

"One. Two. Three. Deep breaths..."

"Mom...the pain..."

"I know, honey." Louise rolled a black pellet between her fingers. "Here now, just chew this."

As the sunlight crawled across the floor, Donna and Ailse brought fresh water, removed fouled blankets, fetched the pot. Donna's world shrank to the congested bedroom.

"That's right, honey. They're closer together now. Won't be long." Louise turned to Donna. "Get that bowl. Slip the knife into the green water."

Donna stared at Sally's convulsing body. Sweat and tears streaked the girl's face. One white-knuckled fist twisted the blanket; the other gripped her mother's hand.

Louise encouraged her daughter: "Soon, now, sweetheart. Soon. You can do it. I know you can."

Sally's body arched and then sagged. Donna saw a bloody grey wriggling creature lifted high into the air. Louise's fingers tied quick knots. A slap on the baby's behind, a brief cry, then Louise swaddled the child in fresh cotton and set it in Sally's arms.

"Well done, sweetheart." Tears glittered on Louise's cheeks. Like an old painting, the light illuminated three faces for a moment: Louise, Sally, Ailse, the triptych focused on the child cradled in the safety of its mother's arms.

Donna ran from the house and puked onto the sand. Bent double, her hands on her knees, she spattered the desert floor until there was nothing left inside.

Orrett stood beside her, wiping his hands on a rag. "You okay?"

Donna wiped her mouth on her sleeve and stood up. "The coche. Is it fixed?"

"Can't say she is."

Donna tried to keep her voice steady. "When will it be ready? A week? A year? When?"

Orrett raised his palms. "Whoa, take it easy. She's ready when she's ready. What's your hurry all of a sudden?"

Crying drifted from the door behind Donna. She thought of Madre's clean blue waters. "I'm going."

"Where?"

"Home." Donna headed toward the hardtop.

"What about your friends?"

Donna didn't answer. She wiped away hot tears and concentrated on the horizon. Her foot found a rock and sent her crashing to her knees; she got up and marched on, ignoring the gashes. The dirt track gave way to glassy fused hardtop. Donna walked on. Somewhere beyond those mountains lay Ciudad Madre.

Orrett pulled up beside her in his truck. "Get in."

Donna didn't turn or answer.

"Will you stop acting like a child and just get in," Orrett said, trying to keep pace but almost stalling the stuttering truck. "You'll never make it."

"Yes I will."

"No, you won't. I'll drive you home, even if it takes a year's gas. I won't have you on my conscience."

Donna took one more step, hesitated, then climbed up into Orrett's truck. Donna scraped the mixture of dried tears and sand from her face. The hot-copper smell of Sally's blood clogged her mouth.

As Orrett aimed the truck at the horizon, Donna stared straight ahead. She could almost feel the waters closing in around her; suspended and inert, she'd never leave Madre. Like the ribbon of hardtop, an eternity stretched before her.

Clean.

Warm.

Numb.

Safe.

Crystalization

by David Gerrold

It's the moment when a liquid solidifies, when the temperature drops and/or the pressure rises. When the slush finally turns to sludge—to mud, to concrete; it stops flowing, it hardens, it becomes impenetrable. It crystallizes.

For the first few hours after the Los Angeles freeway system hardened, most people believed the problem was temporary and that traffic would eventually start flowing again. Even for the first few days, they believed they could eventually chip their way out of the concretized arteries.

The slush of Los Angeles traffic had been slower than sluggish for years, churning through looped spaghetti concrete channels in a lumpy stream of metal and plastic peristalsis, in a persistent state of uncertain hesitation, punctuated only occasionally by forward jerking movements and uneven painful surges, a textbook demonstration of socio-technical constipation and definitely no place for a stick shift.

The city engineers had been aware of the potential for crystallization for nearly two decades, but few of them had taken their own warnings seriously, and eventually they took it for granted that the projections of crystallization were situational artifacts occurring whenever the simulators reached the limits of their ability to process the rapid flows of data.

Unfortunately, only the data was flowing rapidly. One desperate afternoon, even that stopped. The air conditioning broke down in the central monitoring station. The temperature rose uncomfortably. Fans didn't help. The computers began shutting down in self-defense. The screens went blank, or declared, "No signal." Blind and deaf, the traffic engineers could neither monitor nor prescribe.

The rest was inevitable.

Outside, in the place where facts don't care about simulation, events took on a terrifying momentum of their own. It was Friday, early afternoon on a three-day holiday weekend. Temperatures in the basin had peaked at 106 degrees shortly after 1:00 pm. Add to that, a localized gas shortage acerbated by higher than usual oil prices, a high degree of situational stress about the staggering economy, a disturbing series of terrorist bombings in the mideast, and three days of overheated shock jocks nattering about a particularly scandalous high-profile murder trial, and crystallization was no longer a question of if or when, but *where.*

Surprisingly, it did not begin on the freeway. Not exactly. Although a freeway was involved. The first hardening in the traffic flow began in the San Fernando Valley where Burbank Boulevard intersected Sepulveda. Always a sluggish intersection, today it revealed its true capacity for horror. An overweight, overstressed soccer mom with two screaming children in the back seat of her SUV and a cell phone pressed to her ear, her attention everywhere but on the road in front of her, abruptly became aware of a motorcyclist coming up out of the blind spot on her right. Startled, she swerved left, forcing two teenagers in a dropped Honda Civic (don't ask) to brake suddenly. The empty tanker truck which shouldn't have been in the same lane behind them braked, swerved, and jackknifed sideways into a city bus, effectively blocking all three northbound lanes of Sepulveda and the middle two lanes of Burbank.

Almost immediately traffic stopped on both boulevards, backing up on Burbank as far east as Van Nuys Boulevard and as far west as Woodley. Sepulveda froze all the way north to Sherman Way and as far south as Ventura Boulevard. When the traffic at the intersection of Ventura and Sepulveda froze, the crystallization of the surface streets began to spread east and west on Ventura Boulevard as well. In the horror about to happen, there would be no alternative routes.

The 405 freeway stretches north across the San Fernando Valley; the heaviest used access ramps are at Burbank Boulevard, just slightly east of the fatal intersection and up a slight incline. The northbound and southbound access ramps represent two additional intersections to interrupt Burbank's westward flow—it's a wasps' nest of lanes, contradictory traffic signals, and intermittent left-turn arrows. Even at three in the morning, it takes 90 seconds to negotiate this ganglionic nightmare in any direction. During crush hour, wise drivers bring a book or a magazine. Teenage boys change the radio station and readjust themselves in their jeans. Grown men pick their noses and think about business. Teenage girls turn their rearview mirrors and fix their makeup. Everyone else is on the phone, their attention two or ten or a thousand miles away. Watching the road is optional, something only sissies and old ladies do.

On any ordinary afternoon, traffic feeding into the northbound Burbank off-ramp would start backing up by two pm. By five, it would be backed up two miles south, all the way to the 405/101 interchange. This day, however, traffic was even more manic than usual. As soon as the critical intersection of Burbank and Sepulveda hardened, the crystallization of the 405 began spreading southward as fast as new cars arrived and joined the creeping boundaries of the linear parking lot.

Imagine the intersection of the 405 and the 101 as a cross. The entire northwest quadrant is the Sepulveda dam basin. For the next three miles west, there are only two surface routes that will take you north to the neighborhoods beyond, Balboa and Woodley, if you can get to Woodley. For two miles north, there is only one westward access—Burbank. But there are over a million residents northwest of the intersection and their *only* access from the south or east is through this interchange—or through the intersections of Ventura and Sepulveda, or Burbank and Sepulveda. As quickly as Sepulveda clogged, all of the intersections and all of the surrounding surface avenues began to solidify as well. Within forty minutes, an area ten miles square had crystallized.

The 405 and the 101 freeways only exacerbated the situation, feeding more cars into this black hole of traffic from all four compass points. With no place to go, the traffic ground to a halt both north and south on the 405 and very quickly after east and west on the 101 as well.

With the computers down, Caltrans was unable to post warning bulletins on the freeway alert signs. Instead, an Amber alert was posted to look out for a suspected kidnapper driving a black Ford Explorer, license number, etc. It was this particular (alleged) kidnapper's bad luck to be caught on the 101 westbound at Vineland. Traffic came to a halt with the SUV pocketed between a stretch limo on the left and a battered Plymouth pickup on the right, piled high with tree branches, and driven by three Mexican gardeners whose command of English was limited. Behind the pickup truck, however, was a distracted mother in a white Honda Civic, whose 11 year old son had read the Amber alert only a few moments before and who was now intently watching all of the traffic around the Civic on the promise of a ten-dollar bill if he spotted the suspect Explorer, but only if he kept absolutely quiet while he did, so his exhausted mother could listen to her deadbeat ex-husband (who apparently operated out of the bizarre belief that a good excuse is always an acceptable substitute for a tangible result) explain why his child-support check would be late again.

In the middle of this conversation, the 11-year old suddenly began shouting and pointing. Despite his mother's annoyed refusal to accept the obvious—that she now owed her son ten dollars that she did not have—she eventually accepted that indeed, the suspect's vehicle was only a few yards ahead in the next lane over.

By then, owing to a repeat of the same Amber Alert news bulletin on static-riven KFWB, the inhabitants of two other vehicles had also spotted the Explorer. One driver was already calling 911. The other driver and his two passengers, (all of them new enlistees on leave from the marine base at El Toro and on their way to visit the Tarzana-based fiancé of the driver), exited their own SUV, two of them carrying baseball bats kept in the vehicle for occasional trips into West Hollywood for gay-bashing. With traffic temporarily halted—or so they believed (that it was temporary)—they approached the Explorer on foot. The suspected kidnapper panicked, tried to hit the gas, tried to force his way between a lime-green Volkswagen Beetle and a 1988 gray-blue Chrysler LeBaron convertible driven by a harried college student whose car insurance had just been cancelled, and the result was a three-way crunch, with three soon-to-be-ex-marines banging on the hood and fenders of locked Explorer with baseball bats. They had just escalated to smashing windows when the first officers arrived on scene and ordered them to stand down.

From there, the situation metamorphosed into a police standoff as even more motorcycle officers came racing up the still empty shoulders of the freeway, followed by the warbling and flashing cruisers of the California Highway Patrol and the Los Angeles Police Department. Very quickly, this nexus of confusion and rage was surrounded by armed officers, all of them crouching behind automobile fenders with guns drawn, while two police helicopters and three news choppers circled overhead and terrified drivers in all directions evacuated their vehicles, crawling quickly away through the lanes on their hands and knees—including the harried mother, still on her cell phone, and her 11-year old son who whined loudly that he wanted to stay and see the kidnapper get shot. The suspected kidnapper, his vehicle permanently jammed between the Volkswagen and the Honda, was unable to extricate himself from the vehicle and sat there helplessly while police ordered him to get out with his hands up.

The irony of the situation was that the Amber Alert had been posted with the wrong license number. The driver was not a kidnapper, his only relationship to the kidnapping was that he drove a black Ford Explorer. He had only tried to flee, because he had seen three angry men coming toward his vehicle with baseball bats.

Nevertheless, innocent or guilty, this particular blood clot in the arterial flow of urban commerce effectively shut down the 101 in both directions, trapping even more drivers in their cars. Some of them turned off their engines and got out to smoke, leaning against their fenders or lifting themselves up to sit on the still-warm hoods of their rapidly-depreciating vehicles.

Meanwhile, the clotting of the freeway system spread south and east with pernicious speed. East along the 134 toward the 5, and southward down the 101, which was already terminal. It took less than an hour for the crystallization of the system to hit the nexus of the Pasadena, Harbor, and Hollywood freeways. The four-level interchange, one of the first in the nation, was in easy view of the mayor's office in the nearby city hall, a building that, contrary to popular belief, had *not* been destroyed in the 1953 attack of George Pal's Martians and their manta-ray shaped war machines.

With the news media now reporting that the 101 and 405 freeways were impassable and that drivers were advised to seek alternate routes—of which there were either few or none, the best thing to do was find a movie theater or a motel and wait for the weekend. Starting at city-center, the northward crush of traffic tried to force its way up the 5, an overstressed artery that crawled along the east side of Griffith park; the results were predictable and immediate—another nexus of crystallization. Nothing moved. The clotting of the Los Angeles freeway system was now irreversible. Within another hour, the 10, most of the 110, and a large part of the 210 were equally out of commission as were most of the surrounding surface streets. Too many cars, not enough road.

Unable to feed their traffic flows into the northward and westward traffic channels, the 710 and the 605 also began to solidify. Crystallization spread like ice across the surface of a lake, creeping steadily and inevitably toward a frozen stillness. As fast as new cars arrived at the outward edges of the solidification, that's how fast it spread.

And there were still four hours until sunset.

Most drivers, unaware of the scale of the growing catastrophe, unable to comprehend or believe that their trusted freeway system had finally, utterly, and completely failed them, remained in their cars, existing in a state of quiet desperation—or quiet domestication—because most of them still believed that it was just a matter of time until traffic began easing forward again.

The Zen master, Solomon Short, is quoted as saying, "No pebble ever takes responsibility for the whole avalanche." Nowhere was this so evident when the disaster escalated to its next stage.

Start with the sweltering sun. It's the fifth day of an impossible heat wave with no end in sight. There's no wind, the air is stagnant and brown. People are tired, uncomfortable, cranky, and selfish. Unwilling to be uncomfortable, every driver in a vehicle with air conditioning has rolled up his windows and has his air conditioner turned on full blast. To power his air conditioner, he's running his engine. Half a million vehicles. All those engines now create a furnace of additional heat at ground level, encouraging even more drivers to keep their engines running and their air conditioners blasting.

Frozen in time, as inert as the dead air above them, a million and a half cars and trucks and buses, idling impatiently, every second turning tens of thousands of gallons of gasoline into hot exhaust—as the sun's rays bake the day, various chemical transformations occur; the exhaust becomes a rising cloud of air pollution. All those restless waiting vehicles spew a cumulative soup of toxic fumes into the brown smoky air of the basin, aggravating an already deadly miasma that lay across the afternoon like a smothering blanket—and triggering the next stage of the catastrophe.

Sitting alone, stuck and frustrated, desperate and angry, people begin to demonstrate irrational behavior. Some people begin honking incessantly, triggering even more stress in the people around them. Some drivers turn up their music—too loud. The hyper-amplified subwoofers broadcast rhythmic pulses that feel like body punches to people in vehicles many lengths ahead and behind. Arguments begin. Fights break out. Windows get smashed with golf clubs. Ramming incidents occur. Even individuals who are uninvolved experience increased levels of stress. A few have panic attacks. Others suffer respiratory distress. Some go into full-blown asthma attacks. Then it gets worse. Kosh's corollary to Short's observation: The avalanche has already started, it is too late for the pebbles to vote.

Despite the efforts of social historians, an accurate account of the events of the day remains impossible; too many events, too many scattered and confused accounts. What is certain however is that once the cascade of failures began, each breakdown triggered the next; but the most catastrophic of all was the failure of the telephone system.

Stuck on the freeways, with relief from the sun still hours away, people began flipping open their cell phones and calling home, calling for help, calling ambulances and fire trucks and police, even calling Caltrans and the city councilmen and the Governor's office to complain. As the channels overloaded, the system began dumping calls to clear bandwidth; people began calling their service providers to complain. In self-defense, the network went into emergency procedures and shut itself down, increasing feelings of alienation and isolation among those trapped in the crystallized traffic. The arteries became linear madhouses of desperate frustration. Increasing numbers of people lost control of their bladders and bowels, adding to their individual discomfort, both physical and emotional.

As the afternoon wore on, two pregnant women went into labor and a third miscarried. Two people en-route to hospitals died in the ambulances that could not get through. A burly farmworker, one of several crammed into the back of a pickup truck experienced debilitating food poisoning, a combination of projectile vomiting and near-projectile diarrhea that expelled more than two liters of fluid from his body in less than thirty minutes. A 56-year old type-A studio executive experienced crushing chest pains that left him gasping for breath and too weak to cry for help. No help was available anyway. Even where calls for help could still be made from emergency callboxes, impatient drivers had already filled both shoulders of the highway in their desperate attempts to escape. The rescue vehicles couldn't get in and the med-evac choppers had no place to land.

By mid-afternoon, a significant number of vehicles had run out of gas. Even under the best of circumstances, a single stalled automobile in a middle lane could back up traffic in all four lanes for miles. Under these circumstances, with hundreds of dead vehicles scattered throughout the system, and more dying every minute, the crystallization had become complete. The vehicular arteries were solid and terminally impassible. The patient was dead, although it would be several days before any of the specialists would admit it.

But on some unconscious level, some people were already getting a visceral sense of what had happened. Maybe their survival instincts were kicking in, or maybe they were simply overcome by frustration—but it was the final moment of breakdown, the recognition that the system had failed and could not repair itself. Drivers started getting out of their cars. They locked them up, out of some optimistic belief that they would eventually have the chance to come back and retrieve them—and then they left them where they were. They gathered what belongings they could carry and abandoned their metal sanctuaries. First one or two, then a few more, and finally a veritable flood of refugees, hiked between the sweltering lanes toward the nearest off-ramp and their separate illusions of relief.

Not all drivers were that easily persuaded. They sat and waited in desperate hope, afraid to leave, afraid to let go of their attachment to their vehicles, afraid to disconnect from the pernicious false identity—*I am my car*—that pervades Los Angeles culture. Still believing that this was only temporary, they sat in their cars, their engines still running, their air conditioners still blasting. (Even today, all these years later, archaeologists are still finding mummified bodies in some vehicles, including many varieties of small animals.)

Some engineers argue that even up to this point, the Los Angeles freeway system might have been saved, if only the next phase of the disaster could have been prevented. Others argue that the next moments were inevitable from the first beginnings of the crystallization process. Computer simulations have given us no clear answer.

It was this simple. All of those automobiles, all of those desperate drivers too attached to their metal and plastic personalities, unwilling to leave the technological illusion of identity, security, and safety—they sat in their wombs of music, unaware that their engine temperatures were steadily, inexorably rising. The automobile engine is designed to cool itself while in motion; it needs a steady flow of air through its radiator so it can dissipate excess heat. But now, immobilized, all of those engines ran hotter and hotter without any chance of cooling, the temperatures around them rose, and overheating was inevitable. The first vehicle caught fire at 3:31. Like a good idea occurring to many people simultaneously, fires began breaking out everywhere. Within the next half hour, thirteen more vehicles began to smolder—some drivers had blankets and fire-extinguishers in their trunks, some didn't—so very soon, flames were licking out from under the hoods of seven of those vehicles.

But the fire trucks couldn't get to them. The shoulders were jammed. Cars with plastic gas tanks exploded with surprising fury, and the fires began to spread, leaping from vehicle to vehicle with alarming speed. Drivers who only moments before had been completely resistant to leaving the comfort of their sedans panicked and fled. Soon, there were firestorms. The biggest raged on the 405 where it intersected with the 101, at the heart of the first big clot in the system. Another firestorm flickered to life further south on the 405 where it intersected with the 10. A third fire exploded just west of where the 10 intersected with the 110 and also where it fed into the 5. In a very short time, the two fires met in the middle and expanded into a terrifying wall of flame that cut across the heart of the city.

Aerial tanker drops helped to slow down the flames, but it wasn't enough. Before the end of the 7:00 news broadcast, the governor had declared the city a disaster area. All across the world, people clustered around television screens, mesmerized by an event that was both incomprehensible and horrific. Los Angeles was choking to death on its own vomit. Like a great beast shuddering to a halt, the city of the angels was collapsing and shutting down.

Even after the fires were contained, even after the last smoldering embers were extinguished, most of the inhabitants of the city continued to believe that normalcy could be restored, that someday traffic would flow again. Maybe they believed this because there were still pockets of mobility scattered throughout the urban sprawl, quiet neighborhoods where housewives could still drive to the corner market for milk and bread and eggs; but by the fourth day, as the stores began to run out of perishables, the problem of resupply became critical. How could the city feed its stranded millions?

Despite promises from local, state, and federal authorities that the freeways could be restored and working again within a few days, well maybe two weeks at the most—all right, full recovery was probably at least a month or two away, but the city could function and survive, just a little more time, that's all we need—despite all the promises and reassurances, by the middle of the week many Angelenos were beginning to experience growing fear, frustration, and skepticism.

The city hadn't yet succumbed to panic, but the seeds were growing. Many of those who lived on the edges of the city, especially those who had access to uncongested avenues, began evacuating themselves voluntarily to other communities. In the first week alone, Orange County took in over 40,000 refugees, San Bernardino accepted 50,000; many went to the homes of friends and relatives, others went to hotels, the most desperate camped out in tent cities erected on the grounds of local high schools, colleges, and the parking lots of several major malls. But there were still over five million people within the affected areas of the city.

At least twenty thousand came out on motorcycles or motor scooters; while the trip through the surface streets was slow, it wasn't impossible. Many more rode out of the disaster area by train. Metro-

Link borrowed trains from as far away as Seattle to ferry passengers from Union Station to refugee camps in Santa Barbara, San Diego, and Palmdale.

Even more came out of the frozen zone by subway and light rail. The Green Line and the Gold Line and the Blue Line were major arteries. The Red Line funneled people from the eastern edges of the San Fernando Valley down to Union Station, where they could transfer to the other colors of the rainbow, or to other trains which would take them even farther out.

A few people, not a significant number, escaped by helicopter. Van Nuys airport and LAX became hubs of activity for those who could reach them, with planes landing and taking off as fast as the overstressed controllers could open flight paths in the sky. The lack of aviation fuel deliveries to the airports meant that planes had to fly in carrying enough fuel for their outward journeys. All of the airports in the zone were given double-black stars, an unprecedented new classification which meant that travel to or from was at-your-own-risk. It meant limited-to-zero availability of rescue and emergency vehicles and facilities.

But the refugees from deeper inside the disaster zone, where there was no access to rail or air, had the most difficulty extricating themselves. Some refugees walked as far as ten miles to reach a subway station, or a Metro-Link access. Amtrak brought in emergency trains on freight lines, putting up awnings and tents and benches to create makeshift stations at convenient street-crossings and overpasses. The crowds gathered and waited. Many arrived with bicycles, overloaded with their belongings. Red Cross helicopters lowered food and water to the waiting masses.

The disaster maps showed that almost every neighborhood within an area bounded by the 5 on the east, the 405 on the west, the 118 on the north, and the 105 on the south was pretty much immobilized to some degree or other, with tendrils of crystallization extending linearly outward from all of these routes.

While surface streets provided some relief, the spillover from the network of hardened freeways had choked most of the city's major thoroughfares. The streets were full of cars; the only reason the city had functioned before was that not every car was on the road at the same time. Now that the city was immobilized, a panic-stricken populace did the only thing they knew how to do—they rushed to their automobiles to make their escape. Evacuation didn't solve the problem, it exacerbated it. Broadcasting information on viable routes out of the city was self-defeating. As soon as a route was cleared and announced, it clogged up within minutes.

On Thursday, seven days after crystallization, as part of a larger disaster-relief package, the Republican-controlled Congress passed the Insurance Emergency Relief bill, declaring the disaster an act of God, thereby freeing automobile insurers from billions of dollars of exposure. This allowed the state to declare all abandoned vehicles a public nuisance and begin the wholesale removal of freeway blockages. The outrage that followed was not limited to the survivors of the disaster.

Leaders of the Democratic party were quick to point out that the

Republicans had abandoned the protection of property rights in favor of the rights of big government. While not exactly a wedge issue, it did open the door for further political divisions. The Democrats portrayed themselves as the Party of Opportunity and painted the Republicans as the Party of Opportunists. The destruction of a million automobiles was seen as a gift to an automobile industry that would clearly benefit from the need to replace those lost vehicles. The bottom line, the Democrats insisted, was that the Greedy Old Party had no heart, they had abandoned the people of Southern California in favor of protecting the interests of their corporate sponsors. The Republican Congress tried to backpedal, but the damage had already been done.

Meanwhile, estimates of the time to full recovery now varied from six months to three years. The cranes and tow trucks necessary to clear the streets would have to work their way slowly to the center of the disaster and there were no computer simulations capable of the necessary extrapolations. Where to put the extracted vehicles and how to get them there complicated the issue.

The cars couldn't be removed from the freeways, because there was no place to put them. Trying to save all these autos for their owners' eventual return meant finding storage space for them and logging their locations in a master database. Perhaps, the surviving cars could be transported out to some wide-empty space out in the desert, from which owners could reclaim them. For a fee. Maybe. But did anyone really want to risk putting all these vehicles back into circulation where they could just clog the system again? The arguments were just beginning. (Some people advocated that this disaster represented an opportunity to remodel Los Angeles' dependency on automobiles and replace or augment the freeways with more light rail systems. But that particularly expensive alternative was not only an expensive proposition, it was not an immediate solution to anything.)

Even though the Vehicle Reclamation teams were now authorized to pile up cars in great towering pyramids of metal and glass and plastic wherever they found a big enough parking lot, there was enormous reluctance to do so. All those automobiles represented billions of dollars that nobody wanted to discard casually, especially not the far-removed owners. On the other hand, at the present rate of progress, by the time the reclamation teams reached the innermost majority of affected vehicles most of them would have rusted into near-total uselessness.

On the brighter side, the Los Angeles County Air Pollution Control District announced that air pollution levels for the basin had dropped dramatically. The air was cleaner than it had been since 1955 when the county finally outlawed backyard incinerators. An awkward spokesman embarrassedly announced that this was the direct result of taking a million and a half vehicles off the road, except that of course, those million and a half vehicles were still *on* the road. Just not moving anymore. But this was the *good* news. It was now safe to breathe in Los Angeles again.

Despite that incentive, the flood of refugees streaming out of the city continued, straining the resources of surrounding counties beyond the breaking point. By now, the first waves of escapees from the zone were spreading out across the continent, bringing with them sordid tales of non-vehicular terror and enough digital camera photos, phone-camera photos, and handy-cam videos to keep the news agencies happy for weeks. Even after the continuing live coverage abated and regular programming resumed, the networks still scheduled ongoing special reports. This was as much an opportunity as a necessity. Universal, Warner Bros., Fox, Disney, and Paramount all had their lots within the frozen zone. The production of sixteen major television series had come to a halt, including (ironically) several that were set in locations as far removed as Orange County, Las Vegas, Manhattan, Miami, and Boston. Although there were finished episodes of all prime-time series in the pipeline, once those were aired, new episodes would not be available until new production facilities were established, or until transportation to existing facilities could be resumed.

Every news and current events show from *60 Minutes* to *Nova* began multi-part examinations of the collapse of an entire city, with alarming speculations about the possibility of similar crystallizations occurring elsewhere. Real estate values in small towns and rural areas began to climb.

The days stretched into weeks as refugees continued to stream out of the zone, sometimes as many as a hundred thousand a day. The nightly news kept a running tally on the numbers; the flood showed no signs of abating; but each succeeding day, those who had successfully escaped from L.A. seemed more and more despairing and desperate. While not quite ragged, they looked hungry and haggard, thin and wan. Many had gone for a week or more without fresh fruits and vegetables, fresh milk and other perishables. They had exchanged their tan healthy presence for more sallow dispirited complexions. The surrounding counties continued to absorb as many as they could, exporting the overflow to the rest of the nation as fast as transportation could be arranged. Amtrak borrowed Pullman cars from Canada and Mexico, and converted over a hundred freight cars into makeshift passenger units. A number of Jewish families refused to board anything that looked like a box car.

Entering the fourth week of the disaster, as it became apparent that this was the new normal, disaster recovery teams entering the frozen zone discovered a startling fact—some people had created ways to survive their transformed circumstances. The most amazing finding was that some Angelenos had given up their dependency on their cars and learned how to *walk*. (No, that is not a misprint. The word is *walk*.) Computer analysis of urban residential zones revealed that more than 35% of all residential dwellings in Los Angeles had access to supermarkets, pharmacies, banks, and other essential services within a radius of ten blocks or less. For most of these residents, walking might be an inconvenience, but it was easier than giving up their homes. Reports from the zone suggested that in some places, neighborhoods were reinventing themselves as actual communities.

Satellite maps revealed that fully 10% of those who were refusing to leave their homes were planting gardens in their back yards or on their front lawns. Others were creating a new economy using bicycles and motorcycles to trans-ship goods from subway and light rail stations into the otherwise unreachable interior of the zone.

Simulations projected that 20% of the city's population could survive without automobile access, possibly more if enough streets could be cleared so that trucks could deliver goods to local communities—but if enough streets could be cleared, the automobiles would return.

Surprisingly—or maybe not so surprisingly—a small but growing number of people liked the new normal, and were starting to voice the opinion that they did *not* want the automobiles to return. They actually liked being able to see the Hollywood Hills clearly. They liked the way the air smelled in the morning. They liked working in the garden, walking to the corner store, actually talking to their neighbors, and living at a less frenetic pace.

Teams of sociologists who studied the phenomenon—now called disvehiclization—observed that it was not simply a rejection of the automobile, but of the entire technological cocoon that had enveloped daily life. The disvehiclized person was also more likely to leave his or her cell phone off, turning it on only for limited periods each day; the disvehiclized person rarely watched television; he or she also cut back on computer time, accessing the Internet only for essential news or shopping services.

But not everybody could afford disvehiclization; it was a luxury of the retired, and of those who could work from their homes. Those who still depended on day jobs could not survive without transportation. While the subway, light-rail, and emergency bus lines were able to provide some measure of service, they were simply not designed to handle the traffic load, nor did they provide the degree of coverage necessary to the entire basin. In the first month alone, over a million people emigrated from Los Angeles to surrounding counties.

In Orange County, rents soared first. Demand far exceeded supply. Real estate values followed quickly. Automobile sales took off as well, both new and used; individuals who felt their lives were dependent on their mobility were quick to replace their lost cars. For the first few weeks, car dealers all across the nation were shipping as many vehicles as they could into Ventura, San Bernardino, Santa Clarita, and Orange counties.

Commentators have called this influx of additional vehicles onto the avenues and highways of the counties surrounding Los Angeles the "squeezed mud" effect. Squeeze a handful of mud, it oozes out between your fingers; squeeze Los Angeles, and the traffic oozes out in all directions across the state. Caltrans now projects that in the post-crystallization era, California will see at least an additional million vehicles on the highways of the four counties surrounding Los Angeles.

Caltrans officials are also quick to point out that the recent stoppages on the 22, the 55, and the 91 are only localized anomalies, and not representative of any larger process. There is absolutely no reason to fear crystallization in Orange County. Absolutely no reason at all.

Treatments and Complications

Sixty Thousand Dollars Per Hour

by John Skylar

Well, it hurts where my face hit the doorframe, I guess. And I'd feel a lot better without these handcuffs, but...I can't really complain.

You caught me! Must feel pretty cool. I actually think it's great, but we'll get to that. I hope you're not mad, bros—face-mashing aside, you guys are all right.

You wanted a confession, so let's get this on paper.

Last week, and all the weeks before that, I slept on the beach. I've slept on the beach since my grandmother died. They brought the Parkinson's cure to market a year after that. I guess it was five years ago? I was twelve then. I think I'm seventeen now.

I woke up every morning and had a mango, because some guy's estate down the beach had a mango tree. The guy's some retired general, and never shows up at his Hawaiian place unless the weather's great. I watch out for his personal helo on the landing pad. I've only been able to beg or steal doses of insulin, so to make it last I have to have a bunch of sugar with each injection. The mango-a-day plan helps with that.

Well, I guess I don't always sleep on the beach. Sometimes, when a meal gets the best of me, or I run out of vials, or something, I'll wake up in a hospital bed, with no memory of how I got there. People would usually help me out when I collapsed on the street. I'm pretty lucky, I guess. Most homeless Type I diabetics just die, sooner or later.

Sometimes the doctors would tell me how it used to be a lot easier to care for people in Hawai'i, but stuff's just too expensive for them to give away free insurance anymore. Guess I was born too late.

Totally not bitter though.

I got by okay for a while, 'cause you can usually find a good emergency room that will take you. But it sucks. I've spent a lot of warm nights wandering down the street shivering and begging for someone to help me get to the ER. One time, I staggered across town in a funk, only to find that my usual hospital had gone broke and closed. I still don't know how I managed that night.

I guess I'm lucky to live in Hawai'i. People *get* sharing around here. I live on the beach because the beaches are all free. Fong's sushi restaurant lets me nick food from time to time if I run deliveries for them. Sometimes one of the Waikiki hostels lets me use a shower. You know, we help each other.

I surf in the mornings, until it gets too hot. The ocean mostly kept me clean. Then I'd go work at Fong's.

It was pretty okay for a while, but lately...I dunno. When you see all these mainlander haole tourists or you take the bus up to some fancy town you see just how different it could be. Not that I could ever afford a place on O'ahu. Or any of the islands.

I think sometimes about moving to the mainland where it's cheaper, but my parents are here, or at least, what's left of them. I want to stay with my memories. With my ancestors.

Speaking of ancestors, I learned my first programming language on my Dad's rusty old G5. I can't really write software for shit—I have no idea how to do user interface—but I know how to get into the cloud and get out. I'm literate, I guess. It's the only part of him I have left.

He used to program the UAVs at the Navy Base, back when that was a job because they couldn't program themselves. Software's a lot more like animal taming now, I guess, than it was when my Dad did it.

I'm a pretty bad animal tamer. But I *am* a pretty good system cracker. I was good at 12, but I've gotten better on the library machines. There's a beauty to breaking something. I wish I could've been around when the old hackers were alive. You know, like _why and all those folks who lived back when it was an adventure.

Anyway, I know a thing or two about the old code that lies under most systems. It's fun.

This isn't really supposed to be my life story, is it?

Deal with it.

I saw them—that family of mainland haole tourists—for the first time last Monday. I knew they'd never be back because the lady kept bitching about everything. They walked into the Fong's for sushi, and I swear she had the best boobs I'd ever seen. I waited their table just to stare. Plus her LED bikini was pretty cool. Even though she shoulda been kinda old, she didn't look it.

These tourists always get upset when you look but like who goes into a sushi restaurant in beachwear? Whatever.

The other thing that I noticed were the tubes hidden just under their son's shirt. They poked out a little. An insulin pump! I'd heard about them. Doctors always tell me to get one, but I'd need insurance. Do you remember the part where I sleep on a beach?

Seemed weird that a rich kid would have one, though. He should've had a stem cell pancreas by now, and treatment for the autoimmune part of his diabetes. I knew I would be dead before that got cheap enough for me.

About halfway through they ordered a beer for their son. He looked old enough, but I carded him anyway. Brendan Bancroft, just turned 21. This was either a 21st birthday party or his stepmom's honeymoon. I memorized the ID number. Yes, that's where it started.

They paid with an Amex Black Card. You know, the one with a 250k-a-year *minimum?* I swiped the account number when I swiped the card.

The wife was kinda flirty when I brought back the check, but I lost interest. Just another tourist.

It takes a doctor ten hours of work to fully cure someone of Type I Diabetes. Ten hours, and it costs six hundred thousand dollars. I could work at Fong's Fugu Fugue for ten years, and if I didn't spend a single penny, I could pay for five of those hours myself. Eight with tips.

Here's how it works. First they take a sample of your DNA, and start growing you a new pancreas. That takes the first hour. For a few days, the doctor moves on to something else and nurses treat you, if you can pay. That costs more too, but I didn't count it in the ten hours.

Then, two hours before the pancreas is ready, they treat the autoimmune condition that ruined your first pancreas. They totally refactor your immune system with some ultra-expensive stuff that I don't understand.

And then for the next five hours, you go under the knife. Bad pancreas comes out, good pancreas goes in. You see the doctor two more times: once after you wake up in recovery, and once during a follow up appointment two weeks later.

You take some pills—cheaper ones than insulin—for a few months.

And then you're cured, for sixty thousand dollars per hour.

I know, I know—back to the confession, right?

Okay, so I stole a credit card number and a drivers' license number. I took a bus to the Ala Moana Apple Store later that afternoon. I used a computer there to order a few things for pickup at WikiWifi radio shop. I made a room reservation at the Grand Hawaiian, too.

Once I had the hotel room and the computer junk, I cloned the black card to an old credit card I'd found, in case I needed a cash advance. It would take longer for new expenses to be noticed on a no-limit card.

Doctors won't let you charge a replacement pancreas, though, so I had to take out an insurance policy in the son's name. It's cake to do if you have access to all of somebody's state records. They don't look too closely at rich people who buy very expensive plans. It cost less than $600,000, though.

I got a temporary insurance number. I made a fake ID. The whole thing took me two days.

Then I went to the doctor.

Well, first I bought some new clothes, and a whole bunch of grooming. They had to believe I was who said I was. I had enough forged papers and rich kid props to really sell it, though. It's not so weird to see a kid like me with a haole name, really, not with so many soldiers at the base who settle down here. I've got enough different features that I could be any race.

I found a surgeon's office that specializes in stem cell endocrinology, and made an appointment. With my credentials I barely had to wait. They moved other, "poorer" people around so that they could see me. Nobody even asked questions.

The waiting room was full of people who looked worse off than me, but I only had to wait for fifteen minutes. A nurse—a native—called me to an exam room before people who'd waited longer than me. You get treated weird when people think you're rich.

Dr. Liang was already waiting when the nurse took me into the room. She was a good looking lady, for someone her age. Not that way, but she looked smart and healthy. Kind of...warm, with a glow. The way a doctor should be.

She beamed at me and said, "Mr. Bancroft! It's a pleasure to meet you."

I looked at my feet. If it was going to go wrong, this was the time. "I, uh...hi. Me too."

"Have a seat, and fill out this questionnaire." She handed me a clipboard. It asked all kinds of questions, many that I'd never even thought of. Am I on any other medications? No, I can't afford them. How much do I drink? Can't afford that, either.

Dr. Liang smiled at me the whole time. She seemed so nice. Her bangs were going grey, but the rest of her hair was still jet black.

"Here you go," I said and handed her back the clipboard.

She took a quick look over it. "I got your medical records from the California state system, Brendan. It says here you've been using an insulin pump. Can you show me?"

Now I had to think quickly. "Actually, I had it removed so that I could go swimming while I was here. My doctor didn't note that? Well, I guess we knew I was going to get the cure soon anyway."

She frowned, but somehow still managed to look happy. "Well, that explains why you look so ashy. Have you been taking your insulin?"

I looked at the ground again. "Well, see, I uh, just ran out. I could use a new prescription."

"Do your parents know you're here, Brendan?"

I sighed. "No, uh...they do, I mean. I decided to stay after our vacation. I want to volunteer at the aquarium in Waikiki. I'm taking the year off from college." It was a dream I always had. I guess it seemed like the kind of thing a guy like "Brendan" could do.

Her smile returned in full force. "That's so nice! But I see why you need to get the cure now. Okay, here's what we'll do. We'll get you expedited for the operation, which means I'll have to take a skin sample now rather than relying on getting one shipped from

California."

I tried to hide my excitement. I'd dodged a real huge risk right there, and I hadn't even expected it. "Oh. Will it hurt?"

"Only a little. Here, look at the comics on my wall while I get you prepared."

Her office wall was covered in all kinds of cutesy little comics, from the ones people read online to some cut from newspapers, back before those cost $20. A few of them came from old calendars. I didn't really care for them, though. Nobody does comic strips for sick homeless kids.

Instead I looked at a picture of Duke Kahanamoku. He wouldn't have let a medical thing scare or hurt him. Then again, he wouldn't have lied to get medical care.

Really, I didn't notice the sting when she took the sample. She took a little blood, and that hurt worse. Needles are no bueno.

"Okay, Brendan. Do you want me to send you a nurse for the next few days, to handle your insulin? Your insurance can cover a visiting nurse."

"Uh, sure!" I gave her my hotel address. "I don't have a place yet, we're working on that."

"No problem, Brendan. I'll see you Friday."

I walked out not believing it would work. I guess it didn't. Haha, right?

The nurse came. Nice lady. Reminded me of my grandmother. She kept me up on treatments until Friday.

So far I figured the tourists would not notice anything strange, but just the same, I made sure to completely take over their accounts. They could still access and do what they were used to, but I could make changes to keep my moves hidden. They were blowing $2000 a day on restaurants—what's a $600 insurance payment on a statement like that?

I showed up Friday and they didn't waste any time. Everybody gets nervous before surgery and I guess they train the doctors to just be firm. They give you short answers to questions. Dr. Liang was about as different as she could be. Suited up in her surgical gear, I thought she might be smiling, but in that almost-spacesuit, she seemed cold and distant.

I was okay with that. The less I spoke, the more certain I got that my plan would work.

The anesthesiologist asked me to count backwards from 20. I think I hit 16. Everything got kinda fuzzy, though, like snow on a broken television, except it was all my senses.

I came to in the recovery ward and the first thing that I thought about—after I sorted out reality from the drug haze—was how to get out of there. At first I tried to get out of bed, but every muscle in my abs screamed when I tried. Since I couldn't use my abs, I tried to use my chest and neck to lever my way up.

My neck felt like it got stomped by a whole seal. They told me something about that beforehand, that maybe the breathing tube would make me a little sore, but I wasn't prepared for that. I slumped back to the bed.

In a few minutes, the nurse from my hotel room rushed to my side. "Please, Brendan, don't try to get up."

"But I feel like I really need to pee," I whined.

"You probably don't. The catheter can make it feel that way afterwards, but I suggest you take it easy with that for a few hours."

Later, I learned that she meant it would burn like hell when I tried. For about a day and a half.

"We'll move you to your room soon, Brendan. In maybe 30 minutes. Then you'll be able to try moving around." She smiled at me and took my hand. "I bet it's lonely here without your parents."

"Yeah," I said, though she couldn't know quite what that meant. I gazed at the sheets and slowly drifted off.

That night in the hospital was awful. The nurse was right, peeing was hell. I don't ever want to have surgery again.

They woke me up once every few hours. First for a dinner I didn't want to eat. I was hungry, but after about one bite of chicken I felt over-full. Then they woke me up to give me pain killers. "How would you rate your pain on a scale from one to ten?"

I rated it "give me some freakin' painkillers."

The last time they woke me up was at about five AM to take blood for, as far as I could tell, no reason. Well, maybe they just wanted to hurt me for fun. I don't really get hospitals.

So after this night from hell ended I was all set to go home, but I still had to talk to Dr. Liang. It might sound whiny that that all I'm writing about is how they poked at me all night, but trust me, I was overjoyed. Yes, it hurt, and yes, I could barely eat, but whenever I stopped to think about it I realized that I had gotten away with it. The new pancreas was inside me, and working. For them it was routine, but it had totally changed my life.

I guess what *really* made me so impatient was that I knew every second longer that I stayed in the hospital was another second closer to getting caught. I took out a lot of that on the people who had come just to make me feel better. But the poking still hurt.

They told me that I couldn't leave the hospital until Dr. Liang came to see me again, and I didn't ask more than once so I wouldn't attract too much attention. I think it already seemed weird to the staff that my parents weren't involved at all, so I didn't want to push my luck.

She showed up around 10:35 AM, or at least, that's the time I was arrested. She had two cops with her. You guys. I tried to run but I was still sore everywhere.

"SHOW US YOUR HANDS, we don't want to hurt you." Those were the first words you spoke to me. I listened.

Then Dr. Liang spoke. She never made eye contact with me. "We found out that you aren't Brendan. I had to call the police." She looked at the doorway, where I saw a man, a hospital admin I think, with brown hair in a suit. He nodded to her, and she frowned back. Maybe turning me in was his idea.

You guys, the pals that you are, cuffed me to the bed, so I guess that was cool. At least you didn't slap me around too much. The elbow in my face was a nice touch, though. Just so you know, when you press that hard on somebody's cheek they *can* taste their own blood. You can stop trying to find out.

The patient advocate came in with a very huffy look on her face, which got my hopes up, but it evaporated once you explained that I'm a common juvenile criminal who had robbed a perfectly nice tourist family. She helped process my discharge papers.

While you guys took care of all the forms I was supposed to sign, Dr. Liang came over. She still couldn't look at me.

She put an orange pill bottle and a slip of paper on the nightstand. "You have to take one of these every day, whoever you are. It won't do if you–if you get sick in custody. The paper is a prescription for refills."

Dr. Liang turned away and started to walk for the door, but then turned back to me. "I–you remind me of someone I knew once. Someone very dear to me." She paused and looked into my eyes. A lost son? A husband? Someone who could make her eyes well up. I could see the pain of honesty in her, and for that second understood her dedication to kindness.

"What is your real name?" she asked. She could have read the arrest papers, but I guess this seemed better.

"Keona," I whispered.

"The attractive one." She smiled, but I noticed the wet glint at her eyelids.

I grinned. "To some. It also means 'the louse.' Try asking those guys which I am."

Dr. Liang hid her face and scurried out.

So that's my confession, like you wanted. Yes, I impersonated Brendan Bancroft and stole his identity to get medical treatment. Please send me to jail now.

See, I already have my new pancreas. You can't take it out. And the law says you have to spend money on my healthcare. I'll have my pills in prison, and I'll never have to wake up in the hospital with sweet blood again.

It's only about sixty thousand dollars a *year* to keep me in a minimum security prison, but I never had that kind of money before. And it's a white-collar jail. I never hurt anybody. So I'm out in a few years with a new pancreas and some education. Maybe I could get into college after—I think this would make a great admissions essay.

You guys are the best. See you around, keep in touch. Don't you ever change.

Tears, Not of a Child

by Preston Dennett

We were both seventy years old when we closed the gate. It was the same treatment that our parents had gone through, and our grandparents and their parents. Everyone accepts the treatment sooner or later, most people earlier than us. We wanted to experience old age…or rather, David did and I went along. But we didn't want to risk going past seventy. We've all heard the horror stories of people who actually died. So I drew the line of seventy. Besides, as David liked to say, everyone knows the chances of having a bad reaction go down the longer you wait. It was one of his ways of convincing me to wait. Later I learned there is no known correlation between age at time of treatment and results.

"Less than one in a million people have a bad reaction," I told him, making up my facts as I spoke. I didn't want to be old anymore. I was tired of the pain, the lack of energy, and the looks people gave us. I didn't know back then that the accurate number was closer to one in twenty million. In total, there were less than a thousand known cases, another fun fact that I learned the hard way.

"We'll be fine," he told me when I complained to him that we were getting too old. Statistically, the most common age of the treatment was fifty-five.

"People stare at us."

"So? Let them stare."

So we waited. I loved him, it wasn't a big deal. But when the day finally came for closing the gate, I was relieved and excited. Finally, we wouldn't be the freaky old people and we could join the rest of the human race.

The treatment was simple, just a series of injections. Nano-meds would flood our blood stream and invade every cell, repair the damage done to the DNA and remove the random mutations, rebuilding the precious telomeres that controlled aging. By restoring our DNA molecules to their original condition and tricking our cells into thinking they were new, the aging process would be reversed. We would be young again.

We were in and out of Doctor Ander's office in minutes. If he ever mentioned the possibility of a bad reaction, I don't remember it. He may have.

It was a joy to watch our bodies become young. Each morning, I looked in the mirror and saw fewer wrinkles. My breasts became firmer, my stomach was flattening. And watching the auburn come back into my hair…I'm not ashamed to admit that I wept with delight.

David didn't want to admit it, but he was enjoying himself as much as I was. He had started working out again. He had always been handsome with his blue eyes and blond hair. But watching him become young again…I fell in love with him all over. And he was equally stricken with me. We were like two young love-sick teen-agers.

"See Mel, aren't you glad we waited?" he said one morning, right after we had made love. Love, in the morning, before work! We hadn't done that since we were in our twenties. Being old for so long had given me a new perspective on youth.

"Yes," I said. "I'll admit it. You were right. Now, please remove your hand from my breast and let me get dressed!"

David laughed, swept me into a kiss, and dashed into the shower, motioning me to join him. Whew! Had we ever been like this? This was something I could get used to.

And it only got better. The doctor said that the treatment would take effect immediately, and that in about three months, we would be back to a biological age of about twenty-five.

After the three months had passed, we both looked amazing. We went to Doctor Anders and he confirmed that our treatments had been successful. He congratulated us and sent us on our way.

I never thought we'd see him again. After all, these days with the home nano-medkits, there's not a real big demand for doctors.

Soon, we settled back into our routines. The only big change in our life from the treatments was that David and I became closer. We had always been deeply in love, but somehow, growing old and then becoming young again together had bonded us in a profound way.

We did have more energy. Now we were doing all the wonderful things that had caused us to fall in love with each other in the first place. We'd go out dancing, visit the nature preserves, go kayaking and snowboarding. But this time, we appreciated it even more.

Our parents and grandparents were, of course, hugely relieved that we had done the treatments and they started bugging us about having a child.

Both of us had decided that we would put off having our child until we were absolutely sure we were ready. After all, what was the rush? Raising a child was hard, and there were already a lot of people in the world. Yes, we wanted kids, but we were waiting.

I was wondering if the time for a kid had finally come when we first noticed something wrong. David was losing his chest hair.

"I'm sure it means nothing," I said. "It never was thick until he was in his forties."

"Is it still falling out?" asked Doctor Anders.

David nodded. He reached out and pulled out a clump. "It's going quick. Soon there'll be nothing left. I haven't had a smooth chest since I was a teen-ager." He looked worried.

"Hmm," said Anders. "I'm going to order some additional tests, but your wife is probably right. Chest hair is often a feature that comes in later age. It's not unusual to lose it. I wouldn't be alarmed. Of course, as you know, we can restore it. But I'd like to wait until we have confirmed that your biological age has, in fact, stabilized."

"Excuse me," I said. "Stabilized?"

"Well, yes. Trust me, nothing to worry about. It's just a period of adjustment. You both will be just fine."

I looked David. He shrugged. You can't argue with the doctor.

The tests came back normal. Doctor Anders explained that we were simply having trouble adjusting psychologically, that the transformation from old to young was so radical—particularly in our case—that anxiety and fear reactions sometimes took place. We would be fine, he said, once we got used to the fact that our bodies were young.

"See, I told you it was nothing."

"Yeah, well, you're not the one losing your chest hair," he said, smiling.

We were in each other's arms again, finished and basking in the afterglow. We were making love twice a day now. David couldn't keep his hands off me. I wasn't complaining. It felt good to be wanted, desired, to be young.

"You were quick tonight," I said.

David smiled guiltily. "I know. I'm so sensitive. I haven't been like that since I was a…" He looked suddenly pensive.

"The doctor said not to worry."

"I know, but there's something I didn't tell you. Ah…I stopped shaving." He felt his smooth chin. "See? Nothing. I can't grow a beard anymore."

It was then that I noticed a red splotch on his chin. It was a pimple. I didn't say anything. It was just a pimple. It didn't mean a thing.

"Well," I said. "We can see the doctor again if you want. But you heard him. He said you were fine. Why didn't you say anything?"

"I don't know. I guess I was embarrassed. It's not like I even want a beard. It's just nice to know that if I did, I could have one."

"So let me see if I have this straight. You're upset about not having something you don't want."

David tilted his head. "That sounds about right."

"You are so weird."

"Thank you."

"It wasn't a…oh, never mind!"

"Well, this *is* curious," said Doctor Anders. David had taken a third set of tests and Anders seemed hesitant to continue speaking. I wondered how old the doctor actually was. You never could tell. He looked about twenty-five. But these days, *everybody* looked twenty-five.

"Just tell us," I said. "Does David have the disease?"

"It's not a disease," said Anders. "It's best termed a hyper-reaction to the treatment. It's exceedingly rare…so uncommon in fact that it's statistically insignificant. I've never even seen one. We don't know the cause, and there have been only a few hundred cases. But yes, it appears, Mister Perkins, that you are one of the unlucky ones. I'm so sorry."

David looked at me to see how I was reacting. What did he expect? I was furious.

"Are you sure?"

"Oh, yes. There's little doubt. The markers are distinctive."

"What does that mean?" I asked. "What's going to happen to him?"

Anders sighed. "I'm afraid the news is not good. I know this is not what you want to hear. There is no cure for this condition. We do not have any effective treatments either. My advice is to just enjoy the time you have left together. I'm very sorry."

"What? That's it!" I was past furious and bordering on livid. "You're just going to send us home?"

"Well, no," said Anders, "We would like you to come in for regular examinations. As I said, Mr. Perkins, your case is quite rare and it's sure to generate a lot of interest. There is quite a push to discover the causes of this condition. There's always the possibility that a cure might be found. And certainly you'll be eligible for all kinds of assistance with being taken care of."

"*I'm* going to take care of him," I announced.

"Of course," said Anders, given me an annoyed glance. "I'm just saying that there are experts in this area who are willing to assist you, should you need it."

"How long do I have?" asked David.

Anders shook his head sadly. "Not long. The time varies. In a few cases, it's only a matter of months. The average is about a year or slightly more. No one's ever lasted more than two."

"I can't do this anymore," I told David, and pushed his writhing naked body off mine. I shuddered to think what people would think if they knew we were still having sex.

"What? Why?"

"David! You're a teen-ager. Not even. You look like you're twelve years old."

"So? It's still me, Mel. I'm still me."

I shook my head. "I can't. I feel like a child molester." *For God's sake, you don't even have pubic hair anymore!*

David looked hurt. "I'm still the same man I always was." His voice cracked to falsetto, and his face turned red.

"See?" I said. "We both know you're not. You've changed. You're a child now."

"But inside, I'm still the same. I still love you, Mel. I'll always love you."

I began crying, and he put his arms around me.

"I love you, Mel. You know that."

"I know. I love you too. It's just…I can't do this. I can't have sex with you anymore. It just doesn't feel right. You understand that, don't you?"

"Don't cry," said David. "Of course, I understand."

"You do?" I looked up at him blurrily.

He was crying now. I had only seen him cry once before, the day we got married. He had gotten close a few times, after we'd been fighting, the time I was hospitalized after falling down a flight of steps. But never until then had I seen his tears flow freely. "Of course," he said. "I'll move into the spare room tomorrow."

David's reversal went very quickly. Only one month had passed since diagnosis and now he was already at a biological age of eleven. A whole team of doctors were studying him. The experts, they called themselves. Hah! For experts, they were of precious little help. Their consensus was that David had only about two months to five months left. They couldn't even agree upon that.

They hovered around him like locusts. The way they pawed at him! David had become more valuable in his disease (and yes, I'm going to call it a disease) than he ever had been in life.

If the doctors had their way, he would be living at the hospital, with a tube in every orifice. Eventually we both had to put our feet down and kick them out. It became clear that the doctors couldn't help us and we're only interested in watching David's decline out of professional curiosity.

Yes, my husband was a miracle of nature. But he was *my* miracle of nature, and I intended to protect him to the best of my ability.

The worst was our families. Once our parents and grandparents and great grandparents learned about David, of course they insisted on helping. However, when they saw how quickly David had already declined—how young he now was—they were able to provide little more than awkward words of sympathy, words that did little to disguise their pity.

David didn't need that, so we decided that we would allow visitors, but nobody could stay at our home. It would be just us, David and me. I would take care of him myself.

"Does it hurt?" I asked him one morning, when I noticed that he was rubbing his leg painfully.

"Only a little," piped David. "I call them un-growing pains." He giggled. His high-pitched voice sliced right through me.

The doctors had explained to us that the body regenerates all the cells in a few months and with the accelerated process that David was experiencing, there might be severe pains involved as the old bone structure was dissolved and the new one was formed. Thankfully, David was one of the lucky ones; he experienced only minor pains.

We made love one last time. David was in a lucid period and I was not. We probably shouldn't have done it. But nobody had warned me how hard this would be. He crept into my room and slipped into my bed. Before I knew what was happening, we were too far to stop. That night, we slept together in bed. In the morning, it was understood. That would be the last time.

By the middle of the second month, David had reached a biological age of seven. That was when his mind first began to be really affected. He started losing his memories. He began to look at the world through the eyes of a child. He cried a lot more. Tears became common.

The doctors had warned me of this. A child's brain is different from an adult's, they said. The frontal cortex is not fully developed. Your husband will lose certain faculties of perception. There will be memory lapses, periods of disorientation. Stages of decline, of un-development.

They were being kind.

There were times when David still thought he was an adult and he would try to seduce me. Once, he actually tried to attack me. Of course, I easily flung his little body off mine, and I reminded him again that he was a child now, and although we were married, we couldn't do that.

He hung his head in shame, said he was sorry and we hugged.

I often caught him staring at me with a sad longing expression. There was little that we could do together that wasn't awkward. He was becoming more and more dependent on me. I cooked for him, helped him dress himself. When he was lucid, which was rare, we would talk.

We had to unplug the television. Every channel we turned on, sooner or later it was the same thing. *Have you heard about David Perkins? He's the latest victim of the longevity treatments. The poor man.*

One evening as I was tucking him into bed in his room, he looked up at me longingly. "I remember the way it used to be, you know," he said. "When we were old. When we'd just sit and talk for hours. I remember that."

I fought back the tears. "You still remember?"

"I remember a lot," said David. "You're not the kind of woman a man can easily forget."

"Do you remember the day when we first met?" I asked.

David smiled. He had only little baby teeth now. His adult teeth had fallen out a few weeks earlier, the new ones sprouting out like tiny gravestones. "Of course. I will never forget how beautiful you looked. How beautiful you still look. I can't believe I convinced you to sleep with me on our first date. We were quite the young lovers, weren't we?"

He began crying, which opened my floodgates.

"I'm sorry," he said. "I'm so sorry I put you through this."

I shook my head. "Stop it. It's not your fault." Everybody dies, I almost told him, but caught myself. Yeah, everybody dies. The treatments aren't a cure for immortality. They don't actually close the Pearly Gates forever. They only double the life span, giving the average human an average just shy of two hundred years. Somehow, I didn't think David would find that comforting just now.

"It'll be over soon," he said. I started to protest but he raised his hand. "Let me speak. I want to say this before it's too late. Let's be honest, I have only a few weeks before my mind goes away completely. I can feel myself slipping, Mel. I know I don't have long. I just wanted to say thank you. Thank you for picking me. And thank you for taking care of me. Wherever I'm going, I'm going to miss you. I will always love you."

I was a torrent of tears. "Me too," I managed.

That night I cried myself to sleep.

The whole family is in the house now. I can hear them bustling in the kitchen. I smell coffee. They are trying to be quiet, but I'm sure they are also eager for me to be up, to bring David out for their latest appraisal. They haven't seen him in a couple of weeks. They are going to be shocked at how small he is.

Biologically, David is barely one year old. He has lost his ability to speak most words, but in my imagination, his little lips can still utter my name, Melinda. I sit in our room, on our bed, holding him in my arms. Outside, the sounds of my family echo through the house, dishes clanging, footsteps, muffled conversation beyond the bedroom door. They are here to help me, I remind myself. They are here because they care. They loved David too. *Love* David, I chide myself. I refuse to think of him in past tense. Not yet. Not while he still lives.

David's bright round eyes gaze up at me and he coos softly. Despite what Doctor Anders says, I know David still recognizes me, still loves me. Maybe not the same as before, but the love is there in the way he lets me hold him, in the way his little fingers cling to my collar as I feed him his bottle. He is a very cute baby.

I feel his diaper…wet.

I change him and clean him off, giving myself and him a quick bath together. He has always enjoyed bathing together, and this morning is no exception. I dry him off and dress him in his new baby clothes. He smiles and giggles. He is an awfully cute baby.

As I scoop him up in my arms, his wide eyes gaze at me lovingly. He knows who I am, I am sure of it. He still recognizes me. He is my husband, David. And I am his wife, Melinda.

I give him a little kiss and take him out to visit his family.

I stand before David's grave-site as they lower his tiny infant-sized coffin. David is dead. My family stands around me in solemn support. The men are solemn, but my mom and grandmothers weep openly. I have tears in my eyes, but they are not entirely of sadness. Yes, I miss my husband. But I have a wonderful secret.

I feel a wave of nausea, and I look down at my stomach. Soon I will be showing and my wonderful secret will be out. It is David's last gift to me, a gift that will last for hundreds of years.

I consider just blurting out the truth right there. Just let everyone know. Then I hesitate. No, I decide, not now, not yet. I will tell them soon, when the time is right. When I can enjoy the surprised looks on their faces.

No Such Color as Indigo

by Megan Lee Beals

The first ring alerted Holly to the fact that she'd been listening to the same Cinderella overture for the last hour and a half. She pulled the headphones away from her ears and listened, unsure if the ringing came from the phone or from the desperation that comes from two months of waiting. It rang again, and Holly's throat tightened as the adrenalin jumped into her heart. She grasped for the cane kept at her side, but set it down the moment her fingers found it. The phone wasn't far. Just twelve steps across her well mapped apartment. She unfolded her legs from the chair and carefully crossed the floor to the desk where the phone was screaming through its third ring, and she felt the top of its handle, afraid to even answer. Holly twisted her pretty little mouth and shoved aside the irrational need to hesitate. Her hesitation was born of a lifetime of clockwise food and counted footsteps. This one phone call could end that, but only if she fought against her stifling comfort and picked up the damn phone.

"Hello?"

"Ms. Holly Abrams?"

She knew his voice. How did she know that voice? "Yes, this is she."

"Holly, this is Dr. Priest from the Prism Institute. A while ago you signed up for an experimental light transistor to train blind patients to see. Are you still interested in the experiment?"

There, in the dropped consonants, his voice tuned naturally to an f sharp. Marcus Priest, the boy from elementary school who mocked her eyes to hide an embarrassed crush.

"Holly?"

"Yes! Yes, I'm still interested. But my eyes..." she brushed away her bangs and picked a crumb of sleep from the third eye in the center of her face. Should she tell him? No, let him turn her down in person.

"Is there a problem, Ms. Abrams?"

"No." She was unused to lying and the word stuck in her throat.

"How does Saturday sound? We have an opening at noon."

Holly smiled through her nerves and grasped the desk in lieu of her cane. "Noon will be perfect."

Holly met Dr. Priest in the lobby of a cold office building with buzzing fluorescent lights. She could feel the jagged pangs of anxiety roll off him as she shook his hand. He knew her. This was her Marcus Priest, but he said nothing about it. He couldn't have forgotten her. No one forgets a three eyed woman. But he didn't mention her eyes, and he kept up the casual rapport of doctor and patient. Holly took the reprieve and graciously played along. If neither party admitted their knowledge of the other, the experiment could continue.

The light transistor was a relatively non-invasive method of sight augmentation. It involved no cameras, no wires, no open brain surgery. The entire operation resided on a small elastic chip, less than a hundredth of a millimeter thick and about half the size of Holly's fingernail. A small hole would be drilled into her head to place the receiver on her occipital lobe, and eye drops applied to help her corneas zero in on the receiver. Each week, Marcus would remotely reconfigure the transistor through a computer program to aid her brain in comprehending the frequencies of visible light and translate them into optical information. They would begin with the lowest frequencies, and work their way through the spectrum until Holly's vision was on par with the rest of the sighted populace.

"We're not going in and rerouting your eyes to a camera, Holly. We're retraining your brain to use the connections it already has, but never utilized before."

Holly was well acclimated to her brain retraining itself. In the womb, she briefly entertained the idea of becoming twins, and her head began to split in two. But practicality won over novelty, and the unborn Holly decided that the life of one person would be more than enough for her. By the time she realized this, it was too late to put herself back together. Her brain was partially separated into three hemispheres in the front, but only two in back. This gave her the third eye in the center of her face, but the true problem rested in Holly's inability to reconcile her two frontal lobes. For her first two years Holly was comatose, paralyzed by the force of the outside world and all its stimuli. Fortunately, the human brain is an infinitely adaptable thing, and by the age of three, Holly was holding tea parties and getting in fights like any other little girl.

"Do I have to shave my head?" asked Holly.

"Not unless you want to."

"When can we start?"

"If you sign here, we can get started tomorrow."

Holly reached out and grasped Marcus' hand and followed it down to the paper. She felt along the document to find the x and signed wide and loopy, far beyond the rectangle allowed for her mark.

* * * *

"So what do you do for a living, Holly?" asked Marcus on Sunday as he fastened her head into place. She sat in a chair that restricted all movement for the drilling.

"I'm in between jobs. I used to own a bar. Are you familiar with The Otherworld?"

"Like in fairy tales?"

"No. Like in the bar I tended. It was a weird-girl burlesque show on the weekends. It burned down a year back and I haven't done much since. The bar made plenty of money, and I got even more out of the insurance."

"You ever get up and dance?"

Holly barked out the small laugh allowed through all the chin straps. "Hell no. I poured drinks. Had the shelves memorized. Got good tips, too. If I'm honest, though, it was more for this than for the drinks." She closed her outside eyes and kept the middle open. The center eye was larger than the other two, and the iris was milky and stretched wide like a goat's. Holly felt the spike in Marcus blood pressure as he stepped backwards. "It's cool, Dr. Priest. Everyone has that reaction."

Marcus coughed into his hand. "Alright Holly, I'm about to begin. You'll feel a bit of pressure, but the anesthetic should have taken hold by now. There shouldn't be any pain. I just need you to relax. Why don't you tell me what you'd like to see for the first time?"

"What I'd like to see?"

"Well, yeah. You have quite the unique opportunity. You get to decide what your first conscious memory of sight will be. Any ideas?"

"I have no idea." First sight never factored into her dreams of learning to drive. The act of seeing far outweighed the idea of images. Holly racked her brain, but only one thing came to mind. "Tom Selleck."

"Tom Selleck?"

"My mom is always saying how handsome Tom Selleck is. We'll make it that. A great big poster of Tom Selleck."

"And we're finished."

"Already?"

"Already."

…

Holly stayed overnight for observation. She felt no discomfort from the transistor, and it was tuned the next morning through Marcus' computer in under an hour. Holly was given a bench to sit on while she adjusted to the new light. Red struck her as muddy and hot.

Like the smell of undercooked beef and boiling wine. She dredged through the bloody black blur to find Tom Selleck's face peering down at her in shades of red and pink. Holly stared at the poster for five minutes without making a sound, taking in every pore of Selleck's face. It was so powerful, so stark in its symbols. Eyes. Nose. Mouth. The pattern so ingrained that it reached past twenty eight years of blindness to shock her with its unbelievable beauty. A thought gurgled forth from her comatose state, bursting aloud in an ugly grunt.

"Huh."

She fell forward onto the floor. Marcus jumped from his chair and ran to help her. He caught her arm and she briefly glanced at him before screwing all three eyes shut and pitching forward in a dry heave. Marcus steered her toward the bathroom, kicking in the door to let her collapse over the sink. Holly gripped the edges of the sink, using it as an anchor, and slowly opened her center eye to the mirror. Nothing happened. The other two eyes squinted open and a rush of slippery shapes slid into view. Marcus' face pressed in behind her own, and she leaned in even closer to block out its reflection. She pinched and poked her face, putting shapes to the contours she knew so well, and stopped between the twin bridges of her nose, just under the third eye. It looked so much larger than it felt. She closed it, then brushed her hair forward from behind her ears. It fell across her face in a near solid black mass, only broken by faint strands of dark red.

"I thought my hair was blonde. Everyone always told me blonde."

"It is blonde. Kind of a straw color. But right now you're only seeing color on the lowest human frequency. You'll pick up traces of red, or you won't see anything at all."

"So I guess I can't get rid of this thing?" She waved the cane at him, and was struck by the intense beauty of its red paint at the bottom. It cut through the swirl of dark bloody shapes like a single piercing soprano voice among an orchestra of cellos.

"I'd say we can keep your status as legally blind until the experiment is over. But this is already promising. We'll give you a week to let your eyes to get used to red, then if the tests look good, we'll step it up to orange."

"Great." Holly looked back to the mirror and watched her reflection's eyes twitch back and forth. She fixed her bangs solidly over her face to mask the dent over her third eye. "I think I need a drink."

"As your doctor, I'd advise against that."

"No worries, Doc. It'll be virgin. I don't think I'd like to be any more muddled than I already am."

*　　*　　*　　*

Marcus found the right frequency for orange in under fifteen minutes. Holly decided against a poster for the new color, and instead focused on the walking stick as it took on more of a peach tone with the new frequency. Orange was warm and bright, a force of calm in her shoulders and lungs. Ten minutes after the transistor was tuned, she left Dr. Priest at the door of his office. She almost hugged him, awkwardly grinning as the new color lit up the room, but restrained herself to a small quick wave instead. He tried to keep her for an interview, but she couldn't wait to leave.

"I promise I'll answer everything next week. I swear," she called as she ran out to catch the bus back home.

Her apartment was a new and lovely thing when she got there. Everything was tinted peach and gold, and she relaxed into the beautiful luxury of her spartan quarters, content to watch the sunlight deepen and fade against her walls. As the light finally left out the window, Holly turned on the single lamp in her apartment, and dialed the phone to call her mother.

"Mom, what color is my apartment?"

"It's white, dear. Why?"

Holly *hrmed* into the phone and closed her eyes, keeping the center open to test if orange translated to her third eye. It didn't. She tested her vision again, opening all three eyes and focusing on the deep red-orange light her lamp cast into the rest of the room. Everything in the apartment was the same hue, even her shirt and her slip-on shoes. *This is what white looks like when I can't see it*, thought Holly.

"Mom...?"

"Honey, are you okay?"

"I'm fine. Thanks. Love you."

"I love you too, dear."

She hung up the phone and turned off the light. A dull glimmer of red stalked her from a dark corner of the room. "Shut up," she snarled to the walls.

...

Holly thought she would like yellow. She knew yellow from the sun on her arms, and the taste of the word in her mouth. But yellow came with a survey, and yellow forced her into a corner with a clipboard. Her answers against the bright paper looked black and harsh without the upper end of the light spectrum, and she kept her answers short, brushing the pencil so softly against the paper until each response was only a ghost of a thought. "Yes it is effective." "There is no discomfort." "Not much has changed."

Marcus read through the paper in silence, then set it aside and folded his hands, coughing gently to fill the void. "You don't see much difference between blind and not?"

Holly closed all three eyes and tightened her grip on the cane. It hadn't left her side in the last three weeks. She didn't rearrange the furniture of her apartment. She went to the same bar every Sunday night. She didn't buy a television.

"No, there is a difference, but it hasn't changed anything. Do you know what I have for dinner on Monday nights?"

"What do you have for dinner?" asked Marcus.

"Stir fry. I have for the last three years. Do you know what I made for dinner last Monday after I got orange?"

"Stir fry?"

"Bingo. I'm a creature of habit. Being able to see after twenty eight years without, well, it just seems like it would change so much more."

"I think waiting for outside forces to change you is the best way to be stuck in a rut your whole life."

"That's stupid, Marcus. And it's not outside. The damn transistor is stuck in my brain!" She closed her eyes and gripped the cane tighter. "I'm sorry, Marcus. I didn't mean to say that. Just don't get all sentimental on me, okay? I've been made into a 'totem of strength in the face of adversity' all my life. It comes with being a freak. You'd hate the sentimental, too."

Marcus shuffled the survey into a fat manila folder and tossed it onto the desk. "Have you given any thought to going back to work?"

"Yeah. A guy I know wants me to move up to Seattle and co-own a bar there. I guess he's got the location. He just needs more money, and I've got that in spades."

"Because of the insurance?" he asked, with his eyes kindly trained on hers.

"I didn't burn down my bar."

Marcus snapped his eyes back to the manila folder. "And how is yellow treating you?"

"Yellow?" She glanced around the room. Without the sun, yellow was just orange with teeth. Like glee and fear swirled together and shot through the heart. "Kind of forgettable, really."

* * * *

"Do you have a guide dog, Holly?"

"Had. He died when I was in college. A chocolate lab called Diggles. I dropped out shortly after he passed. I never was really sure why I was there to begin with, and after Diggles was gone, I sort of lost all sense of direction."

"There, we should have green now. You can open your eyes."

Holly opened the middle eye before the other two, but no color came to the third eye. Green was cold and warm at the same time. A heavier yellow with a heady organic tinge. Like the smell of rain and compost. Marcus watched her adjust while she marveled at the shockingly green eyes in his yellowy face. The force of color in his eyes hit her stomach and she gripped the walking stick at her side, hoping to transmute its cold metal into an armor against the green.

"Holly?"

His mouth gnashed open, an attack of red and black, and Holly snapped her eyes shut. Matching faces and voices was still an unusual process. The new color only made it worse.

"Why won't my third eye work?"

"Your third eye is a vestige of the activity in your mother's womb. Honestly, I'm surprised it can open and close in conjunction with the other two. It even has eyelashes."

"I'm right here." She opened her outer eyes in suspicious slits. "And it's not just a dead spot in my face. It's cried before."

He reached out and took her hands. "I'm sorry, Holly. I know it's not just a dead spot. But the truth is, the third eye isn't connected to your brain in a way that will work for vision. No matter what I do, that one will remain blind."

Holly shrugged and stared out the window at the dull red buildings, wishing for a bright spot of green to test the new color. A spot outside of Marcus' eyes.

"Listen," said Marcus. "Why don't we make the next survey an informal one? We could meet for coffee. Completely informal."

Holly glared at him, inspecting every inch of his face, but unable to read his expression.

Marcus smiled and squeezed her hands. "Professional, though. It won't be a date."

* * * *

Holly met Marcus at a small café three days after blue. It was the first time she left the five mile radius of her apartment since the bar burned down. She took the bus and stared out the window to avoid the faces surrounding her. Faces were dangerous. Too entrancing to look away from, and the world already demanded so much attention. It wasn't so bad in the first few weeks. Red was close, keeping her vision within an arm length or two, and even yellow only allowed about twenty feet before the world mashed together in a burnt mess of nothingness. But with green she could see trees, and blue opened up the sky. Everything was so much bigger than Holly ever imagined. She held her cane close to her chest as she tried to imagine how tall the tallest tree could be.

The bus came to a halt close to the café and she let the cane drop to the ground out of habit, and counted her steps from the bus stop to the door, tucking away the number thirty-eight should she ever wish to return.

"Holly!" Marcus stood up to greet her when she arrived. Two large mugs of coffee sat steaming on the table. "I was worried you weren't going to make it. I took the liberty of ordering for you."

She sat down and leaned her walking stick against the table. A little brown fern was drawn in the foam of her coffee. She blew on it, swirling the cream and brown. "The bus was slower than expected."

"So how do you feel about blue?"

"It's enormous. I can't get over it. I saw the moon for the first time last night. Do you know how far away the moon is?"

"How far is it?"

"No, I'm asking you! That's just it, I can't even fathom it. And leaves. Have you seen leaves, Marcus? I mean really looked. There are so many leaves, even just on one tree. How can there be so many leaves? How do you get up in the morning without wondering how many leaves you'll see, or how many people or cars. It's enough to make you want to stay inside and waste away into nothing."

"You'll get used to it, Holly. Everyone does."

"Everyone thought being blind was a chore, but I knew everything then. Every place I went had a number. Vision is just a constant reminder that the world is so much bigger than your life could ever be. Bigger than numbers, even. One wrong step and I could be lost forever!"

Marcus touched her hand and kept his eyes on hers, coercing her to look at his face. "Some people find a partner. It makes things easier."

The anxious timbre was back in his voice. A charge of restrained adoration ran from his hand to hers, reminding her of elementary school. Marcus hadn't changed much. Holly took her hand back. "You're getting sentimental again. I thought this wasn't a date."

"It's not. Just an informal survey."

She took a sip of the coffee and placed it down on the table, her hands surrounding the cup palms down, ready to choke the life out of it. Or him. "Alright. What have you got?"

Mark looked to the edges of the table, to the vacant chairs. The absence of a medical file was suddenly and oppressively apparent. Holly clenched her fists.

"This is why you chose me, isn't it?"

"What do you mean?" Marcus shrank back in his seat as Holly rose from the table.

"For the experiment. This is why I was given the go-ahead, over all the two eyed applicants. Little Marcus Priest in Mrs. Martin's class is still in love with the three eyed freak." She spat the last word, daring him to defy her.

"You remember me?" His voice was wavering.

"I don't forget voices, Marcus! They're all I had. And I don't forget how they made my life hell."

He stood and reached out to her, to take her arm and comfort her, and she pulled back from him and sneered.

"Holly, I never meant to hurt you. I'm so sorry. I love you."

"You can't be in love with me, you idiot! This is nepotism! God, how can you be so stupid?"

"Holly, I..."

"Whatever. I'll see you on Sunday. I want indigo and violet in one shot, too. No more of this dragging me along to pretend we're dating crap."

"I don't know if I should do that, Holly."

"I remember the numbers, Marcus. Violet and indigo aren't far off in frequency."

"I just don't want to overdo it and ruin all of our hard work."

"Our hard work? I've been the one adjusting to new colors week by week. I'll decide if it's too much. Sunday. And nothing outside the lab, got it?"

"Got it. I'm sorry, Holly."

"Get fucked, Marcus."

* * * *

Marcus insisted that violet and indigo be set separately, but Holly's defiance eventually wore him down into a silent and unwilling accomplice. He set the computer for the initial tuning and pressed enter. Indigo instantly flashed into her brain and Holly fell out of the chair, pressing her palms into her eyes.

"What the hell did you do to me?" she shouted from the floor, squinting with her third eye. The other two were screwed shut. "Everything is glowing! What did you do?"

"I barely touched the computer, Holly. What could I have done?" He went to help her and she batted him away. He stepped back, but the center eye stayed on him, watching him. "Why don't you try opening your eyes? Maybe they need to adjust."

"No. It only works in this one. I can see outlines of everything. What's going on?"

"Holly, that eye isn't even connected to anything."

Holly opened the other two eyes to glare at him, but the mix of vision collided and forced her eyes to close again. "I don't know, maybe it's more connected than you thought. God this is giving me a headache. Like everything has gone electric."

Marcus fought her hands away and gripped her jaw, flashing a light in her third eye, swinging it left and right. Her eye stayed trained on his face. "It's not reacting to normal light."

"Then what's it reacting to?"

Her third eye glared hard into him and Marcus felt his face go hot. "Um, I think me?"

She pushed back from him and swept her third eye across the room. The lines of objects lit up like candles, but Marcus stood in the middle of it like a halogen bulb. She looked down at her hands and saw the glow echoed in her edges, blue-white and jagged. Her other eyes opened, and the mix of color flowed into her hands and into all the glowing edges around the room. Her third eye closed, and the light shut off, but the faint glow still burned in her mind. "Marcus, did you hook up my third eye to night vision?"

"I think that's impossible, Holly."

She squinted at him. His outline was soft and quivering, contemplative, but it still glowed as bright as her own. "I think it works best on people. Marcus, I think I've got x-ray vision."

"That's definitely impossible, Holly."

She closed her outside eyes, letting the bright blue glow overtake her vision. It hummed in her chest like too much coffee. "Maybe we should try and add violet? Keep fiddling with the transistor and see if we can fix it?"

The outline of Marcus shifted, now a strong and steady glow as he folded his arms over a blank black chest. "Right. I'll see if I can fix it."

Holly could see Marcus' anger in the white glow that jabbed into the keyboard as he set up the transistor for violet. He was doing this for nothing. Holly was useless as a test subject; nothing more than a glitch in the system.

Holly sat in the center of the room, her palms sweaty as the man who gave her sight fumed behind the computer.

"I knew you liked me in elementary school, Marcus." The glow around him quickened, it gave off little spikes around his wrists. She watched him, outer eyes closed, and pushed him further. "You threw things at me on the playground, and made fun of me to your friends, but I could tell you had a crush. People give off little impulses of emotion." He looked up, and a flare of light radiated out from his head. She couldn't see his face, but she could feel his clenched jaw from across the room.

His hand moved across the desk, and hovered over the power switch. "This was a mistake," said Marcus. "I should never have called you. I should shut the transistor down right now." It wouldn't blind her, but she'd be trapped in yellows and reds.

"You could. I'd just go back to what I've always been doing. I've been blind before, Marcus." His outline quickened, anxiety breaking up the steady calm that comes with anger. "You won't shut it off, though, will you?"

"No."

"I didn't think so."

"I don't think I can get indigo out of your third eye, and it's blocked our access to violet. I guess you'll have to learn to live without it."

Holly saw a flare of indigo twitch behind the computer as he exited the transistor program. Fine. Let him keep violet for his trouble. "I never had violet, Marcus. I won't even miss it. We can pretend this never happened, okay? I'll say I've got a camera hooked up to my eyes. You won't lose your license, and I won't lose my vision. Sound good?"

"Sounds good."

"Goodbye, Marcus."

She left his office and counted the sixty three and a half steps to the bus stop, then continued to walk until she lost count. Holly picked up her cane and tucked it under her arm, then asked a man for directions to the train station. The sky was blue, the people glowed, and it was a good day to buy a bar in Seattle.

For the Children

by Jennifer R. Povey

"Your scan is fairly clean, Ms. Blackwell."

I sighed in relief at the counselor's words. "Fairly clean?"

"We'll be wanting to get rid of your myopia, obviously."

Was it obvious? I'd worn glasses all my life, shunning contact lenses as far too annoying. Was it really worth trying to edit out such a minor inconvenience? "Anything else?"

"Well, there's a general edit we're doing. It reduces telomere decay considerably." The counselor rested her hands on the desk. Thin hands. No wedding ring.

I didn't have to ask her what she meant, even without the wrinkles on her hands reminding me. No doubt if she had not known I was a biologist, she would have used simpler, more straightforward language. She meant life extension, which of course, I was not going to turn down for my child. I would benefit from medical technology myself, but my genes were what they were, and this might help my child live longer still…

I just wished that the child would have a father. A living father, not the sperm David had donated before the accident. "Anything on the father's side?"

"Slight risk factor for heart disease, easily enough fixed." The counselor smiled. "Are you ready? We can start right away."

A pause, then. "I would like a son."

That was an easy enough assurance. A son whom I could name David. I could always have a daughter later. There was more than enough in the sample and my genetic rating was certainly high enough to warrant two children. Well, unless certain conservative elements got their way. They were, again, making rumbles to deny reproductive rights to women who were not currently married to a man.

They'd been trying that for years and never got anywhere with it. I did not worry. I left, thinking about the son I would soon have.

There was no substitute for the natural womb. My pregnancy was easy, with almost no morning sickness. No complications. Part of me wanted a c-section, to avoid the inconvenience of labor, but kids born that way were more likely to be delinquents, bullies.

So, they didn't do that unless they had to, not any more. It was discouraged. So was going without genetic counseling and editing. I would not even have thought about going without it, doing the 'turkey baster' thing with a random sample of David's sperm.

None of us would deny our children the right to be healthier and live longer than us. How could we? We would not have been good mothers if we had.

A general edit. They did it to all the kids. Of course they did.

David was average size when he was born. He had his father's eyes almost from the start, a haunting echo of the man I had loved and lost. They asked us, later, if we thought anything was odd about the kids, about this new generation. I honestly don't remember anything. Not to start with, not as he grew and learned and played. I got him the best education I could afford, and David had left me quite a lot of money.

So, he got everything he needed to grow up a normal and healthy boy, and at first I thought that was exactly what he was. He was one of the first to get the therapy, the telomere edit. We didn't know. We couldn't possibly know, couldn't have even the slightest clue was to what was going on with our children.

Even when the first signs showed, I thought it was just some kind of luck. I won't ever forget the conversation, though.

"Mother."

I was in the kitchen, putting together a crockpot supper. That was often all I had time for, but I made sure it was healthy, I made sure and certain that he always got all of the recommendations. Well, except when they got stupid. Sometimes it seemed as if they wanted us to starve. "What's up, David?"

"There's something going on." His voice, from his bedroom. Our house was on one level, no upper floor, and his bedroom was all but opposite the kitchen. It was not like him not to come out. He had always been an active child and even as he hit his teenaged years...

"Okay..." I turned the burner down and then crossed to his bedroom. He sat on his bed, his knees drawn up to his chest. "What is it?"

Honestly, the answer I half expected was for him to announce that he was gay or something. I hadn't asked for any of the genes that increased the risk to be removed, as some people did. Heck, I knew of some parents who had asked for those genes to be added. I wouldn't have done that to him, but I felt it best to leave it up to the luck of the draw.

"I don't know," he said, finally. "I just know something's wrong."

"You're thirteen. Your body's changing. You're growing up." Except he wasn't, and we didn't know that. Not then.

Soon, though. Soon we knew it, soon we understood what we had done to our precious children. I suppose I realized it about a year later.

David still had a high voice, still had no beard. Neither did any of his male classmates. I didn't see a girl who had graduated to a real bra, either. Had the telomere extension delayed puberty?

That was what the doctors, finally, admitted. That our children were taking longer to grow up. And that might be a reasonable side effect of the attempts to extend their lives. I accepted it, hugged David, and gave him his extra time as a child.

He was doing college level work, but he still looked twelve. They all did, our beautiful, beloved children. I was growing old. I never had produced the second child I had once thought I wanted.

One child and a job was enough for any woman to be going on with. I worked and he learned, but he did not grow. Even then I did not suspect.

The truth was a slow realization. And it was not I who realized it.

David, turning from his computer to look up at me. "I can't stay here forever."

"You're still a child," I reminded him. A child with a PhD. What would we do if he did not grow up before I died?

"Only physically."

He was right on that front, too. He was right about so many things. He was smarter than I was, I knew that, his brain making new connections better than a true adult would have. He was twenty-five years old, with the face of a twelve year old and the brain of a genius. They'd stopped doing the gene hack after they realized. They would reintroduce it when they had worked out what went wrong.

My own body...old, tired. I would age and die. He would...stay a child. Not a single one of the children had gone through puberty yet, even those a little older than him. The whispers were that they never would, that we had a generation, even two generations, of eternal children. They could not produce offspring, not without artificial wombs.

But it had been corrected. Just these children, with their youngest siblings normal once more, growing and developing as they should. Human. As I was not sure David was. "If you try to live on your own..."

"I'm not ever going to grow up, mother." He had stopped calling me mom when he was ten. I remembered that keenly.

"And I can't look after you forever, but..."

But. That but.

"This is what we are. These are the bodies you gave us. We have to live with them."

But. But so much had been taken from him. I'd agreed to it without a thought. What mother would let her child die younger than necessary? Now he might live for a long time. We did not know. Our children walked in an uncharted territory. "I know. I didn't know. I swear."

He stood up and hugged me. "I know you didn't, but I'm leaving."

He could legally vote, he could legally drink alcohol, although he didn't. He was an adult in time if not in body. "Where are you going?"

"We're...putting something together. Some of the other children. A sort of commune, I suppose."

Now, that made sense. "Okay."

"And you won't be shut out. Parents are welcome to visit." He smiled. "But I'm going to be busy. We have work to do."

I knew about neoteny. I was a biologist. I knew that David was more intelligent because his brain was staying younger. I didn't grasp how much more. Or what these children could achieve. Some had whispered about them crewing a starship, because they would live longer.

I remembered pointing out that we did not know how long, and could we risk these unearthly children dying in the void, of some sudden onset of old age. For all we knew their lifespans would end up being shorter. For all we knew...and now David was leaving. Later than I had expected when I first held him in my arms. Earlier than I wished. Perhaps they just kept tugging at our maternal heart strings.

Perhaps.

The 'commune' as David had called it was part of an old apartment complex. Most of the buildings had been demolished as obsolete, but they had upgraded the remaining one as best they could. I could see the 'roots' of smart buildings in the landscaped grounds nearby. Soon they would have all modern conveniences, as my grandmother used to say. For now, just the roots, growing slowly as if they were great trees. Landscaped grounds surrounded them, planted with flowering trees and bright pansies. It was a beautiful place on a beautiful day, and I wanted to stay there forever.

Those grounds were full of children. It was a nice day, but they weren't playing. In groups of three and four they had gathered around unrolled screens. Why work indoors, I thought, on a day like this? And working they were. There was something surreal about it. One did not let children work.

But these were not children. Perhaps they never had been. David and his 'something's not right'. What had he really felt that day? I looked for him in the clusters of children, walked over closer to one of them. On the ground, the screen showed part of the human genome. Were they seeking to solve their problem? Or were they happy the way they were?

I realized I had never asked him. Never asked him if he was happy. Another group had a map of the solar system, tracing routes to Mars.

This 'commune' of David's was a think tank. I understood with sudden clarity that they were leaving us behind, moving into even more uncharted territory. That's likely why it happened.

David came walking across the lawn towards me, stepping around his compatriots and their work. I didn't hug him, not in front of them, but looked at him. Still no change, no age, no growth. An aberration that would not be perpetuated. Or would it? Would they, in the end, make more of themselves through us normal humans. In that moment I knew fear, fear of these children. That's why I understand. That's why I understand what happened. They really would have made us second class citizens to preserve themselves, because they had no choice.

Or they would have let old humanity gracefully go extinct once they solved the artificial womb problem.

"Come inside, Mother," he said.

I could hear the capital letter. They would, but they would also respect their mothers. Fathers, of course, they had no need of. Only mothers...and that was the future I suddenly saw with clarity. "Of course."

He led me into the building. "We're working on every problem we have the manpower for. Trying the Mars colony again, although we'll need normals for that."

Breeders, I translated. "And fixing your genetic problems?"

David shook his head. "Not yet. None of us want to be fixed yet. We're working on something else."

"What?"

"The next generation. We don't want to be fixed, but some of us don't want to ever make any more like *us*. And besides, we might be able to..." He tailed off. "I need you to do something for me, mother."

"What is it?"

He told me. Something simple. Something oh so simple. Then he showed me everything else.

Three days later, David was dead. Most of them were. They'd been so thorough, whoever did it. A virus that killed children and left adults alive. Normal adults. Of course, it also killed a lot of ordinary, innocent children. It wiped out most of the new generation, most of the ones we'd made without the gene hack.

Whoever did it did not care. They pulled me in for questioning, of course. I was a biologist, albeit one that worked with animals, not people. That did not last long. Not long at all before they realized my hysterical grief could not be feigned. I wept, I sobbed, I cajoled. And, above all, I hated. I didn't have the ability to find them, but I hoped they would be found. Would be found and punished. I wanted them dead, in truth, but that particular piece of barbarism had been long since rendered obsolete.

I still wanted them dead even as I knew what they had feared, clearly saw it. Even heard the echo in David's voice. "Some of us don't want to ever make any more like us." Some. Not all.

I knew that some of them would have tried for what I feared. Which is why I have to leave.

They're trying the Mars colony again and I'm going. I'm still young enough, with the right drugs, to carry another child. I'm taking it with me.

It?

That was the favor David asked of me. To take one item with me. He knew, or at least he suspected, that they would be killed. And he knew what else the people behind it would do, wiping the computer system they had used. Destroying their work, or most of it. The ship design we're using is one of the things they got out before it happened.

He gave me everything. Everything his group achieved. Not everything the children did, just his group. It's enough. It includes the reason I won't actually need those drugs.

I took it. It worked. I'm going to live for a very long time. And when humanity is ready, everything will change.

Which is why I have to leave.

Saturday Night at the Sickbar

by Shane Robinson

Last night's typhoid is still coating my mouth when I get up. If I had any of the delirium dreams it's supposed to bring, I don't remember them. I flush my system with some disappointment. Don't want to hallucinate my way in front of a car on the way there.

The strident Asian bellwork of my alarm keeps on ringing. By the time I stumble into the wall and turn it off, I'm back to myself, except for the rot in the back of my throat.

I gargle out the crap while I make sure my hair is destroyed in all the right ways. Then it's fumble through the pile at the bottom of my closet. Hawaiian shirt, tan trench coat. I push the sleeves up. The uncaring angle sounds right tonight.

The door whirs and clicks locked behind me.

The night is the same as every night. Warm. Perfect. The streetlights shift colors every few minutes, giving everything a new perspective, keeping the boredom at bay. An unpracticed eye wouldn't be able to distinguish between the crowds of beautiful people strolling down the walks. My eye is very practiced. It's easy to tell those who are just floating from those who get it. It's in the casual drop of a strand of hair, the understated application of a few lines in the face. It's what separates the artists from the rest of them.

Our eyes meet as I walk, me and the other artists. There's nothing so obvious as a nod when I pass someone, but there's an acknowledgement all the same.

Sickbar is wedged in between two big, clean moderns like a piece of food stuck in someone's teeth. The cleanbots stop the place from looking really authentic, sweeping up the cigarette butts and ceremoniously vacuuming up any vomit moments after it arrives on the concrete. Even with every surface cleaned every two minutes, Jonjon's done a great job keeping the place looking beaten up, between the antique-styled aluminum signs and the old, four-pane windows. Or normally it looks good. Right now, I'm unable to appreciate it for the tumor that's sprouted up on the face of the scene.

One of the networking-eggs is floating across the street. A hard terminal for people to log into the social sites at a club or a bar, so you can prove you were there. Hop into the fake world to show how real you are. That's as backwards an idea as I've ever heard. I can't believe Jonjon would have something that tacky installed here.

Still, I can't help but like the design. Modeled like one of those 1960's mod space chairs. A big white egg with a seat in it. Too tacky to be truly inauthentic. Some little girl is inside, laughing and tapping away at the keyboard. I appreciate the tiny plastic dress, but she's not an artist. Her hair is perfect, and so is her skin.

A polite recorded voice informs her that her time is up. The egg bobs slightly as she gets out, and smiles at me as she walks by. Perfect teeth, too. Imagine that.

There are other places besides Sickbar, but none that get the vibe quite so right. No filters for the haze of smoke, the clean-bots shooed out the door with a broom whenever they try to sweep the floor or programmed to not buff out the scratches on the wooden table. It's real wood, antique as hell. Shitty fluorescent lights from the early 21st century, half of them flickering or dead. Sickbar doesn't try to pretty it up. We love the grime. It's why we come here.

My booth is in the back. I'm late. Everyone's here already

Thomas is gorgeous in a black satin shirt. Short-sleeved, of course, showing off the stud at the inside of his elbow. We all have the holes. We don't need them to get sick. The input jack isn't any more necessary than the sparkling pseudo-hypodermics on the table, but the little metal rivet is a sign. *We get sick*, it says. *We like the pain.*

Thomas flips his blonde hair at me in greeting as I come up. Next to him, Myra gives me a begrudging nod. "Hey, Gabe."

There's already a selection on the table. I wonder what Thomas has decided on tonight. We usually follow his lead. The man is a real artist. I've never felt like shit like I have while I was in his company.

I take my place at the table, next to Loreen, who's casually spectacular in a micro-LED dress that casts dramatic shadows on her cleavage, and on a new feature. I toy the input just above the swell of her left breast. "That's clever," I say, because it's the thing to say, but also because I'm impressed by the combination of the lighted dress and the unorthodox placement. The eye is unmistakably drawn to that bit, glinting and casting its own shadow. Much less noticeable is the deliberate placement of the heavy circles under her eyes. It adds an excellent note of desperation to a face that would otherwise be just too damned pretty.

“Thanks,” she says. Her voice is practiced shy, but the flutter of the long lashes–glittered to catch the sparkle from the dress, of course–is practiced turn-on.

I collapse into the seat next to her, and my hand casually finds her thigh under the table. Her skin is warm, no sweat, no shivers. The party hasn’t started without me.

Myra leans in and slides me a bile-yellow vial. I trust her judgment on how to start the night. She's a bitch, but she's a better artist than me. The blue hair is new, a short-and-shaved chopjob she probably did herself. It looks awful; I'm suitably impressed.

I shove my sleeve back, click the needle in, and wait that tiny beat before twisting it to activate. The effects are immediate. My chest heaves and twists, like I've just breathed in lungfuls of sand. I lean back, savoring the weight.

"Good?" Thomas asks.

I try to respond, but my words are broken apart by a battery of coughs. I thump my fist on the table as I push through the attack. "Oh yeah," I manage to get out, my voice crackling like a piece of cooked chicken skin. I don't ask what I've been given. Take the ride, then read the itinerary afterward, that's the idea.

Loreen leans back and sweeps that mane of brown hair off her shoulder, smiling at me. I slide the jack into the hole in her chest, and click it casual as can be, even though I know exactly what she's telling me, having me give it to her instead of taking it herself. I know where I'll be spending the later part of the evening.

It's a game, soon, each of us trying to hold a conversation without coughing. Thomas is the undisputed master of this, and he tells stories of his week with only a gravelly edge to his voice, not betraying the phlegm and blood crowding his airways.

The waitress comes by and deposits a box of tissues on the table. I crack it open and wipe my nose, noting the paint-lines of red that appear with satisfaction.

"Ah, shit," Myra says. "Nancy's coming."

I look up, and sure enough, it's little Nancy with her leopard-print shorts and her explosion of buffed-up red hair, trying just a little too hard.

"Hey guys," she says, coming up to the table. We murmur vague assertions at her; Loreen hacks into her tissue.

"What're you on, then, Thomas?" Nancy says, sliding in next to Myra, either ignoring her dagger-eyes or missing them altogether.

"Consumption," Thomas says. Nancy sniffs contemptuously. "Consumption's not even a real disease."

"Consumption is an old term for the weight loss caused by late-stage tuberculosis," Thomas says. All of us know it, but none of us are about to miss the opportunity to put Nancy in her place. We've all been there, in the newbabe's chair. Shame Nancy doesn't seem to recognize that's where she's sitting.

"Oh," she says. "Well, can I have some?"

Thomas gestures absently at the needles on the table. *Sure, do whatever the fuck you want.* He continues his story where he left off before he was interrupted.

Nancy scoops up a pale blue syringe and sticks it into a jack halfway up her thigh. The hole is new, and she makes sure I see it. One of these days, I'll sit her down and explain that it's not about flashing sex everywhere. It's about looking lived-in, like a real human being.

"All right, we're out." Thomas stretches and feigns a yawn. It's sometime in the half-real span of after-midnight. We've gone through three needles each, and it's showing on his face. His cheeks are hollow red, and the space under his eyes looks like he's been punched.

Thomas ushers Myra out of the booth. Nancy doesn't get the hint right away, and chirps her annoyance as Myra pushes her to get her to move. Thomas ignores the exchange and slides his jacket on.

I stand and clap my arms around him. "Be well," he says. Old joke.

As they exit, Myra takes hold of one of his asscheeks with an iron-taloned hand and gives it a thorough shake. Marking her territory, and damned if she isn't right that we're all staring at it as it goes.

"What are you guys doing now?" Nancy asks Loreen and me. She's still chirpy and alert. Cleared her system, no doubt, and ready for more. So inauthentic.

Loreen just smiles a poor-baby smile at her from behind half-lidded eyes. I shake my head, in love with her ability to stab so deep without saying anything, and pat Nancy on the shoulder. "We'll see you later, babe."

We head back to Loreen's place. There's something comforting about the old New Rich design, all that glass and soft blue lighting. I lift her up onto a swooping curve of plastic that might be a bar or a kitchen counter. The glittery LED fabric of her dress plays its way effortlessly up her thighs.

It's early morning, still dark, when I get up. I keep the latest bout of lactic acid, enjoying the soreness in my muscles. Loreen is draped on the couch, the lines of her traced by the skyscrapers' lights through the full-length window. I don't know if she's asleep or not, but I know that part of the deal is that I not be here in the morning.

I watch her for a minute, letting myself get a bit sad at not being able to lie with her after. It's a good feeling. Genuine. I smile a little. I know she kicks me out for my benefit. Where else am I going to get a dose of regret?

I console myself on the elevator ride down with the idea that she might be a little sad herself, on that expensive couch.

The city's as alive at four in the morning as any other time, but I keep to myself. By now, the social circles have welded together like titanium rings. There's no getting in without too much tedious catchup on the nights' events.

There's plenty of enjoyment to be had in playing the lonely stranger, anyway. Between the Bogart coat, the dark circles under my eyes, and the I've-just-been-fucking hair, I get my share of interested looks.

A night out here sounds like an appropriately melancholy ending to the evening. I sprawl on a park bench, throwing my arm over my eyes. If I'm thinking about Loreen, it's only to maintain the setting.

I'm woken up by the stab of sunlight. Cursing myself for forgetting sunglasses, I shake off and stand, stretching out the kink in my neck where the armrest has mauled it. A cleanbot chirps its eagerness as I get up, and as soon as I'm off the bench it's already wiping it down.

Breakfast comes from a little cart at the side of the 14th Street bridge, an awful burrito crammed with dry eggs, synthetic meat and something orange that tries to claim the title of salsa.This area is downcity, real authentic. No cleanbots here. The garbage stays where people throw it. The graffiti isn't scrubbed off daily.

I dust my hands off on my pants, leaving a smear of orange above one knee. The burrito wrapper I toss to one side, satisfied with the way nothing whirrs along to pick it up.

* * * *

The apartment is paid for out of the trust fund. I only use it to sleep, and occasionally to give good friends a safe, no-sharp-corners place to get out of their skulls in.

No friends around at two in the afternoon. I put on some quiet, beatless nonmusic, strip out of clothes that are now yesterday's, and collapse into bed.

I get up sometime around sunset, startled into wakefulness by the odd contortion my unconscious body has maneuvered itself into. I could kick a bit of adrenaline into my bloodstream and be up in a moment, but the old-fashioned way feels so much better, and I'm in no hurry.

I slump into the shower stall and stab a finger at the hot water button. For nearly a half hour I let the water pound my head back into wakefulness. Then it's a white shirt, grey vest, brown tie. Playing professor today where I played detective yesterday. The outfits are all part of the art.

I debate pumping a minor cold into myself before I leave, but my apartment is too quiet in the orange of sunset, and I'm not in the mood to get sick alone.

There's a message from Thomas on the wall unit. The letters swim up out of the default blue background; I've never bothered to personalize the thing.

Bored, his message reads. *Starting early. Join me?*

Sure, I type back.

* * * *

Despite our best efforts, the new crowd is finding its way into Sickbar. I suppose Jonjon's got to make a living, but it pisses me off to see the waitress walking trays of that designer shit to mewling newbabes who'll move on to some new drug in a week.

Thomas and I have been sticking some recently remarketed strains of flu bug, stuff that hasn't been around for a while. I'm rolling back on it, enjoying the meat-tenderizer ache in my muscles. Thomas is far away, quiet. No philosophical discourses tonight.

Nancy arrives shortly after me, in black leather pants and a tube top that strains her chest. I'm startled to learn it was Thomas who invited her. In any case, she's settled and quiet, watching the two of us like a kitten. She doesn't even ask for any of the stuff on the table. I realize I don't know anything about her. The vintage clothes say she's got money, but the attitude is all wrong. She's too damned *excited* by everything to be from up here.

I think about asking her, but I scrap the question before it gets out of my mouth. I like my idea of her better than I'd probably like the reality. Down kid pretending to be an up kid pretending to be a down kid is a story with a good shine to it. Finding out she's a sheltered tower brat, one of those puritan rich kids playing hooky, would just be a disappointment.

Loreen and Myra show up to interrupt my internal monologue. Myra's outfit is damn near my own, minus the vest; she looks impressively tough and boyish, sleeves rolled up to the shoulders to show off those whip-thin arms.

Loreen, though, is the one who keeps my eye drawn. I'd give her a government grant for the arts, if I could. I'd give her a fucking medal. Her hair is erratic, unwashed. She has the same dress on as the night before. I can make out a couple of spots where the LEDs have burnt out, and damned if one of the dark areas doesn't look kind of like it's in the shape of a handprint. Right on one hip.

Jealousy's a new one for me. I want to enjoy the feeling, but I'm having a hell of a time getting my arms around it.

Nancy huffs as she realizes I'm staring at someone else. Her jealousy is just the pants-kick I need to snap out of mine. I extend an arm to Loreen, and she slides in next to me, accepting the vial of yellow fever I was thinking about starting in a few minutes.

Myra taps her fingers over the array on the table before settling on an orange-yellow vial of tetanus. Impressed by how strong she's starting the evening, I click in some encephalitis in time with her. I'm never quite prepared for the beach-ball swelling of my skull. We grin at each other across the table.

Thomas scoffs at a passing tray of sense-overload cocktails. The newbabes babble about 'ultimate experiences' and 'tolerance thresholds,' but they don't get it, never did. It's about the *authenticity.* It's about communing with the dead, touching a thing that doesn't exist anymore.

"Let's get out of here," Thomas says, sniffing and wiping his nose. "I'm not feeling it."

"But I haven't even hit anything yet!" And there's the Nancy I know. I remind myself that what I'm doing is charity work, and that I was a newbabe once, too, all those ages ago.

I hand her a vial of pneumonia, and she shuts up as she plugs it into the socket. I don't know if we'll ever be able to make her into an artist, but I haven't given up trying yet.

No one else complains. Thomas is the boss. He knows where all the stuff is, he knows what it all does. He puts vials on the table. We all follow where he leads.

*   *   *   *

We're walking down the street, and no amount of cranial pressure is changing the fact that I'm just not riding the train tonight. Everyone is quiet, stewing inside their own heads. I'm debating just calling it quits, heading home.

The peddler materializes out of a shaded area between two buildings. "Hey babes," he wheezes. "Wanna put some real pain in you?"

I'm impressed by his dedication to the bit. His eyes are rheumy and crusted, and his nose is raw. The disheveled balding pate makes me think something academic during the day– librarian, or a professor, maybe. I'd bet a month's trust that receding hairline cleans up nice, with a pair of wire-rimmed glasses to go with it.

"Whatcha pushin', crustfuck?" Thomas says casually, leaning on the man's shoulder.

"I got all kinds," the peddler says. Not to be outdone in cool, he opens his coat without dislodging Thomas' arms. I see Thomas' face catch the low-key rainbow radiating from inside. It's an impressive spread, at least thirty choices tucked into their little holsters. I am humbled by my inability to recognize some of them. A few are obvious–the bubbly green vial is a trademark of pneumonia, and the one with the pretty pewter wolf's-head stopper can only be lupus—but there are others I'm not familiar with.

"You're an authentic kid," he says, grinning up at Thomas with greenish teeth. "That's why I showed you this side of the jacket. None of that new stuff here. Syphilis. Malaria. Cholera, if you want really unpleasant. All the real deal, no holdbacks or additives."

Thomas waves a dismissive hand. "Old hat. What's in this one?" He taps an empty fold of fabric. There's a clink, and a thrill runs through my stomach as I realize the peddler's got a hidden pocket.

The peddler gives Thomas an up-and-down with that watery blue eye. "Oh, that's for the veterans, babe," he says. "You don't want that."

"Oh, I want it," Thomas says. There's a sheen in his eyes I haven't seen since the guy came round Sickbar last year claiming they'd replicated smallpox.

"Shit, you do want it," the peddler says. "Take a look, then."

He rips the Velcro back. All of us shudder a little in anticipation at the noise.

We suck in breaths with the cohesion of one being. Everything has suddenly become real damn authentic. Maybe too authentic.

There's only one thing the vial under the flap can be. There is no decoration, only a plain silver stopper with the stub of info-jack uncovered at the top. The stuff inside is jet black, and swirls of its own volition. A pulse ripples through it at regular intervals, tracing lines of bright red, like veins.

"Is that...?" Thomas reaches out, but softly, softly.

The peddler lets his fingers brush it before he takes a step back, out of reach. "Trigeminal neuralgia," he says.

"The big gun," Loreen says. Her nails are near to drawing blood on my arm.

"Isn't trigeminal neuralgia illegal?" Nancy asks from the back of the circle.

Thomas' head snaps back to her. His glare speaks for all of us.

"Say it a little louder, why don't you?" the peddler says. He steps back, and in a blur of hands, his coat is buttoned again. "I thought you guys were maybe real pain kids. I guess I was wrong."

He's gone into the night before we can chase him down, a practiced shadow.

"Fucking classy, Nancy," Thomas says.

"I wasn't scared," she says quickly. "I was just thinking out loud."

I'm barely listening. I'm thinking about the little man with the shitty hair and the vials of poison in his coat. He wasn't faking; he was a real outlaw. A criminal.

How authentic is that?

"Why's it illegal, anyway?" Nancy asks later. We've been walking around for an hour, with no luck at all.

"God, Nancy, quit being such a newbabe," Myra says.
I hear Thomas click his teeth. "I'm out," he says. "This night bit it till blood came. I don't want to look at people's faces anymore."

"I'll come with you," Myra says.

"Sure, babe."

No one says anything as they leave. Casual, that's the only way to play it. Best way to knock yourself down is to look like you care.

"How about you, Loreen? Want to get out of here?"

She smiles at me. "Two nights in a row?" Her eyes go half-lidded, that beautiful droop that's starting to piss me off.

Not that I say anything. It'll take a lot more than her to crack my cool. She walks away, heels clicking hollowly on the perfect pavement. She's probably picked the shoes just for that sound. I realize I've had the wrong idea about her, the whole time. I thought she was one of the stupid, pretty ones, playing follow the leader. Now I see different. She might be a better artist than Thomas, even.

"Do you...maybe wanna hang out? Just us?"

I'd forgotten about Nancy altogether.

I turn to those puppy-dog eyes, that sniffling nose. I just can't muster up the energy to make a half-decent excuse. Maybe it's the swollen brain. I try for an apologetic murmur as I walk away; maybe it's too quiet for her to catch it.

*   *   *   *

I haven't seen anyone from the Sickbar group in almost a week.

Nancy's called a few times; I've ignored each one. It's not that I'm trying to be cruel; I just don't have the energy to leave the apartment. I try having a couple of friends over...but everyone is busy. No one wants to let a broken link into their circle.

I watch a lot of old movies, spend a lot of time browsing links on the disease forums, reading stuff I've read a half dozen times already.

When the wall unit goes off, I'm glad no one is around to see how quick I'm up and checking it. Not Thomas, I see with some disappointment. Myra.

It's an actual call, too, not a message. Video off, which is good; I can only carry the unwashed, unshaven thing so far.

I catch maybe one word in three between the heaves and the sniffles, but I've heard it before: She hasn't seen Thomas in a few days, could I take a look for her. Then she adds a new note to the song and dance, one I haven't heard before.

"I'm worried he might be in trouble."

Myra cuts the line before I can add anything else. I'm floored with the realization that those might not have been sick noises. She might have been crying.

I check Newpost, Spike, the Waterfront. He's not at any of the normal hangouts. I wander through the parks spaced along the routes from one bar to the next, but there's no sign of him in the grass.

I realize, finally, where I should look. The last place I'd ever expect him to be.

His apartment is across the park from mine, but the buildings might as well have been crapped out by the same giant bird. I ride the elevator up. I've been here a few times before, but never gone farther than the hallway outside his place. This is no-man's land.

I push the button by the door. There's no response.

I'm halfway down the hall when I hear the door stutter open.

He's leaning heavy on the wall as I step inside, hair damp, stuck to his head. He looks like shit, and not in a good way.

"What's the story, newbabe?" I ask. He groans, holds up a hand. "Shh," he says, and weakly beckons me inside.

It's dark in the apartment. I want to turn on a light, but then I realize what's going on, why he's in the dark and telling me to shut up.

"I took it," he says, and sits down on the edge of the bed. He holds his face in his palms, and I notice how heavy his breathing is, how rattled. It must be as bad as they say. A thrill moves through my insides. Trite as it is, I can't help but wonder if he used the whole thing up on himself, or if there's any left.

I sit down next to him. "What's it like?"

He doesn't answer. After a moment, I realize he's crying. I am suddenly sick with fear. I've seen Thomas in the grips of late-stage syphilis madness. I've sat in a private booth with him while we both felt our skin rot from the bubonic plague. But I've never seen him like this, never seen him reduced to...less than Thomas.

"I can't turn it off," he says in a whisper. "It's worse than those migraines we hit that one night. Every time it goes off, it's like someone putting a spike through my head."

"What do you mean, you can't turn it off?"

"I called the doctors. They said they can't do anything." His face twists in a grimace, and he waits for it to pass before continuing, "It's why it's illegal, man. They said it's not a disease, it's a neurological condition, and no one figured out how to shut off the trigger once you turn it- "

His voice turns to a choked groan of anguish, and he falls back on the bed, grinding the heels of his hands to his eyes. I watch, fascinated, the way the spittle shines off his bared teeth in the dark.

I remember all the descriptions I've read of the condition. *Like handfuls of needles driven into your skull, and left there. Like something chewing on your brain.* Repeated continuous attacks on the trigeminal nerve. Talking, eating, light, even touching your face; anything could set it off.

The suicide disease, they called it. Because once you had it, killing yourself was the only way to stop the pain.

I feel like throwing up, and I didn't even have to take anything.

I was so ready to try it. I could have bought one of those needles. It could be me now on the bed instead of him.

"Listen," Thomas says. He's sat half up on the bed. "Listen to me. I can't...I can't do it. It hurts too much. It doesn't stop."

I know what he's going to ask, and I turn my head away. I want to plug my ears, but I won't, not going to break my cool by looking like a kid.

"You gotta kill me."

I sniff out a laugh. "No way, Holiday."

"I mean it, Gabe."

"Call the doctors, man. They'll figure something out." I'm playing with a corner of bedsheet now. I can't look at his eyes, can't see the pleading in them.

"The doctors won't do anything. They're not even answering my calls anymore. I'm a criminal now. I'm nobody."

"I'm sorry, man. I can't...there's no way." I stand. I love the guy, and I can't be near him right now. "This is too authentic. I've gotta go."

There's a long silence. I know I've hurt him, worse than the nerve damage. I'm running out on him, and even knowing it, I'm too scared to stay.

"All right," Thomas says. Too cool to beg me, even now. "Be well."

I want to say it back, but I'm choked with shamefaced tears. I get out of there before the black hole has a chance to eat me.

It's a week before I leave the apartment again. The bugs can't kill me, there are safeguards built all through them, but damned if I don't try. I spend three days caught in the grips of anything with a fever or delirium listed in the symptoms, two or three at a time, trying to drive away anything that resembles a coherent thought. It's a failed attempt. I don't know what stabs me worse—what's happened to him, or how I bolted. Not even like a newbabe. Like a fucking *embryo.*

I finally find relief in more old-fashioned means, drinking bottle after bottle of cheap wine until unconsciousness kicks in. It's another three days of this, waking only long enough to knock myself out again, before I decide enough's enough. He's my friend, my best friend. There's got to be something I can do for him. I'll make calls. I'll talk to the doctors. And if he's right, and not just melodramatic, if there's nothing they can do...

I throw on the first shirt and pair of pants that I can find. Naturally, the more careless I look, the more eyes I draw on the street. I ignore them all, no space in my head for enjoying the admiration.

I could ditch the hangover in a second, but it's keeping me sharp, in the real. I'm not going to go chickenshit again.

I head to Sickbar first. I doubt he'll be there, but Jonjon will be up-to-date if anyone is.

Across the street, I see Myra, leaning up against that goddamned egg, smoking a cigarette. She looks like shit. No makeup, wrinkled clothes. Just like me.

"Have you seen Thomas?" I don't want to ask it. Even as it's coming out of my mouth, I see that her eyes are puffy and red. No tears, though. All cried out.

"Thomas is dead," she says.

There's a splash of cold, and I'm sinking, nothing but dark and the smell of seaweed. "Did...did you?"

She shakes her head. "He asked. I couldn't."

Of course he did it himself. What the hell did I think, he was going to wait for me?

"How?" I ask.

"He jumped," Myra says.

He jumped. I don't ask her where, or when. There's no reason for details. Who cares which windows he fell past? How can it matter which chunk of concrete he painted himself onto?

I collapse into the white egg. It bobs under my weight, and the polite voice asks me to log in. I want to say something to her, but I can't think of a single thing that isn't absolute bullshit. I want to laugh. Leave it to Thomas to strip all my words away.

"I'm going to go," Myra says. "I shouldn't have come out tonight."

I nod, still staring at a space just past her foot. Without Thomas, what is there for me to say to her?

She clicks away. After a few feet, I hear her heels stop. I look up to see her looking at me.

"I....I never really had a problem with you," she says. "You were good to him."

She purses her lips, and nods once, as if her job is done now. The sound of her heels fades away, and then it's gone, and I can only hear the low din of conversation inside the place across the street, a place that used to be a home to me, that I'm not sure I even have a name for anymore.

I sit in the network-pod, drifting through the glittery night lights, ignoring the polite voice that comes on through the little speakers, reminding me that my time is up.

Biographies

Megan Lee Beals lives in the Pacific Northwest with her husband and one-eyed cat. When not writing, she enjoys an ongoing and unconventional education in nearly everything fit to print. Her fiction has been featured online at Weird Fiction Review and Literary Orphans, and in the Stamps Vamps & Tramps and Dadaoism anthologies. Her favorite color is not violet.

Jennifer Brozek is an award winning editor, game designer, and author. Winner of the Australian Shadows Award for best edited publication, Jennifer has edited ten anthologies with more on the way. Author of In a Gilded Light, The Lady of Seeking in the City of Waiting, Industry Talk, and the Karen Wilson Chronicles, she has more than fifty published short stories, and is the Creative Director of Apocalypse Ink Productions.

Jennifer also is a freelance author for numerous RPG companies. Winner of both the Origins and the ENnie award, her contributions to RPG sourcebooks include Dragonlance, Colonial Gothic, Shadowrun, Serenity, Savage Worlds, and White Wolf SAS. Jennifer is also the author of the long running Battletech webseries, The Nellus Academy Incident. When she is not writing her heart out, she is gallivanting around the Pacific Northwest in its wonderfully mercurial weather. Read more about her at www.jenniferbrozek.com or follow her on Twitter at @JenniferBrozek.

Tom Brennan is a British writer living in Liverpool, UK with wife Sylvia and an ethereal white cat called Delaney. He works as an Emergency Dispatcher in the ambulance service and enjoys writing a wide variety of fiction (basically what he enjoys reading). He has a Fantasy novel, Doktor Glass, out at the moment and his short stories have appeared in many small publication web, print and audio.

Miles Britton is a journalist and fiction writer whose work has been published in Radar Magazine, MAGNET, Philadelphia Weekly, and Charleston City Paper, among many others. He studied creative writing at Tulane, holds a master's in journalism from Temple, and is currently pursuing a master's in English at Appalachian State. With a passion for music only rivaled by his love for words, Britton has toured throughout the U.S. playing in various indie rock bands, and song titles and lyrics are the inspiration behind the majority of his short stories. He and his wife, Lizzie, live in the mountains of North Carolina.

Preston Dennett has worked as a carpet cleaner, a fast-food worker, a data entry clerk, a bookkeeper, a landscaper, an actor, a teacher and more. But his true love has always been speculative fiction. Finally he decided to see if he could make his dream of being an SF writer come true. The result has been a string of sales with stories appearing (or forthcoming) in Andromeda Spaceways Inflight Magazine, Perihelion, Encounters Magazine, and several other magazines. He has also earned seven honorable mentions in the Writers of the Future Contest. He currently resides in Reseda, California.

Alexandra Grunberg is a New York City based author and actress. Her work has appeared in Daily Science Fiction, Plasma Frequency Magazine, and Perihelion Science Fiction. Her story "Any Ending" won third place in Fiction Vortex's August monthly contest and her story "Finale in Blue" won third place in their October Horror Contest. She is currently writing a new horror/comedy webseries, "HOUSED," in which she will also be appearing as a lead character. You can find links to Alexandra's stories at alexandragrunberg.wordpress.com .

Wayne Helge was in the Coast Guard for a dozen years, but now writes and works in Virginia. He is also an amateur guitarist, but has finally accepted that he will never be able to play a decent version of the solo from Pearl Jam's 'Alive." His story, "Toca la Guitarra," was written at Viable Paradise XV, and first printed in the January 2013 issue of Perihelion Science Fiction.

Katrina Nicholson grew up listening to gruesome medical tales at the dinner table, so her obsession with infectious diseases was almost inevitable. When she's not reading about Ebola or smallpox, Katrina writes novels, short stories, screenplays, and reviews. You can read more of her stories in the anthologies Futuredaze, Tesseracts Fifteen,

Kisses by Clockwork, and the Speculative Elements series or visit her online at www.katrinanicholson.com.

Sarah Pinsker is a Baltimore-based fiction writer and singer/songwriter. She has two solo albums and one with her band, the Stalking Horses, on various indie labels. Her fiction has appeared in Asimov's and the Magazine of Fantasy & Science Fiction, among other places, and her 2013 novelette, "In Joy, Knowing the Abyss Behind," published in Strange Horizons, was nominated for a Nebula Award. Her website is www.sarahpinsker.com.

Jennifer R. Povey is in her early forties, and lives in Northern Virginia with her husband. She writes a variety of speculative fiction, whilst following current affairs and occasionally indulging in horse riding and role playing games. She has sold fiction to a number of markets including Analog, Digital Science Fiction, and Cosmos and written a handful of RPG supplements, some of which are available from Occult Moon Publishing. She also writes comic books. Her first novel, Transpecial, was published by Musa Publishing in April, 2013.

Shane Robinson is a 28-year-old author of horror and speculative fiction. He lives in rainy, ghost-filled Astoria, Oregon with his wife, Monica. When not writing, he paints, draws, sculpts, and works on shoring up his meager but growing collection of fiction, mythology and folklore.

Holly Schofield's short stories have been published in magazines and anthologies internationally. She travels through time at the rate of one second per second, oscillating between the alternate realities of the prairies and her writing cabin on the west coast. For more of her work, see hollyschofield.wordpress.com.

John Skylar is a life scientist, journalist, and author of both fiction and nonfiction. His work has appeared on Mashable, in The Huffington Post, in Aoife's Kiss Magazine, and in Lakeside Circus Magazine, among others. A full list of John's credits is available on his website, www.johnskylar.com, where he also posts offbeat opinion pieces and tumblr esoterica. He lives in New York, along with his ramen soup.

Ree Soesbee is a fiction writer, game designer, and continuity editor, creating worlds for massively multiplayer online games as well as traditional pen and paper RPGs and CCGs. She has authored more than sixteen novels, as well as a variety of popular short stories. Her credits include writing for Dragonlance, Star Trek, Legend of the Five Rings, and Vampire: the Masquerade. She has writtten and designed multiple RPGs, and her work hs ben included in numerous anthologies and professional literary journals. Currently, she is a Narrative Designer for the award-winning MMO, Guild Wars 2.

Lauren C. Teffeau was born and raised on the East Coast, educated in the South, employed in the Midwest, and now lives and dreams in the Southwest. Her work can be found in a variety of speculative fiction venues. She's a graduate of the 2012 Taos Toolbox writer's workshop, and blogs about the writing life at http://laurencteffeau.com

K. H. Vaughan is a refugee from academia with a Ph.D. in clinical psychology. In his other life he taught, published, and practiced in various settings, with particular interest in decision theory, forensic psychology, psychopathology, and methodology. He is an affiliate member of the Horror Writers Association and a member of the New England Horror Writers. He lives with his wife and three children in New England. He can be found at www.khvaughan.com.

Nghi Vo lives on the shores of an inland sea, and her fiction has appeared in Strange Horizons, Icarus, and Crossed Genres. Her current interests include guardian lions, mourning rituals, revenge tragedy, and baking. She can be contacted at bridgeofbirds@gmail.com.

About the Guest Stars

David Gerrold's work is famous around the world. His novels and stories have been translated into more than a dozen languages. His TV scripts are estimated to have been seen by more than a billion viewers. Gerrold's prolific output includes stage shows, teleplays, film scripts, educational films, computer software, comic books, more than 50 novels and anthologies, and hundreds of articles, columns, and short stories.

He has worked on a dozen different TV series, including Star Trek, Land of the Lost, Twilight Zone, Star Trek: The Next Generation, Babylon 5, and Sliders. He is the author of Star Trek's most popular episode "The Trouble With Tribbles."

Many of his novels are classics of the science fiction genre, including The Man Who Folded Himself, the ultimate time travel story, and When HARLIE Was One, considered one of the most thoughtful tales of artificial intelligence ever written. His stunning novels on ecological invasion, A Matter For Men, A Day For Damnation, A Rage For Revenge, and A Season For Slaughter, have all been best sellers with a devoted fan following. His young adult series, The Dingilliad, traces the healing journey of a troubled family from Earth to a far-flung colony on another world. His Star Wolf series of novels about the psychological nature of interstellar war are in development as a television series. A ten-time Hugo and Nebula award nominee, David Gerrold is also a recipient of the Skylark Award for Excellence in Imaginative Fiction and the Forrest J. Ackerman lifetime achievement award.

In 1995, Gerrold shared the adventure of how he adopted his son in The Martian Child, a semi-autobiographical tale of a science fiction writer who adopts a little boy, only to discover he might be a Martian. The Martian Child won the science fiction triple crown: the Hugo, the Nebula, and the Locus Poll. It was the basis for the 2007 film "Martian Child" starring John Cusack and Amanda Peet.

Gerrold's greatest writing strengths are generally acknowledged to be his readable prose, his easy wit, his facility with action, the accuracy of his science, and the passions of his characters. An accomplished lecturer and world-traveler, he has made appearances all over the United States, England, Europe, Canada, Australia, and New Zealand. His easy-going manner and disarming humor have made him a perennial favorite with audiences. David Gerrold will be a Guest of Honor at the 2015 World Science Fiction Convention.

He is currently completing, A Method For Madness, the fifth book in The War Against The Chtorr series.

William F. Nolan writes mostly in the science fiction, fantasy, and horror genres. Though best known for co-authoring the classic dystopian science fiction novel *Logan's Run* with George Clayton Johnson (*Star Trek*), Nolan is the author of more than 2000 pieces (fiction, nonfiction, articles, and books), and has edited or co-edited roughly twenty-six anthologies in his nearly sixty year career. Nolan is a frequent collaborator with writer and filmmaker Jason V Brock (*Milton's Children*).

In January, 2010 a comic book series and graphic novels based on *Logan's Run* (*Logan's Run: Last Day*) was published by Vancouver, Washington-based publisher Bluewater Productions, and continued into 2014 with *Logan's Run: Aftermath, Logan's Run: Rebirth,* and *Logan's Run: Solo.* The outfit published one other series based on his stories and characters (Tales from William F. Nolan's Dark Universe). In addition, a collection of all-new stories from Centipede Press, entitled *Like a Dead Man Walking and Other Shadow Tales* debuted in late 2013, bringing the total number of his books to over ninety. Adept at poetry and screenwriting as well as nonfiction and short stories (with more than twenty produced scripts to his credit), he was co-writer (with Dan Curtis [*Dark Shadows*]) of the screenplay for the classic 1976 horror film *Burnt Offerings,* and co-wrote *Trilogy of Terror* with his friend, the late Richard Matheson (*I Am Legend*), both for Dan Curtis Productions.

An artist, Nolan was born in Kansas City, Missouri, and worked at Hallmark Cards, Inc. and in comic books before becoming an author. In the 1950s, Nolan was an integral part of the writing ensemble known as "The Group," which included many well-known genre writers, such as Ray Bradbury (*Fahrenheit 451*), Charles Beaumont (*The Twilight Zone*), John Tomerlin (*Challenge the Wind*), Matheson, Johnson, and others. Nolan is considered a leading expert on Dashiell Hammett, pulps such as *Black Mask* and *Western Story,* and is the world authority on the works of prolific scribe Max Brand. Of his numerous awards, there are a few of which he is most proud: being voted a Living Legend in Dark Fantasy by the International Horror Guild in 2002; twice winning the Edgar Allan Poe Award from the Mystery Writers of

America; being awarded the honorary title of Author Emeritus by the Science Fiction and Fantasy Writers of America, Inc. in 2006; receiving the Lifetime Achievement Award from the Horror Writers Association in 2010; and as recipient of the 2013 World Fantasy Convention Award along with Brian W. Aldiss (*Frankenstein Unbound*).

A vegetarian, Nolan resides in Vancouver, WA.

About the Editors

Jason Andrew lives in Seattle, Washington with his wife Lisa. He is an Associate member of the Science Fiction and Fantasy Writers of America, Active Member of the Horror Writer's Association, and member of the International Association of Media Tie-In Writers.

By day, he works as a mild-mannered technical writer. By night, he writes stories of the fantastic and occasionally fights crime. As a child, Jason spent his Saturdays watching the Creature Feature classics and furiously scribbling down stories. His first short story, written at age six, titled 'The Wolfman Eats Perry Mason' was severely rejected. It also caused his Grandmother to watch him very closely for a few years.

His short fiction has appeared in markets such as Shine: An Anthology of Optimistic SF (Harper Collins), Frontier Cthulhu: Ancient Horrors in the New World (Chaosium), and Coins of Chaos (Edge Science Fiction and Fantasy Publishing). In 2011, his story "Moonlight in Scarlet" received an honorable mention in Ellen Datlow's List for Best Horror of the Year.

In addition, Jason has written for a number of role-playing games such as Call of Cthulhu, Shadowrun, and Vampire: The Masquerade. His most recent projects include Hunters Hunted 2 (The Onyx Path), Anarchs Unbound (The Onyx Path), and Atomic Age Cthulhu: Terrifying Tales of the Mythos Menace (Chaosium). He currently holds the position of Developer for the Mind's Eye Theatre line published through By Night **Studios.**

Check out his website at http://www.jasonbandrew.com

Mae Empson has a Master's degree in English literature from Indiana University at Bloomington, and graduated with honors in English and in Creative Writing from the University of North Carolina at Chapel Hill, where she read slush for campus literary magazines, and received the Robert B. House Memorial Prize in Poetry in 1995. She also has a Master's degree in public health.

Her recent publications appear in print in anthologies from Prime Books, Innsmouth Free Press, and Dagan Books, and on-line in The Pedestal Magazine and Cabinet des Fees. Mae is a member of the Horror Writers Association, and of HorrorPNW – the Pacific Northwest chapter of HWA. She is also a member of the Fairwood Writers, a Seattle area writing group which also runs the writing workshop for Norwescon.

Follow Mae on twitter at www.twitter.com/maeempson. Read Mae's blog at http://maeempson.wordpress.com.

About Simian Publishing

Simian Publishing is a small press company devoted to primal dark fantasy and horror fiction. We're interested in seeing how the old gods, monsters, and Jungian archetypes work in the modern world. We want fiction that touches our souls.

With Print on Demand technology, Simian Publishing is able to take chances on a story or novel that might never see the light of day through a mainstream publisher. Currently, we looking for more direct distributors, but for now you can find our products on a variety of online stores.

www.simianpublishing.org

Kickstarter Patron Credits

Justin Achilli

William J. (B.J.) Altman

E. Kristin Anderson

Lisa Andrew

Kerry Beckett

C. Benedict

Len Berry

Riley Crowder

Kimberly Davis

Dhaunae De Vir

Michael Dyer

Herbert Eder

Stephan Empson

Fabio Fernandes

Todd Branch

Jennifer Brozek

Stephen Burnside

J Caldwell

Jason Carl

Buzz Clore

Alicia Cole

Fran Friel

Carol J. Guess

Brad Gunnels

Sara Hart

Danielle Harper

Harold D Hulbert

Joe

Max Kaehn

Rachel Karyo

J Kovach

Yoshio Kobayashi

Dennis Kreinovich

Jen Kuiper

Shaari N. Ladue

Will Laymance

Ed Matuskey

Selene MacLeod

Laurie Meynig

Simo Muinonen

Michael Nazarov

Christopher M. Plambeck

Evaristo Ramos, Jr.

Matthew Sanderson

Diane Severson

Jen "Loopy" Smith

Melinda Smith

Sandra Stewart

summervillain

Michael Teegarden

The V.F.D.

Kickass Thuderfist

Andrew Trujillo

Jetse de Vries

David Wardrop

Cat Williams

Matthew Williams

Kevin Winter

www.ingramcontent.com/pod-product-compliance
Lightning Source LLC
Chambersburg PA
CBHW070822020826
48982CB00014B/341
* 9 7 8 0 9 7 9 4 2 2 1 1 9 *